RUMOR HAS IT

A LIMELIGHT NOVEL

ELISABETH
GRACE

Published by Elisabeth Grace
Elisabeth-Grace.com

ISBN-13: 978-0-9921068-1-2

Printed in the United States of America.

RUMOR
HAS IT
A LIMELIGHT NOVEL

Dedicated to two special men...

To my father, who saw something in me and told me when I was eight that I should be writing. It only took me twenty-five years to take his advice.

To my husband, who (almost always) ignores the messy house, the fact that the kids are eating chicken nuggets for dinner again, and only ever tells me that he's proud of me for pursuing my dream.

chapter one

"Ellie, you shoved your pie right in his face!"

"I did not shove my pie in his face."

"I saw the video. You really did."

"I don't want to talk about this, Katie," I said.

"Can you believe your video already has forty-three million views on YouTube?"

I dropped my forehead down onto my desk. "It's not my video," I ground out. "And I don't want to know how many people have seen it."

"I think we can officially say it's gone viral."

I sighed. There was no use. Katie would do what Katie wanted. We'd become friends since I'd started working this crappy job, but she existed in a bubble of her own creation. She didn't seem to pick-up on social cues. This was the third time I'd told her I had no desire to relive the humiliating video of myself.

As much as she was annoying me, I didn't have it in me to tell her what I was thinking. Katie was a bigger girl with thick glasses. I got the sense I was one of her only friends. Which at the moment was debatable. Instead I glanced up from my computer and said, "I have to get these reports done before Jeff comes back and has a shit fit."

"Enough said." She grimaced, tucked a stray piece of her mousy brown hair behind her ear, and headed to the back of the building.

If there was one thing we did share an opinion on, it was our jerk of a boss. Actually, jerk might be too mild a word for him.

Pompous ass had a better ring to it.

I'd been working at his real estate office for nine months. I'd left Miami, where I went to college, to move to Virginia Beach with my mother and her latest and greatest husband, Ralph. Apparently a degree in Comparative Media Studies didn't scream "must hire" to potential employers. I couldn't afford to live on my own anymore.

These days I worked at Jeff's brokerage, pushing papers, answering phones, and being his gofer the rest of the time. I was still searching for that elusive job that would lead to a career. One that would allow me to pay my own rent, buy groceries, and pay off my student loans. If I was lucky after that I'd have enough to buy myself the odd Starbucks and night out with my friends.

The roar of a car engine brought my attention to the parking lot. Speak of the devil... Jeff raced his silver Mercedes SL65 into a parking spot and slammed to a stop. He got out of the car quickly, his face flushed. Whether from the early summer heat or agitation I couldn't tell. As he approached the doors separating the outside world from my reception desk, I saw his creased forehead and pursed lips. Definitely agitation.

As much as I would have loved to avoid being an outlet for his anger, I was one step up from a Walmart greeter. Saying hello to everyone who came through the doors of Beachside Realty was my job. If I failed my duties I might as well paint a target on the back of my blouse. Maybe if I said hello and looked busy he'd charge on past and find another victim.

Jeff almost ripped the door off the hinges and stalked inside. Show time. I began typing gibberish and concentrated really hard on the computer screen.

"Good afternoon, Jeff," I said brightly.

He stopped in his tracks and spun on his heels to face me. "Ellie."

Shit.

"I just got a call from the housekeeper who takes care of the Oceanfront Avenue property. The idiot locked the house before putting the key back in the lockbox and now she can't get back in. The client who rented the place is due to arrive in the next couple of hours."

"Is there any way I can help?" I didn't mean it, but it sounded like the kind of thing someone who really valued their job would say.

"I have a client meeting me here in twenty minutes." He wiped sweat off his brow. "Have Katie get you the spare key from the safe. Open up the house, find the other key, and replace it in the lockbox."

"I'd be happy to," I said with mock enthusiasm. I'd never get through those files by the end of the day now. That beach house was a good twenty-five minute drive on a day with no traffic, never mind on a Friday afternoon in the summer.

"Go before the client gets there. This guy is a big deal."

"Yes, sir."

"Don't screw this up. I've had about all I can take of incompetent employees today." He glared at me for a moment like the whole situation was somehow my fault, then stalked down the hall to his office.

I forwarded the lines to the answering service and rushed back to Katie's office. She acted as the brokerage's deal secretary but apparently, no transactions needed her attention today. She sat at her desk with her back to the door checking her Facebook account. I'd been avoiding my own page since some loser from my old high school had tagged me in the infamous YouTube video. Ever since my profile page had been loaded with comments from friends and strangers alike giving their unwanted opinion on the whole ordeal.

"Hey." She almost jumped off her seat. It must have been

a good day on her news feed if I'd startled her. She swiveled in her chair to face me. "I heard Jeff's voice. You survive?"

I closed the door for privacy. "Oh, I wasn't the main target—just collateral damage. I need the key for the Oceanfront Avenue property. The housekeeper locked the key inside and another client is due to arrive."

"I wish *I* could get out of this office and go see a million dollar beach house."

"You're welcome to take my place," I deadpanned.

"Sorry. Busy."

Busy, right. With Facebook.

I drove my shit-box car as hard as I could but it seemed the harder I pressed the gas, the slower it went. I didn't want to risk it overheating and end up on the side of the expressway. Traffic wasn't too bad until I got closer to the ocean. The air conditioning didn't work, of course. It was the hottest it'd been all damn year so the windows were down. With traffic barely moving I knew it was going to get even more unbearable. I grabbed one of the elastics I left in the console for such occasions and quickly arranged my hair into a ponytail.

My phone rang. I kept my eyes on the road and reached over to hit the speaker phone button.

"Hello."

"Hi, sweetie, it's Mom."

This was so not what I need right now. It'd been an aggravating afternoon and a conversation with my mother would only add to it. "What's up, Mom?"

"Honey, sorry. I know you're busy."

"It's okay, but I only have a few minutes." By the sound of her voice this was going to be another talk-Mom-off-the-ledge conversation.

"Okay, I'll be quick. When I got up this morning Ralph was already gone. I've called his cell phone and he's not answering."

"And this is a big deal because...?" My mother had a knack for creating drama where there was none.

"We have a morning routine. We get up, make love while we shower, and afterward I make him breakfast. There's got to be something wrong if he left without saying a word. He's never done that." She also had a knack for sharing too much information.

"I'm sure it's nothing, Mom. He probably had an early tee-off time and didn't want to wake you."

"But why not? Do you think he's cheating on me?"

"No. Maybe there's a problem at the dealership and he had to leave in a hurry. I'm sure it wasn't on purpose. He probably forgot to charge his phone."

My mother's latest husband owned a few car dealerships throughout the state. He pretty much let his sons run the day-to-day operations and only got called in when his opinion or his check book was needed.

"I *do* always have to remind him to charge his phone..."

"See, I'm sure that's all it is. Now don't worry. You'll probably hear from him soon."

"You're right. I'm worrying over nothing."

"There you go."

"Why are you out of the office right now? I called there first and it went to the service."

I sighed. "I need to drop a key off at one of the rental houses."

"Why do you insist on working at that place? You should take Ralph up on his offer to work at one of his dealerships."

"I can do this on my own. I don't need any hand-outs from your husband." I didn't add the fact that I wasn't like her; I wasn't going to rely on a man to make things happen for me. Still, I couldn't wait to get a better job so I could move back out on my own. How had *I* ended up as a boomerang kid?

"Fine, suit yourself." She paused for a moment and I knew we were venturing into territory I didn't want to discuss. "You know, I was on YouTube this morning reading some comments on that video—"

"I don't want to talk about the damn video."

"Oh, honey. My cell is ringing. Maybe it's him."

She hung up before I could say anything. More than fine with me. I'd done my daughterly duty for the day. I'd certainly had enough practice over the years. During my freshman year at college I'd taken a week off school to nurse her back to sanity when her fourth marriage fell apart. Yep, fourth.

The turn-off leading to the beach house came into view. A drunk must have run over the street sign. The metal pole lay almost perpendicular to the ground. Thank God it wasn't far now. Sweat began to drip down the middle of my back, making my blouse stick to my spine. Was it possible for this day to get any more annoying?

I pulled into the driveway of the beach house and got out of the car. The sun's rays glistened off the predominantly glass structure. I held my arm across my brow as I approached, then took the steps leading up to the wraparound deck at a frantic pace—keenly aware of the clock ticking down to the client's arrival. I reached the top and bent at the waist, trying to suck in some oxygen. Because of my quick metabolism I didn't pack any extra weight. That didn't mean shit when you couldn't go up a flight of stairs without feeling like you'd run a marathon.

After a minute or two the light-headedness subsided enough that I stood upright. I followed the deck around the house to find the main door. Indeed, the lockbox hung open on the handle, empty. I reached into my purse for the key and put it into the lock. It wouldn't budge. I tried and tried but the metal just dug into my finger. Desperate, I snatched the key out, thrust it back in, and gave it another go.

Katie must have given me the wrong key, or maybe it wasn't cut properly. Who knew if they'd ever used this one before? If I didn't get this door opened before the client showed up the situation would become *my* fault. Not the housekeeper's, mine.

I'd worked for Jeff long enough to see his temper lead to impromptu firings. That would only set me further back. Not an option. I was getting in this house somehow.

I followed the deck around to the back where the house faced the ocean. The Atlantic looked fairly peaceful. No whitecaps, just the sound of waves gently lapping at the shore where water met white sand. A couple of patio sets and chaise lounges sat before the pool and spa overlooking the beach. Apparently the rich didn't like getting sand on their feet and preferred to sit in a sterile pool with a beach view. There were several sets of French doors along the back of the house. I tried them all. Locked.

That left only one choice. There was a small window on the side of the house. I dragged a chair across the deck and placed it below the small rectangular window, praying that since it was high no one had thought to lock it. Setting my purse down, I removed my heels and stood on top of the chair. Of course I'd chosen to wear a pencil skirt today. How perfect. I hiked the beige fabric up my thighs and stretched up to the window. At first it didn't move but when I put more force into it, it finally gave.

"Yes, thank God." I removed the screen and grimaced. Now the fun part. I wasn't a big girl but it'd be a tight squeeze. Still, I was confident I'd make it. I didn't have any other choice.

It took several tries before I managed to get my arms onto the window ledge. I was sweating profusely and cursing the fact that I never found the time to work out. My biceps shook with fatigue but my waist was resting on the window lip. Halfway there.

The window was barely wide enough for me to fit through; maneuvering around enough to get in the house feet first wasn't going to happen. The ceramic tile floor was directly below me and the toilet was to the left.

I'd have to go head first, hoping to break the fall with my hands and not my neck.

Breathing was difficult with the window sill jammed into my midsection, but I gulped one breath down and used my hands to push off. Nothing happened. I didn't have enough upper body strength to propel my bottom half up. The second time I used my feet on the outside wall to get some leverage.

It worked a little too well. I fell forward. My skirt caught on something, and I heard the audible rip as I hurled to the floor below. I bashed my head off the toilet and lay sprawled on the bathroom floor.

All I could think of was how pissed Jeff was going to be if I didn't get that key in the lockbox and scram before the client arrived. I remained on the floor for a minute. My wrist was sore, and my head was pounding but I was inside.

I lifted my forehead off the cold ceramic tile and my vision blurred. I blinked a few times to clear the curious image before me. Eventually my vision focused. A pair of men's sandals were still in front of me.

chapter two

I'd been in the beach house I'd rented for all of ten minutes and already a crazy fangirl had found me. How'd she even know I'd be here? Maybe she didn't know. I'd parked my rental car in the garage. Either way, if my manager booked the rental under my real name he'd fucking hear about it.

I took in the sight of the girl sprawled on the bathroom tiles. It was clear she'd broken in through the window and somehow lost the lower half of her outfit in the process. I was okay with that. Her yellow thong left little to the imagination. She groaned and attempted to see through the mass of a brown ponytail.

Dealing with an overzealous groupie was nothing new to me. I'd never had an actual crazy chick pursue me, but I suppose there was bound to be a first time. My manager always warned me I needed to take my personal security more seriously. "Better safe than sorry" he'd say, and I guess he was right.

"You okay?" I asked.

She didn't say anything but slowly moved into a sitting position. She wore a fitted blouse so I could see she wasn't packing any weapons. Unless a pair of full C cups counted. She lifted her head and her long ponytail swung out of her face, revealing a set of doe-brown eyes. They didn't appear to be fully focused.

"The cops are on their way," I said.

That got her attention. Her eyes widened and she scrambled to use the lid on the toilet to hoist herself upright. On her feet, she gripped the marble counter beside her. Her orange toenail polish practically glowed. My gaze traveled up the olive skin of her legs to the apex of her thighs. Her entire body stiffened. The show was over.

"Oh god," she said. She whirled to grab at the skirt hanging from the window and gave it a few good yanks. It didn't budge. She must have realized she was on display because she whipped around. I guess she didn't like me taking in the view. She eyed the towel rack and hastily grabbed one of the plush towels, wrapping it around her waist.

"Maybe you should worry less about your skirt and more about what's gonna happen when the cops get here." I don't know why she was being so modest. What was the point of breaking into my place if she hadn't planned on letting me in her pants? Hell, if it was a few years ago I would've been happy to see her.

The color drained from her face and for a moment I felt bad. But as cute as she was I didn't want to give this chick any reason to think she'd be welcome during my stay. I didn't need an obsessive groupie trying to insert herself into my life. I was here for one reason only. Relax before my next tour began and find out why the hell a guy who supposedly had it all wasn't content with his life.

"You called the cops?" she asked sounding panicked.

"Wouldn't you?"

"I didn't break in. Honest!"

I looked from her, to the open window and back and raised a brow.

"No really! I'm from Beachside Realty," she said.

"Sure you are."

"The housekeeper was here earlier and she locked the key

inside. My boss told me you wouldn't be here yet and I was trying to get the key so I could put it back in the lockbox for you."

"Well, if you're a Realtor, show me your card."

She blanched. "I didn't say I was a Realtor. I said I'm from the real estate office. I'm a secretary."

"You expect me to believe you don't know who I am?"

She appeared genuinely confused. Maybe she was for real. "Should I? My boss didn't give me a name, unless your real name is client."

I laughed. She had balls. I'd give her that. "Give me your boss's number and we'll see if you're telling the truth."

Her eyes widened even more. "You can't call him."

"Can and will." I crossed my arms across my bare chest. "You'd rather face the police than your boss?"

"Yes. He'll fire me. Let me prove it. That key's got to be in here somewhere. We can find it and you'll see I'm telling the truth."

I probably outweighed her by seventy pounds and towered over her by at least six inches; she was no real threat to me. She really didn't seem to know who I was so I decided to indulge her in the effort to prove herself innocent.

"All right then. Find the key."

She let out a rush of breath. "Thank you." She took a step forward and then stopped. "Wait a minute...how did you get in?" she asked.

"I used one of the French doors on the deck. Why?"

She looked confused. "I checked those and they were all locked."

"Are you going to find that key or not?" It was force of habit to lock the door behind me. Whenever my mom would leave me alone as a kid she'd make sure I'd lock the door after she left. I wasn't about to tell this girl that though.

I motioned for her to go in front of me. At this point I didn't think she meant any harm but I still didn't want my back to her. She scurried past me, and I got a whiff of her perfume. I usually didn't give a shit one way or the other what perfume a girl wore. Something about hers though... I liked it. The slight vanilla and citrus scent left trailing behind her had my thoughts moving in a southerly direction.

She trekked into the great room with its wall of glass and French doors every few feet—a woman on a mission. I'd picked this rental because of the contemporary design on the outside, and more traditional beach decor inside. It featured the expected pale wood floors, white couches and blue accents. The pool on the deck didn't hurt either. I could still go for a swim and maintain privacy if the beach was crowded.

"It's gotta be here somewhere," she said. She scampered around back of the couch and checked the coffee and end tables. When she came up empty she made her way over to the kitchen, searching the black granite counter for the key in question. Her brows drew together after she moved over to the white-washed kitchen table and came up empty-handed.

Those doe eyes of hers darted over to me and panic set in.

"Maybe it's in the bedroom. I'll go check there," she said.

Hell, if this was a ruse to get me into the bedroom with her, it was the most creative I'd seen thus far. And in the past five years I'd seen a lot of shit. I followed her. My suitcases were in there and on the remote chance she did know who I was, I didn't want her stealing my shit to sell on EBay.

I rushed in to find her bent over the nightstand. Before I could imagine what she'd look like in that position *without* the towel wrapped around her waist, she spun around.

"Aha." Her hand flew up in front of her, displaying the key. She winced and dropped her prize, grabbing her right wrist.

"Are you hurt?" I asked, and made my way over to her.

"I'll be okay. I told you I was telling the truth." The smile on her face was triumphant.

"I can see that." Now that I was closer, I noticed a good-sized goose egg forming on her forehead. "Here, sit down on the bed so I can take a look at your wrist and your head."

She stood in place. "What's wrong with my head?"

"You've got a big bump. Do you feel dizzy or anything?"

"I did earlier. I've got a headache, but I'm fine." She glanced warily at the bed, "I'm going to get out of here."

"Sit." My tone brooked no argument and from her swift intake of breath, she knew I meant it. I wasn't trying to scare her but I knew if she had suffered a concussion it could be serious. Experience had been a great teacher. Having a drunk for a mom meant I'd dealt with enough falls to know my way around a first-aid kit.

"I'm fine," she said, but sat down on the edge of the bed anyway.

I liked seeing her on my bed. She was gorgeous in a way that wasn't totally obvious at first. Her appeal didn't scream "look at me" the way most of the women in my world did. At first glance she reminded me of the girl next door, but her lips were a little too plump, her eyes a little too sultry.

She broke eye contact and looked down. When she realized she was looking at my crotch her gaze darted to the floor and a pink flush crept into her cheeks. I felt the stirrings of desire again.

"Wait right here. I'll be back."

Now that he was gone I let out the breath I'd been holding. Holy crap. I'd never been in close proximity with such a stunning piece of male. When I'd first raised my head off the bathroom floor I figured I'd hit it harder than I thought.

He'd been shirtless and on display was a set of muscular arms and a rock-hard six pack. It could have been an eight-pack for all I knew. I *had* been a little woozy at the time. I'd have a closer look when he came back out. My best friend Skye would want details when I relayed this story later, and I was nothing if not a good friend. To push him even higher on the hot meter, tattoos covered both arms from his wrist to his shoulders. When he'd gone into the bathroom I'd seen a huge eagle spread across the rippling muscles of his upper back. His face was chiseled and his green eyes were surrounded by a full set of dark lashes that matched the cropped, dark hair on his head. I'd never seen a guy rock a five-o'clock shadow so well. His look was intense, but he came off as more of a laid-back surfer guy.

I heard him rifling through drawers. Shit, as I stood here mentally undressing this guy the cops were on their way. Jeff was not going to be happy. Never mind how attractive this guy was, I had bigger issues.

"Um...excuse me?" No answer. "Excuse me..." It occurred to me that I couldn't even address dreamboat by name.

He walked back into the room with a first-aid kit in his hands and sat down beside me on the bed. Every nerve leapt to attention. My skin felt itchy like I needed to scratch only there was no one spot that would give me relief. This was ridiculous. I had bigger problems than the fact that my hormones worked overtime around this guy.

"Mason," he said.

"Huh?" Way to showcase my college education with that reply.

"My name is Mason."

"Right. I'm Ellie Wagner. Nice to meet you."

I stuck out my hand to shake his. Seconds after he took my hand in his I wrenched it away; for two reasons. One, because it friggin' hurt my wrist. Two, because the electric jolt racing up my arm when he touched me was unnerving. His eyes flicked up to meet mine. I could see now that they weren't all green. Flecks of hazel around his iris broke up the solid color. The combination made it difficult to look away, but my brain managed to remember the situation with the cops still needed sorting out.

"So, Mason, about the cops. You can call them now and tell them they don't need to come, right? That it was all a big misunderstanding?" I'll admit I batted my eyelashes a little in the hopes he'd see only an innocent girl who in no way deserved an audience with the authorities.

He laughed. He freaking laughed like it was a big joke that I might be arrested. Never mind that when the police called Jeff to check my story, I'd lose my job.

"I don't see the humor in this situation." I was trying to tread lightly but even I could hear the irritation in my voice.

A slow easy smile crept across his face. He had a dimple. Seriously? That attractive and somehow the heavens figured he needed a dimple, too? For what? In case there was a girl alive who didn't want to drop their panties for him upon contact? It was just unfair.

"Easy. The cops aren't on their way."

"But...you said—"

He shrugged one shoulder. "I lied."

"Oh." I sounded so damn intelligent today.

"I didn't have time to call them. I heard the crash and came running and there you were. Pretty girl, pantless, sprawled on the bathroom floor."

Heat rushed into my cheeks. I felt mortified enough that he'd basically seen my bare ass before he even knew my name. Bringing it up again only made it worse. I was saving my mental breakdown for when I got back in my car. Surely I'd exceeded my monthly quota for embarrassment.

"Now, let's take a look at your injuries." He picked my wrist up off my lap and gently turned it over a couple of times to check it out. "It looks like you only sprained it. Nothing is broken or it'd be blown up like a damn balloon right now. It's a little swollen. Ice it when you get home and it'll probably feel a lot better in the morning."

"Okay, good idea."

"I'm gonna wrap it anyways to help keep the swelling down." Instead of moving to get the bandage out of the first-aid kit, he stroked his thumb over the pulse at my wrist. He probably meant it to be soothing. I found it erotic as hell and had to resist the urge to press my thighs together. I said nothing but watched as his much larger hand held mine. My heart was beating so fast I was sure he could hear it. I tried my best to keep my breathing even.

The silence stretched and began to feel awkward so I cleared my throat. Mason let my hand go and searched through the first-aid kit. I found it difficult not to watch the muscles moving beneath the skin on his forearms while he did his rummaging. Who knew I had a fetish for forearm muscles?

"Okay, hold your hand out," he said. He gently wrapped gauze around my wrist, almost delicately. It was surprising a man with so much raw power could be so gentle. "All finished."

"Thanks."

"Let me take a look at your head."

He raised his hand to my face and lightly brushed away stray hairs that'd come loose from my ponytail and tucked them behind my ear. A shiver raced up my spine. As Mason tended to my forehead and the apparent lump there, I used the opportunity to check out his eyes again. They were astonishing. I'd never seen anyone with eyes quite like them in my life. As he leaned in to get a better look at my injury the scent of coconut suntan lotion drifted up and I realized he'd probably been planning on hitting the beach or the pool before I'd come barging in. That must've accounted for him being bare-chested. Of course, if I had a body like his I'd saunter around advertising it, too.

"You have a pretty good bump starting, which isn't necessarily a bad thing, but I want to make sure you don't have a concussion."

"I'm fine. Honest." Uncomfortable again by how close he was, I went to lift myself off the bed. I needed to get out of here before I made a bigger mess of things and he really *did* call my boss, but his hand was on my shoulder exerting pressure to get me to sit back down.

"Sit."

It was clear it wasn't a request so with a sigh I did as he said.

"Do you feel woozy at all?" he asked.

"No."

"Is there any blurring in your vision?"

"No."

"Do you feel tired, like you want to go to sleep?"

"No more so than usual."

"Headache?"

"A little."

"Ringing in your ears?"

"No."

"Feel like you're going to be sick?"

"No."

"You single?"

"Wait...huh?"

He didn't speak. Just pinned his gaze on me; comfortable in the silence and waiting for me to answer. I, on the other hand, was *not* so comfortable. The butterflies in my stomach started because there was only one reason to ask. I was not in this guy's league, I wasn't in the ballpark; hell, I couldn't even afford tickets to watch the game. I wasn't sure who he was but he must be someone of stature based on the mere fact he could afford to rent this beach house for a month.

"Um, I should really..."

"It's an easy enough question, Ellie."

I had a feeling I was at a crossroads and my answer here was going to lead me down either the right or wrong path. I wasn't sure which was which. I could lie to him. I could lie and say I wasn't single and I have a long-term boyfriend I'm madly in love with...but hormones won out. I didn't say any of that.

"Yes, I'm single."

A slow grin crept across his face. "Good to know."

And that was it. That was all he said and then he got up off the bed, took the first-aid kit with him, and disappeared into the bathroom. Talk about leaving a girl hanging.

chapter three

She *was* single. How the hell did that happen? Were the guys in Virginia fucking blind? I didn't date fans, but I was positive she didn't have the first clue who I was. It'd be a nice change to date someone who wasn't trying to get something from me.

Just ask her out. You know you're going to.

What the hell? I hadn't been out with someone without an agenda in years. It'd be a nice change of pace. My goal was to relax, and there was nothing more relaxing than getting laid on a regular basis. Assuming she was into it, too.

I shoved the first-aid kit back where I'd found it and made my way back to the bedroom. She'd gotten off the bed and was standing beside it, tapping her foot, looking like she'd rather be anywhere but here. As I approached her my cell chirped from the great room.

"I'd better get that."

"Sure. Yeah. Okay," she said.

I jogged into the other room and made a dive for my cell.

"Mason here."

"Ah, the prodigal son."

"Hey, Mom." A small amount of trepidation still crept up

my spine whenever I heard her voice on the other end of the line.

"How are you? Where are you?"

"I'm on a little vacay before the next tour gets up and rollin'. How are you? How are Olivia and Justin?"

"Oh, they're good. That's why I'm calling."

"Everything okay?" I asked, the uncertainty in my voice obvious. Justin and Olivia were my half brother and sister, and they meant everything to me.

"Yeah, yeah. But I wanted to call and see if there's any chance you could send more money along."

Prickles moved from the base of my spine up to my neck where the hairs stood on end. My mother asking for money was never a good thing. I was trying to imagine what she'd gotten herself into now.

"What happened to your monthly allowance?" I asked.

"Nothin' happened to it. I've got it but this is for something outside regular expenses."

A plethora of different out-of-the-box expenses went through my mind. Namely cocaine, booze, meth, oxy. I could've kept going but she cut me off before I could ponder any more of her former vices.

"It has to do with Olivia's birthday," she said.

"You sure it has to do with her birthday and not that douche bag ex of yours?" Let her be put off by my tone. I didn't care. Ed was a first-class loser and nothing but trouble. I didn't want him anywhere near my kid brother and sister.

"What'cha talking about?"

My muscles went stiff at her denial. "Don't bullshit me. Jorge told me he's been sniffing around again." Jorge was the full-time sober companion I'd hired for her the last time she got out of rehab so I could make sure her shit was on the straight and narrow while I traveled the globe doing what I do.

"That might be so but I wouldn't give that loser the time of day."

"You sure about that?"

"When are you ever gonna trust that I've cleaned up my act? I've been clean and sober for almost five years now."

Her voice broke in the middle of her sentence. I was upsetting her. There was a momentary twinge of guilt but it was hard to give up the twenty plus years of disappointments my mom had delivered. "What did you have in mind?"

"I thought maybe I could turn the backyard into a carnival with a petting zoo, cotton candy machines, clowns. The whole works."

The house I'd bought my family certainly had enough room to accommodate the idea. Olivia would love it and there was nothing I liked more than putting a smile on her face. "Sounds like a decent idea. How much does something like that cost?" Nothing but dead air. "Mom, how much?"

"Uh...probably fifteen or twenty thousand. To do it right."

"Have Jorge call my accountant. I'll send him a text letting him know it's fine."

"Thanks, baby. I'm so excited. Your sister is going to love it!"

"Good. I'm in the middle of something. I gotta run."

"Talk to you soon."

I knew at some point I needed to extend a certain level of trust to my mother but it was still difficult for me. Five years of sobriety didn't erase a lifetime of neglect. There wasn't a chance I'd let my kid brother and sister succumb to the same fate I'd had growing up. Like hell I was going to see them sitting in a leaky trailer, starving, and wondering if Mommy would remember to come home that night to feed them. Fuck that. I hadn't worked nonstop for years to see that happen. I was going to make sure they were set for life. Whether that life included my mother or not.

I dropped my phone back on the table and turned to see Ellie in the doorway of the bedroom watching me. She had a sheepish look on her face. She must have overheard my conversation.

"I'll just get going," she said. She started to make her way across the wide expanse of the great room.

"Hold up. I'm driving you home."

She stopped and slowly turned around. "My car is out front."

"Well, you won't be driving it. I'll take you home and pick you up tomorrow. Bring you back here to get your car."

"Why would you do that?" She folded her arms across her chest and stuck one hip out to the side.

Lucky for her I didn't mind a woman with a bit of attitude. "You've hurt your wrist, banged your head, and even though you say you feel fine I get the feeling you'd say that whether or not it was true."

"I *am* fine. I appreciate the offer but I can drive myself home."

I could see I was going to have to play my ace to get her to agree. "It's not up for discussion. Unless you want me to call your boss and tell him what happened this afternoon?"

Her arms dropped to her sides. "Fine. I'm waiting outside," she said and stomped out of the room.

I chuckled on my way to the master bedroom to throw on a T-shirt. On the way out I grabbed my phone, took the car keys off the counter, and locked the door behind me. I found Ellie leaning against the outside wall, arms crossed over her chest again. Only now she had on a pair of killer heels that made her legs look even longer than before. Instead of looking stupid, she looked adorable.

"Come on. I'm parked in the garage."

I walked around her and down the stairs to the garage. Ellie's heels clicked on the stairs behind me. I punched the code into the security keypad. The door rose at a crawl and the white Range Rover Evoque I'd be using this month came into view. Damn, I loved this vehicle. If I ever stayed in one spot long enough it might be worth getting one.

"Nice car," Ellie said from behind me.

"Thanks. Hop in."

She moved around to the passenger side, raised one leg up to get in and let out a gasp. "Shit."

"What's wrong?" I asked.

"I still have on a towel. How did I not notice this?"

"Further evidence that driving you home is a good idea. Sit tight. I'll go grab your skirt." I laughed and she turned, eyes narrowed. Her annoyance only made her cuter. I ran up the steps to the side of the house and made my way to the window she'd come through. Her beige skirt was still hanging, half in, half out, flapping in the warm, salty breeze coming off the ocean.

Ellie was waiting for me in the passenger seat when I returned. I jumped in the car and tossed her skirt over to her. "Here you go."

"Thanks." She held it up in front of her to examine it. "Damn."

"What's wrong?" I asked as I turned the key in the ignition and started to reverse down the driveway.

"It's ripped down the side. There's no way I'll be able to wear it again."

I turned my head to look from the driveway directly into her brown eyes. "Oh, I don't know. I wouldn't mind seeing that."

She laughed. And what a great laugh. This girl had already gotten under my skin. I couldn't shake the feeling that it was gonna be about as permanent as the ink adorning the rest of my body.

chapter four

The drive home was quiet. I kept my mouth shut, trying not to make a bigger fool of myself than I already had. I'd rather crawl home than admit it, but I was glad for the ride. My wrist was killing me and I'd swear my brain was pulsing against the inside of my skull with every heartbeat.

Mason had turned on the radio after we'd reached the main road. I guess he'd figured out I wasn't going to be much of a conversationalist because the volume was louder than it'd be if we'd been trying to carry on a conversation. I decided not to mention my headache. The music wasn't making it worse. Besides, one of my favorite songs was playing.

I relaxed into the leather seat, closed my eyes, and inhaled. I'd always loved that smell. Most girls I knew liked floral and citrus scents but I'd take the smell of rawhide over those any day. I was humming along to the song when the volume went way down. I opened my eyes and looked across at Mason.

He was holding a pink package out to me. "Gum?"

"Sure, thanks." I reached over to take the package from him and our fingertips brushed briefly. It was enough for me to become hyperaware of his proximity. I punched a piece of gum out, tossed it in my mouth and returned the package to him, careful not to make contact this time. My reaction to him was freaking embarrassing and I'd had enough embarrassment lately.

I returned to my previous position—eyes closed, head back as peppermint flavor burst into my mouth. Mason turned the music up again and began surfing through the channels. He stopped on a hip-hop song and an aggressive, unhappy sounding man rapped about who knew what. The bass from the song pounded into my body through the seat.

I'd never been a fan of hip-hop. My musical taste had always been limited to rock and roll and the odd country ballad. Based on what I was hearing though, I wasn't missing much. I waved to get Mason's attention and he reached forward to turn the music down again.

"Do you mind if we turn it down, or change the station or something? That's kind of making my headache worse."

The corner of Mason's lips twitched up and what could only be described as a shit-eating grin spread across his face. "You're not a fan of hip-hop?"

"I don't really know anything about hip-hop...but I'm definitely not a fan of *that*."

He stifled a laugh, although I wasn't sure why. "No problem. Why don't you choose?"

"Thanks."

That was nice of him. I was pretty sure handing over control of the radio was a big deal for guys. I raced through the dial until I found a rock station that played mostly classic hits and left it there. It was probably neutral enough to satisfy us both.

"Can you do me a favor and punch your address into the GPS? That way you can relax without having to give me a play-by-play of where to turn."

Hmm. I wonder if he was always this thoughtful or if he was treading lightly because he still thought I might have a concussion. I leaned forward, entered my mom's address into the GPS and relaxed the rest of the way home.

Twenty minutes later Mason pulled his Range Rover into my mom's driveway. My mom and Ralph lived in a traditional-looking Virginia home—two-story, white sideboards, black shutters. It was bigger than the average home and in a sought-after neighborhood. Still, I couldn't wait to be on my own again.

I was happy to see my mom wasn't sitting on the front porch. If I was lucky she wouldn't even notice my car was missing, and I'd get out of explaining the situation. Damn, I'd forgotten about the towel wrapped around my waist. She'd probably notice that.

It was silent in the car for a beat, and I was torn between wanting to bolt and disappointment that I'd probably never see this guy again.

"Well, thanks so much for the ride. You don't have to bring me back to my car tomorrow. I can ask one of my friends to take me over," I said.

"I'll be here at seven." It wasn't a request.

"Okay...well... I'll be sure to set my alarm early then."

"P.M."

"Oh."

"Dress for a date."

"Excuse me?"

"It'll be Saturday night, so it's a date. It's the least you can do after breaking in my house," he said with a grin.

He really wasn't going to let that go was he? "I think I explained that situation."

"And now I'm explaining how you can make it up to me."

"You don't even know me."

"I know enough."

I pressed my lips together. "Really? If you think you so, tell me three things you know about me. If you're right, I'll go out with you."

He laughed and those sexy eyes looked square into mine with a look that said "game on." Crap. He didn't seem nervous.

"One. Your boss is an asshole and you're afraid to piss him off. Two: You prefer rock and roll over hip-hop and pop. Three: You don't like living here and dread coming home."

Damn. This guy was good. I sat silently for a moment, and Mason laughed. I was both impressed and unnerved that he could read me so completely after so little time.

"I could tell you what color your underwear is, too, if you'd like," he said.

I smirked. "I'll see you at seven tomorrow."

"See you then."

He looked like he wanted to say more but the interior of the car was starting to feel like it was closing in. I undid my seatbelt and opened the door.

"Thanks again for the ride," I said and closed the door.

As I made my way up to the front door the towel slipped. Thank God I caught it before it fell to the ground. He didn't need to see any more of me today. I wanted badly to turn around and catch one last glimpse of him. I resisted the urge and instead walked in the house to shut myself off from all that was Mason. At least until tomorrow evening.

A few hours later I lay on my bed listening to music on my iPhone, wrapped in a towel. The hot shower had done wonders for my headache. I'd taken a couple ibuprofen when I first got home and my wrist was still tender, but no longer painful.

When I'd first moved in here I'd been given the guest room. I was grateful I had my own space because I pretty much camped out in it whenever I was at home. It was difficult though, spending so much time in a room that didn't speak at all to my personality. We lived in Virginia but if you looked at this room alone, you'd swear you were somewhere in Florida. A peach and lime green flowered comforter covered the bed, and the furniture was white wicker. Off-white ceramics covered the floor. I'd been waiting for one of the Golden Girls to pop by since I'd moved in.

I'd finally started to relax, when my mom barged through the door. I about leapt off the bed, my adrenaline rushing and heart racing.

"Jesus, Mom. Don't you knock?" I pulled my ear buds out and sat up.

"I did knock, honey," she said oblivious to my irritation. The smell of Mexican food wafted in from out in the hall. "I made dinner. Did you want any?"

"What'd you make?"

"Burritos and homemade nacho chips with pico de gallo." Mom was in one of her phases again. Ralph must be a fan of Mexican.

"Maybe later, thanks."

"Okay, I'll put a plate aside for you." She finished speaking but still stood there. I waited for her to say whatever it was she'd really come in my room for. "When I got back from the grocery store, Ralph mentioned you came in wearing a towel."

"I got a rip in my skirt and needed something to cover me, that's all."

"Oh, okay. How embarrassing." She gave me a big smile and plopped down on the bed. "So you were right."

"About what?"

"Ralph. There was a problem at one of the dealerships this morning. He had to run out quickly and forgot to bring his phone. Silly me for worrying so much."

"Glad to hear all is well."

"Thanks for talking some sense into me, sweetie. I don't know what I'd do without you." She gave me a quick hug and then left the room.

I laid back down and put my ear buds back in. My phone vibrated on my stomach. I lifted it up to see who was calling. It was Skye. We'd been roommates all through college. She'd returned home after college, too, and lived a few towns away.

In a way she was the reason my mom had met husband number five. After my mom's last divorce she'd been beside herself—again—and had ended up tagging along on a visit I made to Skye's over Thanksgiving weekend. She'd met Ralph at some function we'd attended with Skye's parents.

I hit the answer key and the music stopped in my headphones. "Hey."

"Hey, babe. What's shakin'?"

"Oh, another day in the life of Ellie. Capital 'E' for embarrassment."

"You have to stop worrying about that video. I know it looks bad, but it'll blow over. Someone else will do something stupid and put it on the Internet and the world will forget your video ever existed."

"Gee, thanks," I deadpanned.

"You know it's at almost forty-four million views now."

"You do realize that every time you go and check how many views the damn thing has you're just adding to the tally, right?"

"I can't help myself." Skye laughed and I couldn't help but laugh with her. Of everyone in my life I knew she'd have my back. Always.

"I wasn't talking about the video anyway."

"Oooh, this sounds interesting. What gives?"

I filled her in on my day.

"OMG! This guy sounds hot."

"You've never even seen him, Skye."

"Like it matters. I can tell by the way you're talking about him that you're into him."

"I don't know. I guess."

"You're totally holding out on me. He's a hottie."

I sighed. The truth was I had no trouble sharing with Skye...but I didn't know how to describe him. Hottie didn't seem to do him justice. Intense? Sexy? Charismatic? Take-charge and yet gentlemanly?

"He's totally hot." I giggled.

"So are you excited or what? You don't sound excited."

"I guess I am. I have so much on my mind with this damn video and trying to find a job. Not to mention the stress of living here."

"That stuff is all going to exist whether you date this guy or not. You might as well have fun. Do you want to go out with him?"

"I guess."

"You guess you want to go out with him? If it was me I'd be thrilled!"

"Yeah, well, if it was you you'd have to get rid of the jerk first."

"Jerk has a name and besides, we're not talking about me."

"I'm just nervous. We're from totally different worlds. He's clearly got money and some level of success. I'm just...regular."

"Oh, please. That's just an excuse. Maybe he has a rich daddy who's footing the bill on the beach house."

"I guess. My focus has to be on finding a job that'll let me move out of here. I can't take it much longer. My mother has no boundaries."

"Do your job-hunting, and then fit him into the schedule. There's no reason you can't do both."

"Listen to us...it's just one date. He'll probably figure out after that he has no real interest in me."

"Do you *own* a mirror, El?"

"It's not just about looks."

"I know that. And I know you. Therefore I'm an expert on the matter. Once he sees what an amazing person you are he'll be a smitten kitten."

"I don't think guys like him get smitten. They probably just get laid."

"Possibly."

"Okay. Help me figure out what to wear tomorrow night," I said begrudgingly.

"Great idea. I know the perfect outfit..."

After I'd dropped Ellie off, I went back to the beach house and sat on the oversize sofa, watching the Yankees trounce the Blue Jays. I didn't often have time to do this sort of thing anymore. Sit. Think. Drink a beer. Watch a game. The game ran into extra innings so it should've had my full attention, but my thoughts kept drifting back to Ellie. Ellie with her long dark hair, and bottomless eyes. There was something so endearing about her trying her best to explain her presence in my space.

I was looking forward to our date. I couldn't remember the last time I'd gone out on a normal date. It wasn't like I'd been a saint the last couple of years but in my industry people didn't really date. You attended events together, got photographed on the red carpet, hung out backstage, and more than likely got a quick fuck in a hotel room before you packed your shit up, moved to a new city and did the same thing all over again.

My cell began vibrating. It was my manager, Troy.

"Hey, man," I said.

"How's the state for lover's treating you?"

"I've only been here for half a day and I've already had a half-naked chick in my house, so pretty good I'd say."

"Sounds about right. I don't know why you didn't rent a place in Malibu. I mean, Virginia?" His tone of voice implied that I was certifiable for ending up here.

"If I wanted to get my photo on the front of every gossip magazine I would've stayed in Malibu. I'm here to chill, man."

"Well, I'm throwing a wrench in your plans."

I sighed. There was always something. "What's up?"

"I just got a call from the producers at the E Channel. They're looking to do a reality show on the life of a hip-hop artist and your name came up."

I perked up. "Really? What's it involve?"

"Filming would last four months, but they'd start with a test pilot. Probably spin it as a special and see if it gains a following."

"Are we talking something like that family that has all the Ks in their names?"

"Less scripted."

"This might be the opportunity we've been looking for to broaden my appeal. Let me branch out of hip-hop into some of the other areas we've been talking about."

"Exactly my thinking. And they're offering a seven-figure advance."

"You definitely have my attention."

"Good, but it's probably going to cut into your self-imposed sabbatical."

Troy was still pissed that I'd insisted on taking a month off. The fact was, though, I needed it. I'd been working nonstop for five years and I needed a break. I'd learned a while ago that the industry and the people in it will take and take. And after they've sucked all the life out of you, they'll just move on to the next rising star. There's always someone else nipping at your heels in this business.

"No chance we can put it off until next month some time?"

"None, they want to start filming by then."

I rubbed my hand over my face. "What do you need from me?"

"To be available. They're gonna want to meet with you. Next week probably."

I'd planned on relaxation only this month, but this was too good an opportunity to pass up.

"Let me know when and where."

"Good."

"Oh, Troy. One stipulation. I'd want some creative control and I want it clear that my family is not a part of this. They're not going to be on camera and there'll be no discussion on my mom's many issues. Think that'll be a problem?"

"Probably not. We can see if they'll name you as a producer on the show. I don't think it'd be a deal breaker. They seem to be about exposing behind the scenes of the hip-hop world more than anything," he said.

"Great. Let's make this happen then."

chapter five

I paced the front porch and waited for Mason to arrive. I didn't want him ringing the bell because then I'd have to play twenty questions with my mother.

Skye and I had settled on my dark skinny jeans with heels and a basic black tank with a white silk vest over top. I'd worn my hair down and waves cascaded down my back. I had no idea what he had planned but my ensemble straddled the line between dressy and casual.

I was also wearing my period panties. That's what Skye and I called our ugliest granny panties. Those you wouldn't think twice about wearing when Aunt Flo came for a visit.

Skye and I had instituted the ten-date-rule in college. No getting naked before that. Let's face it, college is full of first freedoms, alcohol and a lot of hormones. The last thing either of us wanted to become was a cliché college girl who boinked every guy after she got out from under her parent's thumb.

Most guys didn't make it to date three. It was one of the ways I knew if I really liked someone. If I cringed at the thought that a guy might make it to date eleven, I knew he wasn't for me.

Mason was off the charts hot. Hence, period panties. There was no way, no matter how in the moment or turned on you were, you'd ever let a guy like Mason see you in granny panties. They were a modern-day chastity belt.

A car engine sounded down the street, and I heard the thrum of a bassline. Mason's white Range Rover pulled into the driveway. I made my way to the vehicle with hurried steps, eager to get in the car in case my mom poked her head out the door.

"You didn't have to wait outside for me. I could've come to the door," Mason said.

He was dressed in a pair of distressed jeans with a beige designer T-shirt that was moulded to the muscles underneath. His cologne was an enticing mix of wood and leather. God, the sight of him was enough to make my knees weak. Add in his scent and the female population didn't stand a chance.

Thank. God. For. Period. Panties.

I realized I was staring at him like an idiot. Again.

"Oh, it's no problem. It's a nice evening to sit outside."

He gave me a big smile. "I'm glad you think so. I thought we could eat out on the deck tonight."

I swallowed, hard. "We're going back to your place for dinner?" I asked, hearing the mild panic in my voice.

"If that's okay with you."

I nodded.

"Great."

He reversed the vehicle and in minutes we were sailing down the expressway toward the ocean. The ride to the beach house was quiet because I was nervous as hell and didn't know what to say. Mason let me pick the music again so I was humming along with Neil Young as we pulled into the driveway.

We parked and he opened his door and walked around to open mine. "Come on," he said. I followed him inside the house. He headed toward the kitchen. "Can I get you anything to drink?"

"A beer would be good," I said.

"Coming up." A few moments later he passed the beer to

me, his fingers brushing over mine with the lightest touch. I'd have sworn on a stack of bibles that it'd been intentional. I cleared my throat and took a quick swig of my beer.

"So what do you want to do tonight?" I asked.

He bent down to grab something out of the fridge but popped his head up over the door and raised an eyebrow at me. "Loaded question."

Heat rose to my cheeks at his implication.

He came away from the fridge holding a platter of food and set it down on the granite breakfast bar. "I hope you're hungry."

"I'm starved."

"I picked up some stuff to barbeque: steak, baked potatoes, and corn on the cob."

"Sounds great. Can I help with anything?"

"If you could bring the beers out onto the deck, I'll grab the food and we can chill out there while the food cooks."

I grabbed his beer off the counter and followed him out to the deck. The ocean was quiet and serene and did a lot to calm my nerves. The sun hadn't set yet but it had begun its descent. We didn't get sunsets over the water on this side of the country but that didn't make them any less beautiful. The sky was filled with a golden glow and wisps of gossamer clouds were highlighted in various shades of orange and red.

I chose a chair at the table closest to the barbecue and eased into it while Mason lit the gas and cleaned off the burners. He placed the potatoes inside and came to join me at the table. He leaned back in his chair, looking entirely at ease with his long legs stretched out in front of him.

"Are you from Virginia Beach?" he asked.

"Not originally. I moved here to live with my mom and her husband after I couldn't get a decent job out of college. I was born in Indiana. Where are you from?"

"I grew up in Mississippi."

"Where's your twang?" I asked.

"I've done my best to lose it over the years. It wasn't easy."

"That's a shame. There's something sexy about a man with a Southern accent." My bold statement surprised even myself.

"Dagnabit darlin', you sayin' you don't find me all kinds a sexy without this Southan drawl?"

I laughed. "So what do you do for a living? What brings you to Virginia Beach?"

He shifted in his seat and looked uncomfortable with my question.

"I'm a songwriter."

"Wow. Anything I might know?"

"Doubtful."

I wasn't sure how true that was given the fact he could afford to rent this beach house for a month. The royalty checks must have been rolling in at a pretty steady pace.

"And you're here because..."

"Just to relax. I have a busy few months coming up."

"What's going to keep you so busy?"

"A lot of travel. Nothing that exciting."

I let the subject drop. I was getting the vibe he didn't want to expand any further on the topic. "How are you enjoying yourself?" I asked.

"So far so good." His gaze slid from my face down the length of my body. Now *I* was the one who was uncomfortable. I didn't know what to say but he saved me the trouble when he got up to add corn and meat to the grill.

We chatted about this and that and nothing in particular for the next twenty minutes while he finished cooking dinner. When it was ready we sat across from each other at the table directly overlooking the ocean.

"This is really good," I said after digging into my steak.

"Thanks."

Mason could add barbecuing to his list of impressive qualities. The food was so good I finished everything on my plate. I'd had a brief moment of wondering whether or not I should pretend to be a dainty eater but decided against it. Who was I kidding? I liked to eat and if we spent any time at all together he'd figure it out anyway. Why bother pretending?

It dawned on me that I *was* hoping we'd spend more time together. That surprised me. After my last experience with a guy you'd think I'd be steering clear. I'd known I was physically attracted to him, but now it was more.

Over the course of our short dinner I'd grown comfortable with him, curious about him, and I wanted to know more.

"Ellie?" Mason's voice brought me out of my thoughts.

"Sorry, what?"

"Do you wanna grab another drink and go sit down by the beach?"

"Sure. Let me help you take the plates in first."

"You don't have to do that."

"You made an amazing dinner. It's the least I can do."

I grabbed his plate and stacked it on top of my own. He carried the platter and the empty beer bottles and we made our way into the house.

"Set them on the counter and I'll get to them all later."

"I can throw them in the dishwasher if you want," I said.

"Ellie, I didn't ask you over here so you could load my dishwasher." He grinned.

Was it wrong I hoped there was some innuendo in his statement and that he planned on following up on it later? It was only our first date after all.

He grabbed a couple more beers from the fridge, passed one to me and then led me from the kitchen. His large hand gripped mine as we made our way out onto the deck. I got a thrill from the physical contact. You know the way your stomach starts to feel a little funny and how try as you might you can't help the grin that keeps trying to creep onto your face? That was me.

My heels clicked across the deck as we made our way to the stairs leading down to the beach. It was fully dark out by now but the deck had built-in lights casting a glow several feet onto the beach.

We reached the bottom stair and Mason sat down on it. I

removed my heels, placed them on the top stair, and stepped down into the sand. The soft crystals felt good; warm on the top and cool underneath. I seated myself beside Mason.

The stairway wasn't that wide and our hips touched. I could feel the heat from his body, and I longed to feel more of it but quickly checked my thoughts.

We sat in silence for a few minutes. Normally I'd be looking to fill the awkward stretch of silence that was inevitable after all the bullshit small talk was out of the way. For some reason sitting there quietly with Mason felt comfortable, like we'd done it a thousand times before and would do it a thousand times more.

I finally spoke up. Not out of discomfort but because I really did want to know more about him.

"Do you have any siblings?" I asked.

"Two. Both much younger. Justin and Olivia."

"Your parents sure waited a long time between having you and them."

"Same mother, different father. My dad took off when I was still a baby. Their father only stuck around for a couple years after they were born so it's really just been us and our mom."

"I'm sorry. About your father, I mean." What an idiot. Why had I assumed his parents were still together?

"It's no biggie. All I've ever known. What about you? You have any brothers or sisters?"

"No. I'm an only child. I didn't know my dad growing up, either." I don't know why I'd thought it necessary to throw that out there. Maybe to let him know he didn't need to feel ashamed he didn't know his father? Sometimes the fact that your father hadn't stuck around seemed like a reflection of you, even though logically you knew it wasn't.

He didn't say anything, angling himself to look me in the eyes. His look said he understood what it meant to have a piece of yourself floating around out there, without any means to find it, or understanding why it wouldn't want to find you.

It didn't bother me anymore. Growing up, whenever I'd ask my mom about my father she'd shut down and wouldn't tell me a damn thing. I could tell it upset her when I asked and eventually I figured out she was never going to tell me anything and stopped asking. I'm sure that sounds weird to most people, but when that's always how it's been, you don't even stop to think it might be strange—not when you're the one living it.

"So what do you do at the real estate office?" he asked.

"Nothing much. Watch the minutes tick by until I can go home."

Mason laughed. "Passion for your work, I see."

"It's a means to an end. I'm trying to find a job in the field I graduated in."

"What did you study?"

"I got my degree in comparative media studies at U Miami."

"Impressive."

"I thought so, too, until I graduated and couldn't find a job," I said wryly.

"I have to be honest. I have no idea what a degree in comparative media studies will get you."

I laughed. "Most people don't. Basically it means I can work anywhere from radio, game design, online, film or television. It's pretty broad, which I thought would help me because I'd be able to apply my skills to a lot of different industries."

"Not the case so far?"

"Unfortunately, no. The economy still isn't great and employers are hiring candidates with proven experience."

"That's frustrating because how do you get the experience if no one will hire you?"

"Exactly. I know I'll get a decent job, it's gonna happen, but patience has never been my strong suit."

"So why are you in Virginia Beach if you went to school in Miami?"

"Because my landlord in Miami wouldn't accept my charm as payment for rent. I had to move in with my mother and her latest husband."

"Ouch."

"Yeah. That's putting it mildly."

He reached behind me and placed his hand at my nape and squeezed in what I think was supposed to be a reassuring gesture. "I'm sure something will come up." I found his touch more provocative than reassuring but he could have been giving me a root canal and that'd still be the case.

"I hope so. Moving back in with my mom after being on my own for four years hasn't been the highlight of my year. Where do you live?"

"Pretty much wherever my work takes me."

"I didn't realize songwriters had to travel around so much."

He appeared momentarily uncomfortable and I wondered what I'd said wrong.

"Sometimes." He took another swig of his beer and I could tell it was the end of that line of conversation. Mental note to self. Mason does not like to talk about his work.

"Would you like to go out again, Ellie?"

He'd caught me off guard with his quick change of topic. "Oh, um...yeah. I'd like that."

He moved closer to me and the heat radiating off his body mirrored my own. He leaned in, one hand moved to my lower back, the other bunched my hair at the side of my neck.

He was going to kiss me. I was equal parts ecstatic and scared as hell. What if he didn't like how I kissed? What if *he* wasn't a good kisser? That would totally ruin the hot as hell image I had of him.

His lips touched mine and in an instant my insecurities vanished. He pressed my lips lightly at first and ran his tongue along the seam. I parted my lips to give him access. The moment our tongues met my hormones went into overdrive.

I wasn't the only one. He pressed me closer. His tongue slipped over mine and the pace increased until the kiss became almost frantic. We couldn't get enough of each other and it was like we were trying to devour one another whole.

He pulled away and I immediately missed the feeling of his body close to mine. Our heavy breathing and the pounding of the surf were the only sounds. He fixed his gaze on me with half-closed lids, grabbed me by the waist and lifted me so I straddled his lap.

I should have been offended or afraid. In truth, I liked how he manhandled me. I'd probably put the feminist movement back twenty years with my enjoyment of his display of physical strength and the blatant male satisfaction on his face when he saw I was impressed by it.

Not wanting to be outdone I pushed him until he leaned back on the staircase. The stairs probably dug into his back but he wasn't complaining. From the feel of his rigid shaft underneath me, complaints probably weren't on his mind.

We picked up where we left off. He fisted my hair and groped my ass, pushing me against him so I could feel how much he was enjoying it. Tension built in my lower half and I ground my hips down on him to get some relief.

He started to ease the white vest off my shoulders when I came back to my senses. I knew those period panties would come in handy.

I pulled away. "Wait, wait."

"What's wrong?" He looked confused. His eyes darted from side to side like he was trying to assess the problem.

"I can't do this. I'm sorry. I have a rule." I was panting.

"Can we talk about your rules later?" He moved to pull me into him again.

"No. Stop," I mumbled against his lips. I'm sure he was used to girls dropping their drawers the instant he said go but I wasn't going to be one of them. No matter how badly my body was insisting I should be. "Ten dates. That's my rule."

"Come again?"

His choice of phrasing had my mind swimming in images of the two of us and I fought to keep my line of thinking straight. "I won't sleep with a guy for at least ten dates."

He flopped back against the stairs with a defeated look on his face and scrubbed his hands over top of his shaved head.

"I'm sorry," I said and moved to get off him.

He grabbed my arm and pulled me back down, lifted me by the waist and twisted me around so I was sitting in between his legs. His arms came around me and squeezed me close.

"You don't have anything to apologize for. I won't lie and say I'm not disappointed though."

"Thanks for understanding." I was embarrassed that I'd blurted out my rule to him, but his reaction put me at ease.

"I understand but you can be sure we'll be having all ten of those dates as soon as possible," he said and laughed. "Clear your calendar."

"Has anyone ever told you you're a very wise man, Mason?"

"Save your praise until I figure out a way to shove ten dates into one day and you hear all the great ideas I have that involve you and I."

"Mmm...I'm sure most of them involve us being horizontal," I said wryly.

He nuzzled my neck and spoke low and slow into my ear. "And in the pool, against the wall, in the shower, on the kitchen counter... Stop me when you've heard enough."

Wow, Mason was a dirty talker. I'd heard enough to fuel my fantasies for years. "Enough," I said. I laughed and swung my elbow back into his gut.

We relaxed for a while, not speaking. Just enjoyed each other's presence and the view of the moonlight reflecting off the water. It was comfortable. My nerves had evaporated entirely.

I sunk back into Mason, enjoying his warmth and felt my eyelids getting heavy. The next thing I knew Mason was nudging me gently to wake me.

"Ellie, come on. You should get home. It's late and you're falling asleep."

"Okay," I said in what I could hear was a sleep-laden voice.

"Unless you want to spend the night here. You're welcome to but I have to be honest, if you do I'm not sure I'll be able to keep my hands off you."

It pleased me to know I had that effect on him. I wasn't sure what that said about me but to be honest, right then, I didn't care.

"Tempting but I should get home. I didn't tell my mom I wouldn't be home and even though I'm twenty-one she'd worry if I wasn't there in the morning."

I grabbed my shoes and walked barefoot across the deck, Mason leading me along with his hand on my lower back. He walked me to my car. When I got to the driver's side door he pinned me to the car with his arms on either side of my shoulders.

"I had an amazing night, Ellie. The best I've had in years."

Holy crap. This guy was making it super difficult for me to stick to my ten-date rule.

"I had a good time, too."

"Let's do it again."

"Okay." What else was there to say really? I wasn't into games, which was why I was always upfront about the ten date thing. I wasn't going to play coy or pretend I didn't want to see him again.

He cupped his hands on either side of my face and he kissed me. It was different than the frantic kissing we'd shared on the deck. This kiss was a slow burn; the fire between us building and building until it was a raging inferno and difficult to control.

This time he pushed me back. "You'd better get out of here before I force you to stay." He rubbed one hand over top of his head.

I nodded, got into my car and started it. He knocked on the window. I rolled it down and he passed me his phone.

"Here put your number in."

I did as he asked and when I scrolled up to save it I

noticed that instead of adding me in his phone under Ellie Wagner he'd added me as WORTH THE WAIT.

Damn. This guy was trouble.

chapter six

It finally looked like things were turning around for me. I'd gotten two great calls. Technically one was a text but semantics, whatever.

I had a job interview in Richmond for the programming department at a local cable station. It was only a small station—that was okay. It was a foot in the door leading me to better things, unlike my current job. I hadn't earned my college degree to pour coffee for rich people overspending on beachside homes.

When Mason texted to ask if I wanted to go out with him again that night my day went from great to awesome. Damn straight I wanted to see him again. He intrigued me. There was more to him than his six-pack abs and charming persona and I wanted to find out what.

I was only a few minutes from leaving work for my job interview when Katie came strolling up to my desk. I'd told Jeff I had my annual physical knowing he wouldn't inquire any further. The only thing that made men more uncomfortable than the topic of vaginal exams was period talk. Katie knew where I was really headed.

"How you feeling? Nervous?" she asked.

"A little. I'm sure it'll get worse the closer I get to Richmond."

"Probably."

Friggin' Katie.

"You have to promise if you get the job we'll still be friends," she said sounding really concerned.

"It's just one interview. It'll probably turn into nothing."

"Bullshit. You're a smart girl, a good worker, and any company would be lucky to have you."

Aw, that was kinda sweet because I knew she meant it. For better or worse, Katie said what she meant. "Thanks. And of course we'll still be friends." Despite her rough exterior, she was growing on me.

An hour later I was in the Program Director's office in Richmond waiting for her to come in to conduct the interview. I sat in the plush leather chair, legs crossed with my foot bobbing up and down. I'd chosen to wear my navy suit with a white blouse underneath and had pulled my hair back into a twist in an effort to look more sophisticated and mature. I'd achieved it. When I'd walked into Beachside Realty that morning Katie had asked why I was looking so matronly.

The Program Director walked into the office with an air of authority wearing her own nicer and clearly more expensive, pale yellow power suit. She may have only been running a local Virginia station but she had an air about her like she was running a multi-billion dollar corporation in New York or Los Angeles.

She walked around to her side of the desk, leaned over with her hand outstretched and introduced herself.

"Claire Ambrosa."

I shook her hand. "Ellie Wagner. Pleasure to meet you."

She squinted and tilted her head when she looked at me. "Have we met before?"

"I don't believe so." I'm not sure why it didn't dawn on me where our conversation would eventually lead, but it just didn't.

"Hmm," was all she said before she sat down and began perusing my résumé.

For the next twenty minutes or so she went through the standard interview questions: where I went to school, what previous jobs I'd had, what made me the right candidate for the job, blah, blah, blah. I'd had enough interviews by this point that I could probably recite the answers in my sleep. She was direct but pleasant and I had a feeling she liked me. I thought I really had a shot this time. Until she finally realized where she recognized me from.

"All of this looks really good, Ellie. I have a few more candidates to interview later this week but I hope to have a decision made by early next week. Are there any questions you wanted to ask me?"

Now I have a philosophy that when an interviewer asks you this question (and they all do eventually), you must come up with something. Otherwise it seems as if you don't give two shits about the job. There was nothing people loved more than talking about themselves, and by extension the company they worked for.

"I do, I was wond—"

"Wait! Now I know how I know you." Her eyes were wide and she pointed a finger at me across the desk.

My stomach dropped and did a somersault. My chest tightened. *No, no, no, no...*

"You're that girl from the YouTube video."

Damn it. What did I say to that?

"The one that went viral," she continued.

"I can explain..."

"No explanation necessary. I think we're through here." She began tamping together the sheets of my résumé, put it in a folder and proceeded to throw said folder into the recycling bin. Right. In. Front. Of. Me.

I tried to keep my composure in case there was any way to salvage the situation. My cheeks were flushed in anger, but maybe she'd think it was from embarrassment. "Miss

Ambrosa, if you'd let me explain."

"Save it. I'm not hiring you. Not only do your actions in that video reflect poorly on you, but I wouldn't take the chance someone else in the media found out you worked here and tried to use it to their advantage. This station doesn't need any bad press. A huge portion of our operating budget relies on donations from the public."

I kept my mouth shut and willed the tears that had begun to burn behind my eyes not to fall. I refused to give her the satisfaction of knowing how she'd affected me.

She leaned across her desk toward me and lowered her voice. "Let me give you a tip, Ellie. The world of media is a cruel one and has little tolerance for screw-ups. It's even harder for women because unfortunately, there *is* still an old boys' club. Buck up, get rid of the emotion I can see in your eyes, and get used to it. If you want any kind of success in this business you're going to need to grow a thick skin. It's every woman for herself."

Jeez, why was it always the women who were the cruelest to other women? We didn't need to worry about men oppressing us; we could do it just fine ourselves.

"Thank you for your time." I rose out of my seat and left as quickly as my feet and my three-inch heels could carry me. I reached my car and leaned over the steering wheel and sobbed. I didn't give a shit what she said. This moment deserved a good cry.

One mistake. One instant of not thinking before I acted was affecting every aspect of my life. It didn't seem fair. Everyone made rash decisions sometimes but it seemed that thanks to a camera phone mine was able to play out over and over again to anyone with a WIFI connection.

I pulled my phone out of my purse to check the time and saw that Skye had texted me to see how the interview had gone. I typed her a quick rundown, hit send and started my car to begin the drive home.

I'd been on the freeway for a few minutes when my phone

rang. I hit the speaker button knowing it'd be Skye.

"That bitch!" came blaring through the speaker. "I can't believe she said that to you."

"It was harsh but she's probably right."

"I don't care if she's right or not, that was just plain rude."

"I'm so sick of that stupid video following me around. It's been over a month now. When will people forget it?"

"We've all done things we regret." The tone of her voice was serious. She sounded like she was talking from experience.

"Is everything all right?" I asked.

"Of course. Anyway, don't worry about it. Next week some dancing baby will take over your spot as the newest viral sensation and you'll be old news."

"I hope so."

"Listen, what are you doing tonight? Want to get shit-faced and drown your sorrows?"

"I can't tonight. I have plans." Thoughts of my plans with Mason helped to perk me up a bit.

"Plans. What plans and why wasn't I informed of them?"

"Mason and I are going out again." Even in my crappy mood I got a small thrill saying it. I grimaced as the squeal from the other end of the phone came through the speakers.

"That's so awesome. What are you guys doing?" Skye asked.

"He wants to take me to Catch 31."

"Nice! Okay, then let's go for drinks tomorrow night and you can give me the lowdown on your date."

"Sounds good. The only thing is Katie from work already twisted my arm to go out with her tomorrow night. Are you cool if she's there, too?"

"Hell yeah. I like that girl. She cracks me up at her blatant disregard for social etiquette."

"Alrighty then." Seems Katie had a fan.

"Are you wearing the PP's again tonight?"

That was *the* question. Mason was only here for a limited

time. Did I really want to play coy for the next few weeks, following a self-imposed rule? I really liked him. If I waited until our eleventh date that'd only give us a week or less of bedroom antics before he left. I couldn't imagine that'd be near enough. Besides, my life could use a little fun at the moment.

"I'm still undecided."

"Woohoo! If this guy is as hot as you say then I don't blame you."

"I said I'm undecided."

"Yeah, yeah, we both know you won't be wearing them."

She hung up and a small grin crept onto my face. Damn, that girl knew me too well.

chapter seven

I met Mason at the restaurant since I'd agreed to cover part of a shift for the night secretary and had returned back to the office after the interview. She'd needed to take her kid to an appointment and I'd needed someone to cover part of the afternoon. It worked out for both of us. Well, except me because the job interview had been a bust of epic proportions.

I'd changed into a lilac silk dress with spaghetti straps that hit mid-thigh. Skye had suggested pairing it with my cream peep-toe platform heels and a pearl necklace. Of the fake variety, obviously. The sides of my hair were pulled back with bobby pins. Overall I was happy with the look. I even felt a little sexy, truth be told, which helped brush off my earlier mood.

Katie had stayed late and caught me changing in the restroom. She'd been supportive and seemed to be excited for me. Hell, I was excited for me. Mason was sex incarnate, and I hadn't worn my PP's tonight. Anything was possible.

I arrived at Catch 31 Restaurant on time to see Mason waiting outside for me. My stomach got that half sick, half excited feeling it did every time I saw him. He wore beige linen pants with a white button-up short sleeve shirt, his broad chest evident underneath. The tattoos on his arms were a nice contrast to the clean cut look.

Mason smiled wide as I approached. "You look...exceptional," he said.

I blushed. "Thank you."

He leaned in and gave me a chaste kiss on the cheek. I inhaled his familiar scent. Heat immediately pooled between my legs.

He led me into the restaurant with a warm hand pressed on my lower back. I tried concentrating on where I was walking so I wouldn't stumble in my heels and make a fool of myself. All my attention was focused on the hand on my back. It was difficult to think anything other than naughty thoughts when he made physical contact with me.

We approached the hostess table where an attractive and stacked blond stood. Her eyes ran over Mason like he was on the menu and she hadn't eaten for days. He asked for a table and she smiled wide and pushed her chest out. As if he could miss the double D's pushed up to her neck. I bit back my irritation as she sashayed in front of us to show us to our table.

She stopped at a table with an ocean view. "Here you are. Let me know if there's anything I can do for you."

She was looking directly at Mason when she said it. Her tone held the implication that if he wanted to stick his dick in her later that'd be no problem.

Mason didn't seem to notice and thanked her without sparing her a glance. Her sultry look turned to disappointment, and she looked me up and down, clearly wondering what the hell he was doing with someone like me.

You're preaching to the choir, sister.

Catch 31 was one of my favorite restaurants. The soaring ceilings, white table tops and ultramarine blue accents always gave me the feeling of being under water. My favorite part was the outdoor patio. Set in close proximity to the beach, it had a section of tables that circled various fire pits. I'd spent a few nights there sipping cocktails with my friends listening to the surf. It was a popular restaurant and the place was busy, even for a Thursday.

After we'd gotten our drinks and placed our food orders we settled in to talk. Mason took a sip of his drink and set it back on the table. "Do you miss Miami at all?" he asked.

"Definitely. There's always something to do there, always something going on. I'm thankful that at least I ended up by the ocean." I motioned with my hand toward the water.

"You like the ocean?"

"There's something so calming about it. Even when the waves are crashing against the shore it feels peaceful to me. It makes me feel small, like just one tiny piece in this puzzle of a world. It makes my problems feel small, too." I shrugged. "It's silly, I know."

"It's not. Have you ever gotten up early enough to see the sun rise over the ocean?"

"Not lately. I saw it a few times in college. Not because I'd planned on it though. I just wasn't coming home until dawn." We both laughed. "Did you go to college?"

"No, I never got the chance. I started working right after high school."

"How does someone get into something like song writing?" I asked.

Mason shifted in his chair and looked away from me for a second. "Usually someone in the industry hears your work and likes it. That's how it happened for me anyway."

"Don't you ever get writer's block?"

"Not normally. I've always found it pretty easy to express my feelings on paper. That's all a song is, your feelings put into words, then those words get put to a beat or music."

"Still it must not be easy to keep coming up with new material all the time."

"You just have to look for inspiration."

"Oh? Where do you usually find yours?"

"Right now it's sitting across the table from me." His eyes locked with mine and he stared at me with intensity. I couldn't look away; those eyes of his drew me in. A few seconds later I was aware of someone beside us clearing his throat. Mason broke eye contact first.

"Here you are. Enjoy," the waiter said as he placed our appetizer on the table between us. I'd convinced Mason to try the raw oysters since he'd never had them before.

"Thank you," I said to the waiter and then turned my attention to Mason who was staring at the oysters like they were a science experiment gone wrong.

"I don't know about this," he said. "There's a reason I've avoided these things for twenty-three years." He'd grabbed a fork and was pushing against one of the oyster shells like he was trying to see if it was still alive.

I laughed. "Come on. A big tough guy like you afraid of some oysters?"

"How do we go about eating these...things?" He scrunched his nose up and creased his forehead in disgust.

"Here I'll show you. The easiest way is to take your small fork and move the oyster around in the shell to make sure it's detached, bring the shell to your lips, tilt your head back and let it slide into your mouth. You might have to kind of suck on it a bit if it doesn't come in your mouth right away. Then swallow. Like this." I demonstrated and put the shell back on the plate. "It's really yummy but it'll taste a little salty."

Mason's eyes were heated and his cheeks flushed. "Forget everything I said about not wanting to try the oysters. I love oysters. My new favorite food. We're having them every time we're out together."

"What?" I asked, not catching on.

"Ellie, that was hot."

"Hot?"

"Can you really not know what it does to a man to watch you explain how you eat an oyster and then demonstrate the process so well?"

I thought back to my explanation. I put my hands over my face when I realized what he was referring to. "Oh my god. I didn't mean it like that," I mumbled from underneath my hands.

Mason leaned across the table, grabbed one of my wrists and pulled it away from my face. "I didn't mean to embarrass you." He chuckled and I started laughing, too.

Maybe I was *too* comfortable around him. I needed to start thinking before I spoke. "It's okay. I can't believe I didn't realize what I was saying when the words were coming out of my mouth."

Mason raised an eyebrow. "You really need to stop saying the word coming if you want to make it to the main course. A man only has so much self-control."

We both laughed louder than we should have, drawing the attention of some of the other diners.

"Are you going to try it?" I asked when I could catch my breath.

"Let's give it a go." Mason was a quick study. He did everything right up until the oyster hit the back of his throat. At that point his face curled up in disgust and he began coughing and gagging. His face went red and he grabbed the napkin off his lap and spit the oyster into it.

I did my best to stifle my laugh. "Not a fan I take it?"

"I'm sorry. They're just so...gooey. I didn't expect them to be like that. My throat just refused to open."

"That's okay they're not for everyone," I said still chuckling a bit.

"I feel like such a pussy."

"Don't. They can take some getting used to. Are you sure you don't want to try another one now that you know what to expect? It'd be a shame to waste them."

Mason leaned in across the table, cupped my face in his hand and ran his thumb back and forth over my cheek. "Oh, Ellie. You're going to finish every one of those oysters, and I'm going to Love. Every. Second. Of. It."

chapter eight

Halfway through dinner I started to notice that a few of our fellow diners kept stealing glances at our table. I'd only been recognized a handful of times in public since the video had been released so it struck me as odd, but I was immediately self-conscious. Were they waiting for a repeat performance of the last time I was out on a dinner date with a guy? Well, they could keep waiting. I'd learned my lesson.

I tried to ignore the eyeballs piercing through my skull as I ate but it was distracting as hell. Maybe I was being paranoid thinking everywhere I went people would recognize me because of what had happened at the job interview.

"Have you noticed people looking at us?" I asked Mason in a hushed voice.

He looked at me from across the table like a deer in headlights. "What do you mean?"

"I just feel like everyone's checking us out. It's strange."

He let out a big sigh and ran a hand over his shaved head. "Ellie, there's something I need to—"

"Oh my god! I'm so sorry to interrupt your dinner but I had to come over and tell you that I'm one of your biggest fans!" A girl about eighteen or so with long blond hair stood beside our table looking at Mason. She was practically vibrating with excitement.

"Well, uh, thanks," Mason said, eyeing me across the table, looking a little chagrined.

What the hell was this girl talking about?

"I was sitting over there with my family, and I kept telling my brother it was you, but he was like 'no way he'd be here,' but I knew it. I knew it was *the* Mason Nash sitting here in front of me. I can't believe it!" She put an emphasis on *the* like the name Mason Nash meant something big. Something definitely wasn't adding up here.

"I guess you can ride your brother for the foreseeable future that you were right then."

She laughed. "I loved your last album. It was killer. I'm totally buying tickets to your tour when it comes through town."

Mason looked over to me with pleading look. It seemed to beg me not to spew out the obvious questions I had for him while this girl was standing at our table.

"It's great to have fans like you. I appreciate it." He smiled a thousand-watt smile at her and I swear to God I thought the girl was going to turn into a puddle at his feet.

"Will you sign something for me?"

"Sure."

The girl looked around the table for something that Mason could sign. She leaned over to me and took the white table napkin from my lap and placed it in front of Mason. She turned back to look at me, "Sorry, you don't mind do you? It's not like I expected to see him here tonight or I would have come prepared."

"Now why would I mind?" I said in the sweetest, sing-song voice I could muster. I even threw in a head tilt for good measure.

"Thanks." She seemed oblivious to the fact that my eyes were throwing daggers. She grabbed a pen off the tray a waiter was carrying past our table. Mason signed the napkin and she finally left us alone after her parting shot to me. "You must feel so lucky to be out with him."

"It's like a dream, I can't even believe he's real," I said with as much sarcasm as I could put into my voice.

Clearly Mason was more than just a songwriter.

"Ellie, I can explain," he said as soon as she was out of earshot.

"Why weren't you honest with me?" I crossed my arms over my chest.

"I was. Sort of. I *am* a songwriter. Just not in the context you thought I was. I do write songs for other people, it's just not what I'm best known for." He rubbed his hand over the stubble at his jaw.

"And what are you best known for, Mason? I can call you that right? It seems to be your real name."

He ignored my jab. "I'm a hip-hop artist."

My mouth hung open. A hip-hop artist? I wouldn't have guessed it. Ever. He didn't strike me as that kind of guy. I knew it was a stereotype but when I thought of hip-hop artists I had visions in my head of guys saying "yo" with big gold chains around their necks and the crotch of their pants hanging down to their knees. That most definitely was *not* Mason.

"So, you're famous?" I asked.

He paused and blew out a breath. "Yes," he said finally.

"How famous?"

"What's the scale?"

"Low end of the scale: you struggle to find gigs to pay your rent each month, high end of the scale: paparazzi camp outside your house to get pictures of you on your morning walk."

"Probably somewhere a little over the midpoint then."

My jaw slackened. Again. This was not good. It probably would have been good for a lot of girls, but not me. I was trying to fade from the spotlight, not be thrust into it.

"So is this a regular occurrence? Girls coming up to you at

restaurants to fawn all over you?"

"It can be."

"Why didn't you tell me who you were?" I could hear the hurt in my voice.

"It's gonna sound lame."

"Try me."

He rubbed his hand overtop of his head and blew out a big breath of air. I was starting to recognize his tells when he was uncomfortable. "It was nice not to be recognized. You have to understand...for years I've been surrounded by people kissing my ass. Either because they work for me or want something from me. It was nice to get to know someone who thought of me as Mason, not Mason-Nash-hip-hop-artist. Normally when I meet someone for the first time they know who I am and already have preconceived notions of what that means."

I was pissed that he'd lied to me but I could understand why he'd done it. How was it any different than when people had seen my video and decided they knew me from that one act? The fact that I understood where he was coming from made it hard for me to stay angry with him. Which made me angry with myself.

I sat quietly processing the information. I wasn't sure what to think. On one hand he'd been dishonest with me. On the other hand I could totally relate to why. I was also trying to wrap my brain around the fact that he was a real life, honest-to-God celebrity. I'd never seen, let alone had a make-out session with someone famous before. It was unnerving.

"I understand why you kept it from me. I don't like it though," I finally said.

He reached across the table and took my hand in his. "I'm sorry. I wanted you to get to know me. The real me. People don't treat you the same when you're famous. That sounds pompous to call myself famous I know, but it's the truth. People are just...different when they know you're in the public eye."

The public eye. I hadn't even gotten that far in my

thinking. Mason must live his life in the public eye.

"Ellie, I really am sorry. I would have told you soon, after you knew me a bit better. I didn't want you to find out like this but I did want you to find out. I never planned not to tell you."

"How did you get into hip-hop?"

Mason visibly relaxed now that I was engaging him with questions about his career. "When I was a teenager, money was tight. I was always good at putting rhymes together so when I saw there was a free-styling competition in our area I decided to compete. I won the first one I entered. The crowd was really into it, cheering me on and screaming whenever I got a good diss in on the other guy. It was a good way to earn a few extra bucks and it didn't involve selling drugs like most of my other friends were doing, so I'd compete in any contests I could get to. I won most of them and somehow word spread to Troy—he's my manager. He sought me out, offered to rep me and show me the ropes. That was more than five years ago."

"Do you like it?"

"I like the position I'm in now better than the one I was in before, I'll say that."

"I'll bet. It doesn't hurt having attractive girls come up to your table to talk to you." I tried to keep the irritated tone out of my voice but wasn't sure I was entirely successful.

"You're wrong about that. I'll admit, at first it was cool. A good ego boost. But after a while you realize that even though the fans think they love you, they really don't even know you. They love the product and the packaging you provide them with. The product is my music, I'm the packaging. They love the persona they see reflected in the media."

I was trying really hard to be angry with Mason but the more he explained himself the more I understood his thinking. The lack of privacy would make me crazy. I'd had trouble coping with the small amount of attention I'd gotten from the viral video. I can't imagine the drain of dealing with that on a daily basis. "Does that happen often? People coming up to ask for your autograph?"

He shrugged. "It does. It depends what city I'm in."

"And here I thought all those people were looking at our table to see what the fish special was."

Mason laughed. "I didn't think anyone would recognize me tonight. Not that I was trying to keep it from you, I just didn't want our date to become all about the fame thing."

I knew what he was saying. I'd had a couple similar experiences the odd time I'd been recognized from the video. Once a person put two-and-two together it was like that's all they can focus on. Like the rest of you ceases to exist except the fact that "OMG, I can't believe that's *you*."

"Well, then, let's not make it about that," I said.

Mason smiled and I felt a twinge of guilt. I'd enjoy the rest of our date. We were here now in the middle of dinner and I'd already seen what could happen when you had a strong emotional reaction in a public place. There'd be no part two to my infamous video.

I'd enjoy the rest of the evening but after it was all said and done, I knew what I had to do.

chapter nine

I drove Ellie and I back to the beach house after dinner cursing myself. I knew it'd been a bad idea to go for dinner in public, that there was a chance of me being recognized. But I hadn't wanted to invite her back to my place again in case she thought my M.O. was to get her naked.

Her reaction when she'd learned I was famous was another one of the reasons she intrigued me so much. Most girls would've been ecstatic and had dollar signs in their eyes. Ellie had been the opposite. She hadn't said much about it but she'd seemed disconcerted by the whole thing.

I pulled up the long driveway and turned the vehicle off.

"Ellie, is everything okay? You've been quiet since we left the restaurant."

She blew out a breath. "I've been running the fact that you're famous over in my head and thinking about all that means."

Which didn't sound promising. "What does it mean?"

She looked across the car at me with regret in her eyes. "For one, it means you probably date super models and other celebrity types."

I was confused. "I'm not seeing anyone right now if that's what you're asking."

"I assumed you weren't although I guess I probably should have asked. What I mean is, you're probably used to dating beautiful women."

"I still am dating a beautiful woman."

"You know what I mean."

"I'm not gonna lie, I'm no saint, Ellie. My first three years of fame I probably fucked my way through half of Hollywood and the Victoria's Secret catalogue. But I haven't been like that in a long time."

She flinched at my honesty, but there was no point in lying about it. The gossip rags had documented most of my trysts anyway and she'd only need an internet connection to read about it.

"I wasn't implying you're promiscuous. I don't understand why you'd want to go out with me when you're used to dating women like that," she said in a soft voice.

Was she for real? I reached out and ran my thumb along her cheek. "You're one of the most beautiful girls I've ever met. You've got something none of those other women ever had."

"An extra twenty pounds?"

"Don't even get me started on how bangin' your body is, or we're gonna end up in the back seat. You know who you are. You're your own person."

"What does that even mean?"

"Some of the women *you* probably consider the most beautiful in the world are so vile in character it would make your head spin. They have no heart. No soul. They think only of themselves and what they can get with no consideration for anyone else. They'd sell their soul in a minute if it meant they'd land the right gig, or get on the right magazine cover. They'll step on anyone and everyone without a second thought to get where they want to go."

"How do you know I'm not the same?"

"I saw how you reacted back at the restaurant when you realized who and what I was. You weren't impressed by it, in fact I think it's the exact opposite. It's working against me. Isn't it?"

She shifted uncomfortably in her seat and looked down to her hands. I tucked my hand under her chin and brought her eyes back to me. She looked conflicted and tears had formed in the corner of her eyes, ready to fall at any second.

"Tell me. What is it that's bothering you so much?"

"It's really embarrassing."

I scrunched up my face in confusion.

"Okay, here goes," she said more to herself than me and took in a big breath. "A little while ago I was seeing this guy. We'd been on five dates together and I was really into him. He seemed nice, treated me well, said all the right things. I thought we were a good match and it could turn into something serious."

I fixed my gaze on her. It was irrational to feel as irritated as I did listening to her describe how much she liked another guy, but there it was. Rational or not.

"Anyway, one night we were back at his house, you know, making out and things were getting a little hot and heavy. That's when I told him about my ten-date rule. He seemed okay with it at the time and I figured we were good.

"The night of our sixth date he took me out to a restaurant. He'd seemed a little off all night but halfway through dinner he let me know what had been bothering him. In a big way—he unleashed on me. He began telling me what a cock tease I was and how if he'd known how long it would take him to get in my pants he wouldn't have taken me to all the nice places he did. He called me a gold digger, said I was only dating him to get him to foot the bill for all the places I wanted to go."

"I don't know who this guy is but I want to strangle him. Still I don't see what that has to do with me. You already know I'm okay with it."

"He wasn't quiet, and someone overheard then decided to take out their phone and record the whole thing. I was so pissed I picked up my dessert plate and shoved it into his face. Followed quickly by a drink in his lap. The video ended up on YouTube and went viral, it got connected back to me through Facebook, and I've had to deal with it since."

Of all the things I expected her to say *that* was not it. "What's the problem? That asshole deserved what he got."

"I thought so, too, but I shouldn't have let my temper get the best of me. If the food hadn't started flying it probably wouldn't have gotten so much attention. The comments people have sent me have been less than kind."

"How so?" I asked.

"They agreed with him—called me a cock-teasing gold digger who got caught and that was the only reason I was so pissed at him."

"Is that what you're worried about? That I'd find out about the video and think all that stuff was true?" I pulled her in for a hug and rubbed her back. She fit perfectly and rested her head in the crook of my neck.

"I'm worried because I want nothing more than to fly under the radar. I don't want to be in the limelight. I want it all to go away. If we keep seeing each other the chances of that happening are slim."

What could I say to that? It was true. If the paparazzi ever saw us together they'd make it into something it wasn't and wait around until they could manufacture a scandal. It only took one phone call from some enterprising individual.

"Ellie, I—"

"You don't understand how much those comments affected me. I lost out on a job today because of it. People I don't even know are having debates about what a horrible person I am. I can't put myself in a position like that again. I'm sorry."

"There's no—"

She pulled away from me and held up a hand. "No, Mason. I've made my decision. I can't see you anymore."

"Ellie—"

"I think it would be best if you just took me home." Her voice was devoid of emotion. She'd erected a wall I wasn't going to be able to penetrate. At least not tonight.

I said nothing as I started the car and backed down the driveway. Inside I seethed with a mix of anger and regret. Anger that some asshole had treated her so horribly, and now I was the one paying the price.

The regret was the strange part. It was the first time since I'd gone from being piss poor to skyrocketing to fame that I'd actually felt some measure of regret. Where I felt that maybe all the money, fame, and opportunities it provided were actually keeping something of value from me.

We didn't speak on the ride home. I didn't even turn the stereo on. The silence was deafening.

As her mom's place came into view I tried to think of something to say. Some logical reason why everything she'd said about my life was wrong, but I couldn't come up with one.

I stopped the car in the driveway and she immediately unbelted herself. She couldn't get away from me fast enough.

"Thanks for tonight, Mason. I'm sorry about everything but it was really nice meeting you. Good luck with everything."

She didn't wait for me to respond. She bolted from the car into the house, out of my life for good.

chapter ten

Skye, Katie and I had decided to meet up at Preston's Pub. It was a down-to-earth place with a comfortable vibe and inexpensive food.

I was already sitting with Katie at one of the high tables in the bar area when Skye torpedoed into the room. She looked great as always with her long blond hair pulled back into a high ponytail. She wore a boho chic sundress with a cropped denim vest over top and metallic gladiator sandals. I'd admired her sense of style since college, which was why I always solicited her advice on what to wear on dates. That girl knew how to put an outfit together.

Her blue eyes sparkled with mischief as she plopped her purse down on the empty chair and took a seat at our table. She looked to the bartender across the room. "Rum and Coke please," and turned back to our table.

"Hey, Skye, good to see you again," Katie said.

"Same here," she said to Katie and then swiveled her head in my direction. "Now. Tell me you didn't start spilling your guts before I got here. Because if you did you're just going to have to back that train up and start from the beginning again."

I chuckled but my heart was still heavy from last night's events.

"I've been trying to pry it out of her but she only wants to tell the story once so we've been waiting for you. You were late," Katie said in her typical blunt fashion.

"I know. Sorry, guys. Vic and I got in an argument before I left." She waved it off with her hand like it was no big deal but I saw a shadow pass over her face.

"Everything okay?" I asked. She'd been seeing Vic for a while now and I wasn't a fan from the get-go. I'd found him possessive and controlling, and I worried for her. She always insisted he was just misunderstood.

"Peachy. Now, how was date number two?" she replied.

I hesitated for a moment.

"Uh-oh," they said in unison.

I sighed and then filled them in on all that had happened. When I was done rambling the other two were quiet for a minute until Katie broke the silence.

"Holy shit! He's *that* Mason Nash? Hip-hop superstar?" Katie just about yelled through the bar.

"Shhh," I said, looking around to make sure no one had overheard us. "I take it you know who he is?"

Skye sat with a stunned look on her face. I don't think she'd blinked at all for the duration of my story.

"Of course. Don't you?" The tone of her voice implied that I was an idiot for not knowing exactly who Mason was when I met him.

I shrugged. "Not really. Only what he told me. And that he's famous enough that people came up to the table to get an autograph."

"You seriously need to Google him. He's got awesome tunes. And he's dated some celebrities you'd definitely recognize."

"Wonderful." Equal parts jealousy and insecurity worked their way through my system as I pictured him with an actress or a model on his arm. Which was the exact reason I hadn't Googled him yet. I wasn't a masochist by nature. The last thing I needed was a stream of candid shots of him with a plethora of different women running through my head all day.

"He's one fine piece of ass. Why the hell would you tell a guy like that you don't want to see him? Are you crazy?" Katie asked.

"Have you forgotten what my life has been like since that video came out? I can't even go on social media for fear of what people are saying about me. The last thing I want is to be dating someone who makes that kind of attention look like a drop in the bucket."

"If that was me I'd be all over it. *All* over it if you catch my drift," Katie said.

"Drift caught," I deadpanned.

I looked over to Skye who had finally recovered from her stunned state and was sipping her drink through a straw; the level of the drink going down and down, without her taking a breath.

"You must understand where I'm coming from?" I asked her.

"I'm still processing over here. I can't believe you've been dating a real celebrity," she said.

"I'm not dating him. Haven't you been listening to me at all?"

"Okay, whatever. Past tense then," Skye said to mollify me.

Katie piped up again. "Come on, Skye. You can't really think she has a good reason not to date this guy?"

I looked to Skye to back me up. She looked sheepish. It seemed I was outnumbered.

Skye spoke to Katie. "Honestly, I don't see what the big deal is. I can see she likes him...a lot. So what if he's a celebrity? He's only here for like, what, a month or something? Why doesn't she hang with him while he's in town and have some fun?" Skye asked.

"Exactly. It's not like they're going to end up on the front of *US Weekly* as the celebrity couple of the year. They're not going to be walking red carpets together," Katie said. "It's this whole video thing that's got her so freaked out."

"I know. And I get it, but it shouldn't hold her back from enjoying her life," said Skye.

"Exactly. If it does then every asshole who wrote some idiotic comment about her without knowing her wins," Katie said.

"And you can't let assholes like that win," Skye agreed.

Apparently I'd been dismissed from the conversation. I sat back in my chair and sipped my drink while they continued to discuss me as if I wasn't there.

A part of me knew they were right. How much press could we really get hanging out in his beach house for a few more weeks? More than anything I didn't want to end up in the news, on the internet or wherever else gossipmongers posted their shit; but we didn't have to go out in public.

Another part of me, which I'd refused to acknowledge up until now, worried that Katie had nailed what was really holding me back. I didn't have any illusions that I could hold a candle to the women Mason must associate with in his normal life. Don't get me wrong. I had self-confidence. Before a bunch of random strangers decided to have an opinion of me on every social media channel available I'd had quite a bit. For a regular girl I was attractive, but I didn't come close to the models or celebrities Mason was used to.

Once Mason's time in Virginia Beach was over he'd be wheels up and back to his regular life, with me only a vague memory. Was that what I was really afraid of? That I'd fall too deep to shrug off our time together and move on with my life?

Damn, I didn't know. My mind was moving a mile a minute and Katie was still going on to Skye about how swoon-worthy Mason was. I'd have to sort my own thoughts out later.

"So you're both saying that I should keep seeing him?"

"Yes!" they said in unison.

"What about the press?"

"Screw the press," Katie said. "Stay inside. And horizontal, I say."

I laughed. You never had to wonder what she was thinking.

"At least consider it. How often do you meet someone like him? It'd be a great opportunity to get past the shit-head you dated last," Skye said.

Shit-head being my co-star in the infamous video.

"I'll think about it."

"I'm just gonna put it out there...if you do sleep with him, I want a full debriefing," Katie said. I raised one eyebrow at her. "What? I have to live vicariously."

"Oh, oh, oh! What she said." Skye pointed frantically at Katie.

I pushed my chair out from the table and headed to the bar. I needed another drink if I was going to listen to this the rest of the night.

chapter eleven

The next morning I sat on the patio in the backyard wearing my favorite bikini trying to improve my tan. I saved this bikini for those occasions when there was no chance I'd be getting wet. I'd learned the hard way that even if a white bathing suit was double layered, that didn't mean it wasn't see-through when wet.

It was one of those amazing days where the sun sat high in the sky but there was still a nice breeze. It was perfect. Or it would have been if I hadn't been sitting there replaying the last time I'd seen Mason over and over in my mind.

The doorbell rang interrupting my pity party. My mom and Ralph had one of those god awful doorbells that played an entire melody so loud it startled you every time it rang. It was hard to miss, even in the backyard.

I rose from the lounger and went through the house on my way to the front door. I couldn't imagine who it would be. I wasn't expecting anyone and my mom and Ralph had gone golfing.

I swung the front door open to find Mason on the other side. Before I had a moment to react to his presence he started speaking.

"I'm not letting you do this," he said and stepped past me into the house.

I suddenly felt very naked in my bikini and wished I'd thought to put my cover-up on before getting up to answer the door.

"Mason." It was all I could say, he'd taken me so unawares.

His eyes roamed my body as if noticing for the first time I had more skin showing than not. His muscles tensed and his gaze heated as he took me in.

I tried to ignore my own body's reaction to being this close to him with only scraps of fabric covering my most intimate places.

"Did you hear what I said, Ellie? You're not doing this."

"Um...why don't you come in? I was just tanning in the back." I motioned the direction to go with my hand and waited until he started for the back of the house, being sure to follow him and not the other way around. I did *not* want him following me while I wore what now felt like an entirely too revealing bikini.

Mason was dressed casually in a pair of black basketball shorts, a grey T-shirt that stretched across his biceps and broad shoulders, and a white baseball hat.

By the time we'd reached the back deck I'd recovered from the shock of seeing him on my doorstep and was able to carry on a conversation once again.

"Can I get you something to drink?"

"No thanks. I'm only here for one reason."

I swallowed past the growing lump in my throat. "What's that?"

"I've already said. Stop playing coy."

The words alone sounded rude but I could see it wasn't how he meant them. He was intense. He was looking at me as if he wanted to shake me and ravish me in equal parts. If I'm honest it gave me a bit of a rush to know that I'd elicited such a reaction in him. So sue me. I'm only human.

"Because you're not going to let me do this..."

"That's right. I know you're attracted to me and I get why you don't want to be in the public eye. Believe me, I fuckin' get it."

"My being attracted to you doesn't change anything."

"What can I do? What can I do to convince you that we can figure out a way to explore what's between us without it meaning our business being splashed all over the internet?"

"Unless you can disable every smart phone in the country I can't think of anything." I crossed my arms over my chest to show him I meant business but quickly changed tactics after I realized it only pushed my breasts closer to spilling out of my bikini top.

"What if we laid low and stayed out of public?"

"How'd that work for you before?" Obviously not well because he ignored my question.

"If you can look at me and say that you don't feel the pull between us like I do, I'll leave and never come back." He took a step closer.

It was on the tip of my tongue to say just that but something stopped me. I couldn't do it. It wasn't the truth.

"That's what I thought. You're the most refreshing person I've met in years, Ellie. You're not working an angle, you're intelligent and you're so goddamn beautiful in a way that grabs me by the throat and makes it hard to speak. And I sling rhymes for a living so that's saying something."

I was speechless. I'd never had anyone describe me quite like that. The descriptors of me in YouTube comments were "cocktease," "cockblocker" and another "c" word that even I wouldn't repeat.

The best part was that I could tell he meant every word.

Every. Damn. Word.

The images in my head of the two of us splashed across the front of some tabloid were even more painful with that realization. I opened my mouth to tell him that none of that mattered, I still couldn't see him, when his phone rang.

He let out a frustrated growl and pulled his phone from the pocket of his shorts and glanced at the screen.

"Damn it," he nearly yelled, hit a key on his phone and brought it to his ear. "What?" I had no idea who was on the other end but his body language changed almost instantly. His muscles became tense and rigid. There was a tick in his jaw as he clenched his teeth together.

"You'd better be fuckin' kidding me," he said into the phone, and his voice rose with anger. "How long has she been in there?" He paused for a second and then, "No...no. I'll come down there to deal with her. We need to have a conversation."

His voice was heated and menacing. Call me Miss Obvious but it was clear he was pissed. Beyond that there was a weariness and sadness in his eyes. It pained me to see him like that. Vulnerable almost. It didn't seem right that someone like Mason could be made to feel like that. It reminded me of every time my mother told me she was getting a divorce growing up. I always knew it was coming, but somehow I still held out hope that maybe that day would never come. This husband would be the one that stuck.

He hung up without saying goodbye and looked over to me, his face drawn.

"Everything okay?" I asked. I didn't know what else to say. He was intense when he'd arrived here but the phone call had brought him to a whole new level.

"I've got to go," he said and started to walk past me.

I reached for his arm and he stopped at my touch. "Wait. Are you okay?"

"Fine. Nothing I haven't dealt with before."

"You're upset."

He paused, seemingly deciding whether or not to share with me what was bothering him. "My mother's fallen off the wagon again. Ended up in a holding cell for drunk and disorderly and property damage. I have to fly to Texas to bail her out and deal with her shit. Again."

I don't know what possessed me to say it. Maybe it was the look in his eyes that I recognized so well—the disappointment in the one person you're supposed to be able to rely on, or his little speech about me prior to the phone ringing, but I blurted it out before thinking.

"Do you want some company?"

The surprised look on his face told me that was the last thing he expected to hear. "You'd come?"

"If you think it'd help."

Twenty minutes later I'd changed, left a note for my mom that I'd be back sometime tomorrow, and was boarding a private plane to Texas. What the hell had I gotten myself into?

chapter twelve

I couldn't believe she'd done it again. I don't know why I was surprised. My entire life my mom had been delivering one disappointment after another. It shouldn't even faze me anymore.

My brother and sister didn't deserve any of this. After all the opportunities I'd given to my mom....FUCK! She'd had access to the best rehabs, the best sober companions, the best counsellors. I'd moved her to a ranch the middle of nowhere in Texas. It had everything she could ever want and yet she still managed to attract every douche bag within a fifty mile radius to drag her down. She was a heat-seeking missile when it came to finding the dregs of society.

The private charter plane I'd hired had landed a half hour ago in Austin. The driver who'd met us on the runway was heading to the police station in Hays County. I'd get the details of what had happened from the lawyer I'd hired when I got there.

I knew how this was going to play out. I should. I'd done it enough times. I'd either be greeted with the apologetic mom who couldn't tell me enough times how sorry she was, how she'd never do it again...or the angry, beat-down version who lashed out at everything and everybody. I wasn't sure which was worse. Listening to the empty promises spill from her mouth, or dealing with the insults she hurled my way after all I'd tried to do for her.

"What're you thinking about?" Ellie asked from the seat beside me.

"Just how sick of my mom's shit I am."

"This isn't the first time this has happened I take it?" she sounded regretful. I wanted *something* from this girl. I hadn't figured out what, but it definitely wasn't her pity.

"Far from it. It was a pretty regular occurrence growing up. Back then I didn't have money to bail her ass out of jail though. Sometimes I waited days for her to show up at home. If I was lucky one of our neighbors would notice she wasn't around and take care of me while she was locked up or off on a bender."

Ellie's hand was over her mouth and unshed tears glistened in the corner of her eyes. She looked stricken by the image I'd painted of my childhood.

Not much I could do. It was all true.

"That's awful," she said quietly. She looked down to her lap.

I grabbed one of her hands and gave it a squeeze. "Thanks for coming."

"You looked like you could use the support. Now I understand why."

Damn. I couldn't remember a time in my life when *I'd* had someone to lean on. Growing up there was no one. That hadn't changed any when I'd become famous.

I gave her hand another squeeze. "How much longer?" I called up to the driver.

"Only a few minutes, sir."

We pulled up to the police station and I exited the car before it had stopped. The driver flashed me an irritated look but I wanted to get this over with and get back on the plane. The more miles between my mom and me the better. He let Ellie out of her side and she walked around the car to stand beside me.

"Ready?" she asked, her eyes full of sympathy.

I nodded and led the way into the police station. We walked through the double doors; it looked like we'd stepped into a time warp. It was clear not a dime had been spent on the place since the seventies. A balding overweight man in a brown oversized suit approached me holding a briefcase. This must've been the attorney I'd hired to handle my mom's bail.

"Mr. Nash, I'm Gary Smyth," he said with a slight Southern accent. He held out his hand. "We spoke on the phone."

"Mr. Smyth, this is Ellie." I said shaking his hand.

He took Ellie's hand. "Ellie, pleasure. Your mom is all set. We've had the bail hearing. All that's left to do is for you post bail and she's free to go."

"What happened?" I asked with a hard edge to my voice.

"Apparently she and a male friend were at the local watering hole. When the bartender refused to serve them any more drinks they took to throwing some bar stools and other items around."

"So what happens now?" I rubbed my hand over my face, already weary from the troubles my mom had caused.

"A trial date will be set. We'll see if we can get her off on community service or rehab."

"She's been down that road plenty of times already. It hasn't worked." There was steel in my voice as I spoke.

"I don't want you to worry about your mother, Mr. Nash. I'm sure we can work something out to keep her from serving any time."

"I'm not worried about my mother. I'm concerned about my siblings. She may be a fuck-up but she's still their mom and they'd be crushed if she went to prison. You'll get a phone call from my lawyer in L.A. He'll work with you to make sure this thing goes away." Ellie's hand came to rest on my lower back. I instantly felt some of the tension leave my body.

"Yes, sir."

"Can I see her?" I asked.

"Of course. Let's post the bail and then we'll get you a room where you can speak to her in private."

After I paid the bond Ellie and I made our way through the rows of desks where several officers milled about. The lone conference room was in the back of the police station. We sat in the hall in a pair of uncomfortable-looking chairs that'd been duct-taped several times to keep the stuffing from spilling out.

Ellie turned to me, seeming concerned. She opened her mouth to say something when her attention was drawn to something behind me.

I turned to see a middle-aged officer with a beard that looked like it belonged on the Unabomber standing behind me. He must have been a detective because he wasn't in uniform.

"I hate to bother y'all..." I knew what was coming after the first words were out of his mouth, it was always the same. "...but my daughter is a huge fan. Would you be able to sign something for me?"

"Of course." I tried to give him a smile that said I didn't mind signing shit for fans while I was waiting for my mom to get released from jail. Really, there was nothing I'd rather do.

He shoved a notebook and pen in front of me.

"What's her name?" I asked.

"Mary-Beth."

I wrote a quick note on the sheet thanking Mary-Beth for being such a great fan and returned it to the officer.

"Much obliged. She's gonna be so excited."

After he'd left I turned back to Ellie. Before I could ask what she'd wanted to say Gary the lawyer came walking down the hall with my mother in tow.

She looked like hell. Which I suppose was appropriate after spending the night in a cell and waking up hung-over as hell. Her long dark hair was stringy and unbrushed, her clothes crumpled and dirty. I knew by looking at her she wasn't strung out. At least she'd only hit the hooch last night and not the hard stuff. Small thing to be thankful for in this whole messed up situation, but thankful I was.

Seemed I'd be getting the repentant version today. Her head hung low as she walked down the hall. She didn't glance up once to look at me before Gary brought her into the conference room.

Ellie grabbed my arm. I turned to look at her. The concern was still in her eyes.

"I'll wait out here. Take as long as you need."

How was it possible this girl I'd known for such a short time knew exactly what to say? I was glad for her company but I didn't want her to witness what was undoubtedly going to be an ugly scene between my mom and me.

My hand went to the back of her head and I pulled her in and kissed her forehead. "Thanks. This won't take too long. I'll be doing all the talking."

I walked into the room. There was one small table in the middle with four chairs around it. My mom sat across the table beside the lawyer. She looked up. The dark circles under her eyes were evidence she hadn't gotten any decent sleep in at least a few days.

"Mason—"

I held my hand up while I tried stemming the rage threatening to overflow. "Stop. Before you even start spewing your bullshit. I don't want to hear it."

"Honey, I made a mistake..."

"I said STOP!" I shouted.

What color was left in her face drained and her eyes widened.

"Who has the kids?" I asked, my voice low and filled with venom.

"The nanny was there when I went out last night."

"I'm only going to say this once, so listen good. The only reason I'm doing this is them. It has nothing to do with helping you out of another mess you've created for yourself. I'll make sure you get off without serving any time, which you might have had to do considering the fact this isn't your first run-in with the police."

She opened her mouth to say something but I shot her a glare that must've spoke volumes because she quickly shut it.

"From now on Jorge will be living with you rather than visiting every day. I need someone to keep an eye on you and make sure you're in line. You'll do outpatient rehab. I'll pay to have the counselor come to you if there isn't anything around here."

She looked devastated. "For Christ sakes, I don't need rehab. It was a one-time slipup."

"Well, I'm going to make sure that's all it is. Don't bother arguing, it's non-negotiable." She let out a huff and crossed her arms over her chest. "Unless you'd rather be cut off."

She was quiet for a moment. "You'd never do that to your brother and sister."

"You're right, I wouldn't. But if I cut you off, they wouldn't be living with you anymore."

"You can't take my babies away from me!" she yelled.

"Really? Would you have any money to fight me in court if that's what I wanted to do? Who do you think a judge would side with—an addict who can't get her shit together, or a celebrity who'd be able to provide nothing but the best for them?"

I could see I'd defeated her and she'd given up the fight. I felt like a bastard having to do it, but I needed her in a spot where she knew there was no option but to sober up. If I could take those kids out on the road with me I'd do it, but it was no place for them. She didn't need to know that.

If it wasn't for Olivia and Justin I'd leave her to rot in a jail cell and not feel a lick of guilt about it. But, for better or worse, she was their mother and they loved her. I'd managed to cover for her all these years. They weren't aware of her addictions. It'd been easy to hide when they were younger but they were getting older now.

I turned to the lawyer. "Gary, can you take her to a hotel

or something to shower and clean up? I don't want her walking in the house looking like that. The kids will know something is wrong."

"Of course. No problem."

"Thanks. Just add it to my bill. I'm going to stop by the house to see Justin and Olivia before I go."

I turned to walk out of the door without sparing a glance at the woman who gave birth to me. She said my name when my hand turned the door knob to leave.

"Mason, I really am sorry."

She was so quiet I could barely hear her. There was so much I could say back to her, instead I left without looking back.

Ellie was still sitting in the tiny hallway, probably having gotten an earful. She turned her worried eyes to me.

"Everything okay?"

I shrugged a shoulder. "As good as it can be considering. Come on, let's get out of here."

She stood up from the chair. "Isn't your mom coming with us?"

"No." I placed a hand on her back and led her through the desks to the front of the station. I felt the need to touch her. Her heat underneath my hand calmed me. As stupid and as fucking cheesy as that sounds.

We walked out the doors of the police station and were blinded by flashbulbs. There weren't many of them, maybe three at most but I knew the pictures would still go to the highest bidder; it didn't matter if there were three or thirty.

"Motherfuckers," I hissed under my breath.

Ellie had stopped in her tracks, her eyes wide. "How'd they find us?"

"Just get to the car," I said, sounding more annoyed with her than I intended. I knew the deal. The longer we stood here the more shots we were giving them to sell.

We rushed into the back of the hired car. I gave the address to the driver and he sped off as fast as he could with the photographer's lenses pressed up against the windows.

"Mason, how did they know we were here?"

"Fuck if I know. Someone must have called them."

"But who would do that?"

I chuckled because she sounded genuinely confused. Her naivety was endearing. "Anyone who wanted to earn a few bucks. One of the cops, our driver. Could've been anyone."

Her jaw dropped and her eyes widened. "That's horrible. With all that you're dealing with, your mom...that's cruel."

I shrugged. "I'm used to it."

She scooted closer to me, our hips touching and she grabbed my hand with a squeeze. "You shouldn't need to be." She leaned her head on my shoulder.

I turned to kiss the top of her head.

"Where are we going?" she asked.

"I want to stop by and see my brother and sister for an hour before we leave. Is that okay with you?"

"Of course. I can wait in the car."

I shifted away and her head came up off my shoulder. I could see she was serious, which only pissed me off more.

"You're not waiting in the car, Ellie. You're coming in the house."

"Oh...okay. I wasn't sure if you'd want me meeting your family, that's all."

Did she think she was my dirty little secret or something? I tucked her back under my arm. "Of course I do."

chapter thirteen

We pulled up to a set of wrought iron gates and Mason hopped out of the car briefly to enter the security code. He told the driver to continue along the road until he reached the main house. We passed a smaller dirt road that forked off to the right.

"What's down that way?" I asked.

"That road leads to the stables."

Of course. The stables. How stupid of me.

After a meandering drive down the road past rolling hills of green we pulled into a circular driveway. We got out of the car and I stood staring up at an enormous ranch house that looked like it could span the length of a football field.

"This is your house?"

"Technically, but I bought it for my family. I've never lived here." He placed a hand at the base of my neck. I was starting to really like that habit of his. "Come on. Let's go inside."

We walked through a large set of wooden double doors into an expansive entryway. The home looked to be a nice mix of wood cabin meets contemporary with large exposed logs leading up to the cathedral ceiling but modern-looking slate flooring. A wide hallway ran between twin staircases at either side of the foyer.

The sound of bare feet slapping against tile came from the back of the house, getting closer and closer. A young boy and girl ran into view. The little boy resembled Mason a bit with the same dark hair and jawline, but his eyes were dark brown. I guessed him to be about ten. The little girl looked maybe six or seven and had green eyes more reminiscent of Mason's but dark blond hair pulled back into a ponytail.

"Mason!" they shouted in unison. They plowed into him, hands extended, and almost knocked him over with their exuberance. Mason's face lit up. He hugged them fiercely back, then turned to face me.

"Olivia and Justin, this is my friend Ellie. Ellie, this is my brother and sister."

"Hi, Ellie." Olivia said, jumping up and down on the spot.

Justin smiled at me then turned to Mason again. "We thought you were Mom coming home. She didn't come home last night." He looked worried.

"I know, buddy. Mom wasn't feeling well so she went to the hospital to get looked at. She's feeling better now so she should be home soon." Mason ruffled Justin's dark hair and Justin leaned in to give Mason another hug.

"Let's go in the living room. I want to show Mason the new dolls Mom got for me," Olivia said. Justin didn't seem to like that idea because he rolled his eyes at his little sister. Olivia grabbed Mason's hand, tugging him in the direction they'd come from.

The group of us made our way through the large foyer past an open dining room. The table looked like it could seat twenty. We entered a large living room decorated in neutral tones. A massive stone fireplace was the focal point of the room and was set between two massive panes of glass overlooking the green landscapes and sloping hillsides.

An older woman with grey hair and a round body was standing in the room and greeted Mason with a worried look.

"Is everything okay?" she asked, clearly aware of what had happened.

"It will be," was all Mason said in response. "Greta, this is my friend, Ellie."

"Pleasure to meet you, Ellie." She gave me a reserved smile.

"Same," I said.

Mason turned to me. "Greta looks after Olivia and Justin when my mom isn't around. Greta, why don't you go relax for an hour? I can't stay long but I know you probably haven't had a break since yesterday. I'll be here for a bit."

"Very good," she said and headed out of the room.

"Mason, Mason! Sit down. Come play with me," Olivia said.

"No. Let's play war. I don't want to play with stupid dolls," countered Justin.

Mason didn't seem fazed by their bickering in the slightest. "Listen, you two. We'll play with Olivia's dolls first but we'll make sure to play war for a bit before I have to leave. Okay?"

"Okay," Justin said petulantly.

I was surprised to feel a tiny hand grab mine. Olivia was tugging me toward the floor where she had a collection of what I was pretty sure was American Girls laid out.

"Come on, Ellie. I'll let you play with my new one if you want."

"Wow. That's really nice of you, Olivia."

"Here," she said after we'd all sat on the ground, and pushed a blond-haired blue-eyed doll my way. No wonder every girl wanted to have blond hair and blue eyes; we were practically conditioned since birth to think it was the ideal.

"Thanks," I said.

Mason grabbed a doll as did Justin, although very begrudgingly.

Olivia had appointed herself the mommy and the rest of us played her babies. We'd all been playing the roles that Olivia had assigned us for a while when she blindsided me.

"Are you Mason's girlfriend?" she asked.

I felt the heat hit my cheeks and I'm pretty sure my eyes probably looked about ready to bug out of my head. I didn't know what to say so I looked to Mason for help.

He was chuckling softly but after a couple of seconds took enough pity on me to answer his sister's question.

"Ellie isn't my girlfriend, Olivia."

"How come?" she asked innocently.

God, this kid was cute but she was killing me.

"We only just met a little while ago."

"But you must like her if you brought her here. Do you want her to be your girlfriend?"

I seriously wanted to crawl up the chimney and disappear from sight. Lately my life seemed to be one long string of embarrassing situations after another.

Mason smirked at me and then addressed his sister. "Olivia, it's not polite to ask questions like that."

"How come?"

"Because you're making Ellie uncomfortable."

I really had no idea how he felt about me. He'd shown up at my house earlier today apparently to tell me we were still going to see each other but we'd never finished that conversation. I figured the fact that he was avoiding his sister's question gave me the answer. Even though I'd been the one to tell him we couldn't see each other just days ago, it still stung to know that he felt nothing for me beyond a casual acquaintance.

"I think it's time to play war now isn't it?" I said wanting to get off this topic of conversation.

"Yay!" Justin yelled and got up to run across the room to pick up a play sword and shield. "I get Ellie on my team."

Mason clutched his heart in mock pain. "Buddy, I've been replaced so easily?"

Justin just shrugged. "She's prettier than you are."

Mason chuckled. "I'll give you that. She sure is."

That gave me a warm feeling. I smiled and walked over to Justin who was now holding a play bow and arrow.

"Here. You can use this," he said.

"Thanks, kiddo." I took the toys from him and felt something hit me in the back.

I turned and saw a foam grenade on the floor next to my foot. Justin grabbed my hand and raced to jump over the back of the couch. I followed and we crouched down behind it. I heard Mason make a pretend exploding sound from the other side of the room.

Justin turned to me, the excitement practically oozing out of him. "That was close. Come on, Ellie. Let's sneak around the other side and ambush them."

We eventually called a truce after it was clear there would be no real winner. Mason was like a big kid himself. It was a nice change from the distant, cold Mason I'd seen this morning around his mom.

We stood at the front door saying good-bye, Olivia wrapped around my legs.

"It was nice to meet you," she said looking up at me with those eyes that reminded me so much of Mason's.

"It was nice meeting you, too. I had a lot of fun playing with you guys." I pulled Justin in for a hug, as well, which he let me do.

When the hugs were over Olivia pulled away and asked, "Will you be back again soon?"

Left speechless again at the hands of his sister and unsure what to say I looked to Mason for help.

He saved me by saying, "Come here, you two, and give me a hug before we're off."

They wrapped themselves around Mason, squeezing hard. I could tell they were sad to see him go. Justin's face and demeanor suddenly turned anxious.

"Is Mom really okay?" he asked.

Mason seemed to be a bit taken back by the question and had to compose himself for a minute. That cold veneer was back. "Mom will be just fine. She should be home any minute. Don't you worry."

"Okay," Justin said, but I sensed he understood there was more going on than Mason was telling him.

"All right, you two, we gotta go. You guys be good for Mom today. She's probably still not feeling that great."

The kids called after us as we made our way to the car, yelling their goodbyes again. I could tell they loved Mason very much. He must still be a doting brother even if he didn't live with them because there was definitely a little hero worship going on. I was starting to understand exactly why.

chapter fourteen

We were back on the plane Mason had chartered, somewhere in the air between Texas and Virginia. It was late evening but we managed to get a meal on the plane. Not crappy airline food either. It goes without saying that I'd never been on a private plane, but I was still surprised by the quality of our meal. We'd had chicken served over a pesto pasta and it was as good as I'd had in any restaurant. Probably better than most of the places I frequented, if I was honest.

Mason had been quiet since we'd left his mom's house so I was surprised when he said, "Will you come back to my place when we land?"

I'd been getting more of a piss-off-and-leave-me-alone vibe, than a please-spend-more-time-with-me one, but nevertheless I was concerned about him. He'd been quietly brooding for hours.

"Sure. If you want," I said.

He looked up from his plate where he was cutting a piece of chicken. "Do you want?" he said, eyebrows arching.

It was a simple enough question but it was a loaded one.

"Yes," I said simply.

He didn't say anything and went back to cutting his meat. A few minutes later he was done eating, seat reclined, and looking out of the window with vacant eyes. I wanted to say something to comfort him but I didn't know what. I didn't know him well enough to know if this was his usual reaction to dealing with his mother, or if it was something more than that. Did he like to talk when he was upset, or did he like to be left alone?

His low voice brought me out of my thoughts. "We'll get you a bathing suit at the airport so we can swim when we get back to the house."

It wasn't a question. He wasn't even looking at me when he said it so I didn't bother responding.

After we landed we ducked into the airport gift shop. Mason had put on a baseball hat, reflective sunglasses and kept his head down as we made our way through the store. I quickly picked out a light blue bikini. It was a little skimpier than I'd normally wear but there hadn't been a huge selection to choose from. It was either this or a one piece mid-aged mom bathing suit with a built-in skirt at the bottom. I opted for slutty over matronly given the company.

Mason still hadn't said much and I told myself it was because he was trying to lay low so no one would recognize him but I could tell there was something more. This was a side to him I hadn't seen. He'd always looked intense to me, now his mood matched my original assessment of his looks. I wasn't sure what to make of it but I was hopeful that the other Mason would make an appearance soon. I wasn't sure I was a fan of this one.

I felt like an asshole. I'd barely spoken to Ellie since we'd left my mom's place and she certainly didn't deserve my moodiness. She'd been supportive and understanding the whole time we were in Texas. When she'd first offered to come along I'd felt an immediate sense of relief at not having to deal with the situation on my own as I had for so many years.

Once we'd left to head back to the plane I felt only extreme self-loathing and anger that I'd let her see that side of my life. If she'd looked me up on the internet she'd already know I had a recovering addict for a mother, but the spin my manager had put on it for the media and the reality of the situation couldn't be more different.

The press had been led to believe that I was supportive of my mom's recovery and understood that her addiction was a disease...blah fucking blah, total bullshit. I was pissed that she still couldn't get her act together. I may support her financially but there was no part of me that understood how she could do that to Justin and Olivia. She'd already screwed up royally in raising me but she had a chance to do it over and do it right this time. The fact that she couldn't stop her hand from raising that glass to her mouth, or the joint or whatever vice she was nurturing at the moment filled me with such rage I found it hard to contain.

Which is why I didn't say much to Ellie. I was afraid I'd be unable to control myself. For years, when it came to my mother, I'd been afraid to let even an ounce of emotion through the dam I'd built in front of my feelings. If I let even the smallest crack form I feared the whole thing would come crashing down, destroying everything in its wake.

Ellie was still in the bathroom changing into her swimsuit when I came out of the bedroom so I made my way outside. I stopped in the great room to turn on the lighting built into the decking and the lights in the pool.

I dove into the deep end of the pool and swam under water to the shallow end where I stood up and wiped the water out of my eyes.

God. Damn.

Ellie stood ankle deep on the pool stairs in a light blue bikini. You know the kind where the top half is only two triangles covering the boobs? Even in my shitty mood it was impossible not to notice the way her tits looked as if they were begging to be touched. Her flat stomach was on display and I could see now that she had a belly button ring. The soft amber light from the pool gave her skin a gold glow.

Asshole. Here I was gawking at her when she probably didn't want anything to do with me. She'd likely only come back here because she felt sorry for me. Attempting to be at least a half decent human being I moved my gaze up her body to her face.

I stifled a laugh. Instead of looking appalled at my blatant appreciation for her body she was returning the favour. Her wide eyes darted around my chest, abs and biceps and I could see she held her breath.

I broke the spell. I didn't know how much longer I could keep it up without wanting to strip her clothes off and pound into her.

"Thanks for coming with me today. I'm sorry you had to deal with all that crap."

She made her way down to the bottom of the steps.

"I was happy to do it. I'm glad I was there."

I let out a sarcastic laugh. "I'm sure. It's not your problem. I shouldn't have let you come. I'm sorry."

Her forehead creased. "I offered. I *am* glad I was there. I enjoyed meeting your brother and sister."

"Yeah, they're great. The rest I'm sure you could have done without."

She tucked a strand of her hair behind her ear. "I won't lie and say I was entirely comfortable."

"Exactly. See...shit. If you don't want to be here, Ellie, I can take you home."

"Why would you say that?"

"Why would you want to be here now that you've seen how fucked up my family is and the shit I have to deal with?"

"Mason—"

"You have no idea what it was like growing up with a mother like that."

She stood silent for a moment and she looked almost...angry. What the hell? Finally she spoke.

"You think you're the only one who didn't have the perfect life growing up? You're right. I don't know what it's like growing up with an addict for a mother. But I do have some experience growing up with a mom who has issues."

Tears had pooled in the corner of her eyes, and she turned to make her way back up the stairs. I felt like a dick. Again. I wasn't trying to upset her but I'd gone and done just that.

"Ellie, wait." She stopped halfway out of the pool.

"I'm sorry. I know I'm not the only one in the world who's had a shit deal."

She turned back around. Her look was wary.

"What was it like? Growing up?" I asked.

She came back down the steps and moved into the corner.

"My mom is what you'd call co-dependent. She can't function without a man in her life. She's always been that way. I told you I don't know my father. Growing up, the men in her life would dote on me. Looking back I can see that it was only to win my mom's affections. I was young and without a dad of my own so I'd look up to them as a father figure, then one day they'd be gone from our lives without warning. She'd be on the hunt for the next love of her life and in would come my new daddy. There was no stability. No way for me to feel secure that if life was good today, it would still be good tomorrow."

She paused but I didn't interrupt her. The look on her face said she was a million miles away, deep in her memories.

"The worst part was watching her change herself into whoever she thought they'd want her to be. If a guy was conservative, she was conservative. If he was wild, she was wild. I don't even think she knows who she is anymore she's been pretending so long. It always seemed so degrading to me."

"That's rough," I said.

"Don't get me wrong. I love my mom. That's why it's so hard to sit by and watch."

"You don't have to explain it to me, Ellie. I understand perfectly what you mean."

"I suppose if anyone would, it'd be you. What was it like for you? Growing up?"

"I grew up poor. In a trailer park. I know, cue the violins. My mom would go on benders and leave me for days at a time. If I was lucky a neighbor would notice before I got too hungry and look out for me until she came back. She used to have men come by the trailer and she'd turn the TV on really loud for me to watch. She told me they were going to go visit together in her bedroom. When I was small I always hated when they came because after they'd leave she'd have cash to burn and that either meant a trip to the liquor store or a dealer's house. I only realized as I got older that she was whoring herself to feed her habit."

Ellie brought her hands up to cover her mouth. "Oh, Mason."

"Anyway, I'm sure you could tell today that my mom and I have our issues. I wanted to explain why so you didn't think I was completely heartless."

"I wouldn't think that. Especially after seeing you with your brother and sister," she said in a soft voice.

"Those two are the only reasons I have anything to do with her still. I can't stomach the thought of them having to deal with any of the bullshit I had to growing up. Up until this week my mom had been sober since I got her into a great facility. That was five years ago."

"You're an amazing brother. And son."

Her words felt like they were ripping open an old wound. I'd carried so much rage and hostility toward my mother for so long, I couldn't comprehend how Ellie could think I was a good son.

"You don't have to say that."

"I know I don't but it's true. How many sons do you think would stick by a mom who'd done all that? A lot of people with your money would walk away and never look back. Or maybe just send money and feel like they'd done enough to help. That's obviously not the case with you."

"I told you...it's not for her."

"You can tell yourself that, Mason, but I saw the look on your face when you saw her today. You were in pain. You were concerned for her."

I couldn't deny it. It'd been years since I'd seen her like that and it had brought me back to when I was young. I refused to let my emotions get involved anymore where my mom was concerned though. There was only so many times you could allow someone to tear you apart emotionally like that.

"I've been protecting them from her since they were born. It was easy when they were younger but they're older now and if she relapses..."

"Hopefully she'll get the help she needs."

"Let's not talk about this anymore. We never got to finish our conversation at your place earlier."

Ellie looked away from me and down at the water. I didn't take it as a good sign.

"I like you, Mason. I just—"

"I like you, too. That's all that matters then."

"Wait. Let me finish." She took a deep breath and soldiered on. "I'm sure you can understand why I have no desire to put my life in the spotlight any more than it's already been lately."

I nodded.

"I've decided I do like you and we should keep seeing each other while you're in town."

I took a step toward her. She put a hand up to signal me to stop.

"That said, I want to try and keep it on the down low. I'll deal with the fallout, if there is any, but the less the better for me."

I smiled. I didn't understand why the hell she'd want to associate with me after what she'd seen of my life today, but I wasn't stupid enough to question it.

"Can I kiss you now?" I asked.

Her tongue darted across her bottom lip and she nodded her head. This day just got a whole lot better.

chapter fifteen

I stood in the corner of the pool as Mason crept toward me; going so slow his movements only caused the faintest ripple on top of the water. Those ripples reached me and splashed up over my breasts and I could feel my nipples tighten. Mason noticed, too. His eyes moved from mine down to my chest and I saw his nostrils flare as he took in a breath.

To my dismay when he reached me he didn't touch me. He lingered close enough that I could feel his body heat, only an inch or two away, and I wanted to launch myself on to him. I was desperate for the feel of his skin against mine.

He reached one hand up to the nape of my neck. I thought he would pull me in to kiss him and my body tensed, ready for it. Instead his other hand came up to my breast and moved the triangle of my bikini top to the side so that my breast was exposed. He'd done it in such a way that he'd barely made contact with my skin. I let out a small moan from the back of my throat out of frustration.

"Quiet. I want to take you in."

Normally I'd be offended by a guy telling me to be quiet but he did it in such a way that it only made me hotter. He repeated the process with the other breast and I couldn't help it. I let out a soft moan again.

"You keep making sounds like that and I'll draw this out even longer. Is that what you want?"

"No. God, no," I whispered.

He stood admiring my breasts. "Beautiful. God, you are so damn beautiful."

Finally after what felt like forever he leaned down and took a nipple into his mouth, his hand on my neck gripping me harder when I tried to close my eyes and move my head back. He ran his tongue around the puckered nub and pulled it out with his teeth as he backed away. I let out a little cry at the pleasure the slight pain had given me. He looked up to me and his eyes were fierce.

"Quiet, Ellie. I don't want to hear a sound out of you until I tell you or I'm going to stop what I'm doing. Understand?"

I nodded. I didn't dare say yes out loud for fear he really would stop. That was the last thing I wanted him to do.

He moved to my other breast and paid it the same attention. The hand that had been at my neck skimmed my stomach and moved beneath my bikini bottom quickly finding my most intimate spot. He gently applied pressure and began moving his fingers flat against me in a circular motion. I bit my lip to keep from crying out at the sensation. I couldn't help but grind my hips into him, my hands clutching at the hard muscles of his shoulders. Tension began humming in my core and I was close to the brink. He must have known because he moved his hand further down and pushed one of his fingers inside me.

"Fuuuck," he moaned.

He moved up from my breasts to take my mouth with his in a crushing, possessive kiss. Our tongues both fighting for control until I acquiesced and let him set the pace. His tongue darted in and out of my mouth mimicking what his two fingers were doing in my core. My hands moved over his head trying to get a grip but there was nothing to grab, his hair was shaved to short.

I was near to bursting. The ministrations of his fingers had me almost there but I needed some pressure on my clit to take me home.

Suddenly his mouth and his fingers were gone, nothing but an empty void left behind. I opened my eyes in panic and Mason grabbed me around the waist and hauled me up onto the edge of the pool. He grabbed the sides of my bikini bottoms and wrenched them off. I lifted my butt off the decking so he could get them all the way down my legs. He was in a hurry now, a man starved. He threw the bottoms behind him without any regard for where they'd end up.

His strong hands pushed my thighs apart. Instead of feeling self-conscious I felt sexy, ready for anything. He looked into my eyes, his own heated and full of lust.

"Now you can make noise. I want to hear you scream my name when you come for me."

Holy. Crap.

I started to move my hands behind me so I could lay down when he grabbed my wrist.

"No. Sit up and watch." He placed my legs over his shoulders and leaned in, licking from the top to bottom of my sex. I moaned. Loudly.

I sat there with my breasts out of my bikini, looking down as Mason's head moved in between my legs. It was the most erotic thing I'd seen in all my life. His perfectly shaped head between my thighs, his tongue lapping at me.

His mouth moved up to concentrate on my clit and he slowly slid a finger inside me again, then two.

"Oh, Mason." I had his head in a death grip while my hips moved rhythmically against his face. His fingers plunged in and out of me at a punishing pace. He sucked my clit in between his lips and it was all too much. My orgasm took me hard and fast and I bucked against him, crying out his name.

I'd only received oral sex a couple of times before, and I'd never been able to finish from it. I'd always been mildly embarrassed about receiving it and couldn't seem to stay in the moment and relax enough to orgasm. I hadn't had that problem with Mason. In fact, I couldn't get enough. I'd just had the orgasm of my life but I still wanted nothing more than for him to bury himself deeply inside me.

He moved back a bit, taking me by the waist and pulling me back into the water. He pressed against me and kissed me passionately, gripping my hair with both hands. I could feel his stiff arousal pressing against my belly and I moved my hand down his rock hard abs toward the prize.

He abruptly pulled away. "No, Ellie. Tonight is just about you."

"But I want you," I said reaching out and trying to touch him again. I could hear the slight whine to my voice even in my lustful state.

He grabbed my hand and put it down by my side.

"I can't tell you what it means to me that you went to Texas with me today. You didn't have to put yourself in the middle of all that and deal with my family shit." He straightened my bikini top so my chest was covered once again.

"The look on your face when you got the call. I just....I know what it's like to have your mom disappoint you. To feel like the parent to your own parent."

"I know you do." He brushed a stray hair off my cheek and tucked it behind my ear, then leaned in to kiss me. This kiss was tender and full of emotion and understanding. When we were done he placed a light kiss on my forehead.

I was a goner. The forehead kiss was like my kryptonite and whatever feelings I had been trying to deny came rushing forward.

"I should take you home. It's late and you've had a long day," he said.

"I don't want to go home." I put my arms around his neck and looked into those hazel and green eyes that brought out the minx in me. My nipples were still hard and I brushed them against his bare chest. I knew he could feel them through my bathing suit.

His hands were on my hips trying to push me away. "Ellie, you don't have to do this."

"I know I don't. I want to." I didn't have any time to spare. He'd be gone in a few short weeks and I wanted to cram every ounce of pleasure into them that I could. At this point the ten-date rule was a distant memory.

His ran his hands over the top of his head and blew out a breath.

"I don't have any condoms. Usually I'd carry some on me but I didn't really think I'd need any on this trip."

I tried my best to ignore the part about him normally having them around and all it implied. I felt more disappointed than I should and I knew my bottom lip was sticking out like I was two years old.

Mason threw his head back and laughed. "Sorry, babe. My bad."

"Well, I still don't want to go home."

"You can stay the night. No problem there but no guarantees I'll be able to keep my hands off you. You might not get much sleep."

Satisfied, I pushed up onto my tippy toes and gave him a quick peck on the cheek. "Good answer." I sauntered out of the pool and made my way across the deck to the chair with the towels on it, my bikini bottom still floating in the pool.

chapter sixteen

I awoke to a lush, warm body next to me. Ellie was draped across her side of the bed, stomach down. The t-shirt she'd borrowed to sleep in had ridden up to her waist exposing her bright pink thong and perfect ass.

Yesterday had been one hell of a ride. I needed to figure out how to deal with my mom long-term but I wasn't going to dwell on that now. It only brought out the worst in me. I'd wait until Ellie left to think about it.

While she warmed my bed I wanted to worship at the altar that was Ellie. My hands itched to run over her ass and taste what lay between. Last night had been beyond what I'd hoped for on the plane ride home. We seemed to be in a good place at the moment. With my schedule nothing could last between us, but I wasn't going to waste time worrying about it. *Carpe diem*, and all that.

Ellie looked peaceful with her dark hair spilled across the pillow. I wondered if she was a morning person. Did she wake up chipper and raring to go, or was she grumpy until she got her first cup of coffee? There was so much I wanted to know about this girl it was ridiculous.

I could think of a few really interesting ways to wake her up. Maybe with a back massage...or maybe I'd pull that pink thong down her legs and nibble between her thighs...or I could push that t-shirt all the way up and over her head, roll her over and massage her front. Great, now I was hard.

I can't believe I hadn't brought condoms with me. It had to be the first time I hadn't had any on me since I was fourteen. What an idiot. I'd sure as hell be visiting a drug store today.

Nothing more physical had happened when we'd gone to bed. We'd had a long day so I settled for having her tucked into my body as we drifted off to sleep. There was something nice about that, too.

My cell phone's shrill ring echoed from the bathroom counter. Ellie shifted on the bed and murmured. I bounded off the bed, trying to answer the call before it woke her up. I couldn't have that. Not if I wanted to enact one of my carefully thought out fantasies on how to wake her.

Rushing into the bathroom I grabbed the phone and hit the answer button before looking to see who it was.

"Mason," Troy boomed through the earpiece.

"Hey, man. What's up? I'm kinda busy right now."

"What the hell is going on? Why weren't you answering your phone last night?"

"I was busy. Why?" I said with an edge to my voice. Troy may have been my manager but he wasn't my caretaker and I didn't like when he treated me like I was *his* employee.

"Oh, nothing much. I just got a call from the *National Examiner* asking if I had any comment about your mom being picked up for drunk and disorderly and property damage. Not to mention they wanted to know about the girl you were with. What. The. Hell. Is. Going. On?"

Shit. I'd meant to give Troy the heads-up yesterday but I'd had two very different women on my mind and for two very different reasons. Still, it wasn't like me to forget to inform my manager of a potential PR nightmare coming our way.

"Sorry, man. I was gassed after everything with my mom yesterday and I forgot to give you a call."

"Well, we need to talk to your publicist to figure out how we're going to handle this situation with your mom. The girl...who's she?"

"Her name's Ellie. But I don't want that released. In fact I want you to do whatever it takes to make sure none of this gets out. I don't want my mom's issues becoming tabloid fodder. If it hits the papers Justin and Olivia are bound to find out. There were some photographers taking pictures when we left. Buy the pictures. Tell them Ellie's a sober companion or counselor, whatever, and that her picture can't be in the media to keep the privacy of her clients."

"Didn't take you long to find a fuck buddy in Virginia did it?" He laughed.

Troy never did treat women with any respect. I hadn't been perfect, either—I'd had my share of one-nighters. I gave them whatever amount of respect they demanded for themselves. I was always honest. At times Troy treated them like they were lucky to be in his presence.

"Whatever, man. Just make sure those pictures don't see the light of day."

"I'll see what I can do."

"Don't see about it, do it. That's why you're my manager. To manage shit like this."

"Fine. You're gonna love the next phone call I got," he said the sarcasm in his voice evident.

"What else could there possibly be..."

"I got a call from the E Network. They're also considering Little Mac for the reality series."

"That waste of skin?" Most people remember the whole east coast rapper versus west coast rapper drama from the 90's. Well, that was a pretty apt description of the situation between Little Mac and me presently. He was my biggest competition in an already competitive industry. That's not why I had no love for the guy. I can admit he puts out some good beats. We'd both grown popular around the same time and for some reason the guy loved to try to get under my skin.

He was a total poser acting like some hard-core gangster rapper, when the truth was he was from Orange County and grew up with a silver spoon in his mouth. He subscribed to the theory that all media attention was good so he'd say shit about me to the press and try to get me to respond, or purposely date someone I had. He was the guy who was always competing with someone, even when he was the only one in the competition.

"They're trying to cover all the bases."

"We can't let him get that show. What do we need to do?"

"I'll provide damage control and let you know how I make out."

"Keep me updated."

Troy hung up and I walked back into the bedroom to see Ellie gazing at me with sleepy eyes. She pulled the covers up over her waist. Damn. As I strode toward her she began stifling a laugh to the point that she covered her mouth with her hand to hide her grin.

"What's so funny?" I asked with a smile.

She nodded toward my lower half and I looked down to see my junk standing at full attention underneath my white boxer briefs. Guess my lower half was still thinking of Ellie in bed while I was on the phone.

I bounced onto the bed beside her, careful not to crush my junk. "You can take credit for that. I was lying here thinking of all the ways I could wake you up before my phone rang."

She laughed again. God, I loved seeing that gorgeous smile on her face. It sounded cheesy as hell but it really did light up the whole room.

She looked a hesitant then said, "Who was on the phone? You sounded angry...was it about your mom?"

"It was my manager, Troy. The E Network is doing a reality show based on a hip-hop artist's life. I was at the top of their list, now they're thinking of offering the job to Little Mac."

"Oh, I'm sorry." She grabbed my hand and gave it a small

squeeze. "I'm surprised you'd want to do a reality show. I didn't get the impression you like having everything about your life on display in the press."

"I'm not excited about having a camera crew follow me around twenty-four/seven, that's for sure. But it's a great way to find a larger audience. I don't want to be a middle-aged man slingin' rhymes for a living. I want to branch out. Get out of the pigeonhole I've been put in, show that I can do more."

"What else do you want to do?" she asked.

"Act, direct, maybe run a clothing business. It's cliché as hell, I know."

"I don't think so."

"If I could use the show as a platform to show there's more to me than just the hip-hop persona, I think it'd help to get people in the industry to take me seriously. That, and the pay is killer."

Ellie scrunched her nose up in the cutest way. It was all I could do not to pinch her cheeks it was so endearing. "Can I say...no, never mind."

"What?"

"Nothing."

"Ellie, tell me what you were going to say," I said, my voice firmer now.

"Well, from the looks of the house in Texas you bought your mom, and the fact that you charter a private plane, and you can afford to rent this house for a month...I'd say money didn't exactly seem like a problem for you."

"No, but—"

"That came out all wrong. It sounds like I've been adding up your assets in my head," she said.

"I understand what you mean. What I was going to say was that no, money is not a problem, but I want to make sure that Justin and Olivia are set up. For life. I don't ever want them to have to want for anything. I want them to have the freedom to do whatever they want when they get older."

Ellie was quiet and sat there thoughtfully. I felt the need to keep talking and fill the void, fearful of her judgment.

"I know that sounds ridiculous. It sounds ridiculous to my ears but you'd be shocked at how easy it is to burn through money, even when you have a lot of it. There's a reason there are so many broke ex-athletes and child stars. You can get caught up in the lifestyle. If there's more than enough in the bank, it won't matter what happens. They'll be safe and secure. No matter what."

Ellie raised her hand to cup my cheek and the sweetest smile crossed her face. "I get it," she said. "You're trying to give them the life you never had growing up."

As soon as I heard the words escape from her plump lips I knew they were true. I'd never thought of it that way. How was it that this girl got me so completely?

I turned my head and kissed the inside of her palm. "I guess, Yeah," I said softly. A small smile crept across her face and she looked into my eyes, her deep brown ones pulling me in until the only thing I was cognizant of were those deep pools of chocolate. "What are you doing today?" I asked and leaned down, brushing her hair away from her neck and kissing her lightly.

She let out a soft sigh and my dick twitched, wanting nothing more than to bury itself in the heat in between her legs so that I could elicit more sighs like that one.

"I have a bunch of résumés that I have to get out. I...ahh, Mason..." she said as I stroked and nibbled on her neck with my tongue. "I...I didn't have a...mmm...chance to get...oh, Mason...to get any out this week." Her hands scratched lightly down my back as she enjoyed my ministrations.

Feeling bolder, and I suppose, horny as all hell, I pulled the sheet down to her waist and moved my hand under the T-shirt she wore. There was something innately sexy about seeing a woman wearing your shirt, and not much more. Some primal part of me loved seeing it, like it was some kind of proclamation that this girl was mine.

I grazed lightly over her nipple and felt it harden further. I rubbed it between my thumb and index finger and she arched with a moan. I moved my mouth along her jaw line and met her lips with a crushing kiss. She responded by wrapping her legs around my waist. My eyes rolled back in my head as she ground herself against me. Minutes later she pulled her lips away from mine and I missed the contact immediately.

"What time is it?" she asked in a breathy voice, panting heavily.

"Hmm?" I'd heard her but couldn't get my brain to function properly to answer her. Most of the blood in my body was headed south of the border at the moment.

"Time, the time?" She unwrapped her legs from around my waist and moved from underneath me. I groaned my disappointment. Sitting up against the bed frame she grabbed her phone off the night table to check the time. "It's ten o'clock. I should probably be going." Disappointment hit me fast and deep. I wanted to spend time with her, even if it meant I only got to hang in her company.

"We were just getting to the good part." I wagged my eyebrows up and down.

She giggled. "The good part will have to wait. My mom's already texted me a couple times to see where I am."

"Mind if I have a quick shower before I take you home?" I needed either a cold shower or to take care of myself on my own, the second option seeming more likely.

"Of course. Mind if I make some coffee while you're in there?"

"You could join me," I said in my most cajoling tone.

"If I join you I don't think I'll be getting home any time soon," she said getting out of the bed. I followed her.

"That's the point." I smiled.

She looked down to my waist. "Actually, I think that's the point."

She laughed and went to make her way out of the room. I came up behind her and wrapped my arms around her front, pinning her to my bare chest.

"Mason," she said in a voice that was half playful, half warning.

I bent my knees and rubbed my obvious arousal across the globes of her perfect ass. Her breath hitched and she leaned her head back against my chest.

For whatever reason at that moment the possible leak of the pictures from the day before popped into my head. It was like having a bucket of cold water thrown on me. I pulled away from Ellie and spun her around to face me. Her eyebrows scrunched together, clearly wondering what was up.

"My manager said something else you should know about."

"Okkkaay," she said, seeming to sense my trepidation.

"*The National Examiner* called him to get a comment about the girl I was with in Texas."

"Those photographers..."

"I'm trying to put a lid on it, make it so the pictures won't be published but I can't promise it'll work."

She took in a big breath and nodded. "Okay, I knew this was a possibility."

"You're not angry with me?"

"Why would I be angry with you?"

"I know you're trying to fade out of the limelight...not be thrust back into it."

She put her hand on my cheek again. It was an intimate gesture and I loved that she was sharing it with me. "I told you last night I'll try to deal with whatever happens. Besides, you think after the orgasm you gave me last night you're going to get rid of me that fast?" She chuckled.

I pulled her into my chest and hugged her fiercely. It was the first time in a long time that I didn't feel the giant weight of responsibility on my shoulders. Oh, it was still there lurking in the background. People were still counting on my success: Justin and Olivia, Troy, the record company, the people who worked for me. Somehow it all seemed easier to handle, though, with Ellie by my side.

chapter seventeen

It was a couple of days before I could see Mason again. It took me longer to get my résumés out than expected and Monday night I had to work late and went home and crashed.

Saturday night had been remarkable. The time spent in the pool, or ahem, on the edge of the pool, was epic. We'd shared a connection beyond the physical...it was intimate and comfortable. Maybe it was because we both understood what it meant to have a less than ideal mother and we didn't have to explain exactly what that meant.

It was clear Mason struggled with his feelings toward his mom. I'd already dealt with my issues, accepting a long time ago exactly who my mother was, but Mason couldn't say the same. When the subject of his mom came up he was intense and steely; like the window to his emotions had closed and was impenetrable. I wished there was something I could do to make him feel better but I knew nothing I said would make up for a childhood with a mom he couldn't count on.

I shook the negative thoughts from my head as I knocked on Mason's door. My mom had had dinner ready when I'd gone home to change after work so I'd eaten with her and Ralph before heading over to the beach house. I didn't know what Mason had planned but I hadn't worn the PP's tonight.

I'd gone back and forth on that, but after what had happened in the pool the last time I was here, what was the point?

Mason opened the door with a giant grin. He was wearing dark grey cargo shorts and a light blue V-neck t-shirt. He made a quick appraisal of my beige shorts and fitted white tank top and pulled me in for a kiss. He smelled like high-end cologne, and the feel of his muscular arms around me made me want to press my thighs together.

I curbed the urge and let out a small sigh as his tongue came into my mouth and I tasted him again. It only fueled my desire and I forced myself to pull away from him to try to maintain some semblance of respectability around him. I didn't want to jump him with one foot in the door like a cat in heat.

"I needed that," he said as he took my hand and pulled me into the house. "It's been a long couple of days."

I laughed. "Didn't you come here to relax?"

"Yeah, but then I met you and since then that's been the furthest thing from my mind."

We were in the kitchen and he backed me up against the fridge and kissed me again. He placed his hands on either side of my face. He started off slow and began building from there until we were both breathing heavy and clutching at each other.

He leaned his forehead against mine. "It really has been torture not seeing you. I was left with just the memory of you and the memory isn't near as good as the real thing." He kissed my forehead before turning around to grab something out of one of the cupboards.

That damn forehead kiss again. What the hell did I find so endearing about it? I was pretty much putty in his hands when he did that.

"I remembered that you'd ordered red wine when we were at the restaurant that night so I picked some up for you."

"Thanks. That was sweet."

"Care for a glass?"

"Absolutely."

He poured me a glass and went to the corner cupboard and reappeared with arms full of every confection known to man. "I thought we could watch a movie tonight. I didn't know what type of munchies you liked so I got a little of everything."

"Boy, I'll say. You look like you robbed a convenience store." I laughed.

He started spreading our options out on the granite counter. "Let's see, we've got popcorn, chocolate, pretzels, chips, cheesies... I even picked up some assorted nuts."

It was likely childish that I had to try so hard not to blurt out the naughty joke that was ran through my head at that moment. "Chocolate, always chocolate."

"Done. I'm going with the chips."

We grabbed our treats and our alcohol and made our way into the great room to get settled on the couch. Cuddled up to Mason all night? Yeah, I could definitely handle that. Besides, everyone knew that movie was basically code for making out, and that sounded good.

We settled into the couch and Mason grabbed the remote off the coffee table. "Any requests?"

"Don't worry I won't force you to watch some chick flick."

"Chick flicks can be okay depending on who's in them," he said.

Realization dawned that it wasn't improbable he could have dated one of the actresses in whatever movie we picked. I wasn't sure I could handle watching him watch a movie with a woman he'd dated, or more likely slept with before. I'd be distracted the entire time, thinking of him watching her on screen reliving some memory they'd made together.

"I only have one request," I said. It was petty and juvenile but I didn't care.

"Shoot."

"I don't want to watch any movie starring an actress you've dated."

"Ellie, that's not how I meant it."

"It's not a big deal. I just don't want to be distracted the whole time thinking of you and her...you know...instead of watching the movie."

Mason pressed his lips together and seemed about to argue with me. He must have thought better of it because he just nodded and turned his attention to the TV. He began scrolling through the list of available choices when he passed a comedy I'd been wanting to see for a while.

"Oh, what about that one. Have you seen it?"

"No, but...um..."

"Never mind." I knew what that meant. Rather than dwell on it and let it ruin my night I tried not to think about it.

A couple of minutes later he whizzed by a blockbuster action flick that looked interesting.

"Oh, that one's supposed to be good."

He turned his head and without saying anything I could tell he'd been involved with the actress in it. Seriously? She was a huge star. We're not talking B list movie actress here. I was pretty sure I'd read somewhere she made twenty million a picture. I rolled my eyes at him and let him continue scrolling through the list.

Eventually we settled on a romantic comedy and a few minutes in I'd forgotten all about my earlier insecurities. Instead I decided not to let anything ruin our night together. We were on borrowed time and this was our first real date where everything was out on the table. No more secrets, or omissions of truth. He knew my story, I knew his.

I wrapped my arm around his hard waist, settled my head into the nook of his outstretched arm and heaved a contented sigh.

"Everything okay?" he asked as those sexy eyes of his looked down on me.

I returned his gaze full on. "Perfect."

The movie ended and we headed into the kitchen to refill our drinks. I poured myself another glass of wine while Mason grabbed himself a beer from the fridge. I took a seat at the centre island and sipped my wine.

"What do you want to do now?" I asked him when he leaned against the breakfast bar beside me.

"Hmmm..." He brushed my hair behind my shoulder and leaned in to nuzzle my neck. "I can think of a few things we could do."

The whiskers on his face tickled me and I giggled and brought my shoulder up to my chin. Mason moved away to face me.

"Not the reaction I was hoping for," he said wryly. "Do you wanna watch another movie?"

"Nah. Let's do something more fun," I suggested.

"More fun, eh? Hmmm...we could go skinny dipping in the pool."

I raised my eyebrows at him.

"Don't like that one. Okay, I could check your body for any strange-looking moles. You can't be too careful about skin cancer living in all this Virginia sunshine, you know."

I grinned at him this time.

"Damn, you're a high-maintenance girl. What about beer pong? We could play a few rounds."

"What, are we fraternity brothers now?" I laughed.

"No, but we could always make it interesting. Make up our own rules."

That piqued my interest. "Such as?"

"Such as if you miss you either have to drink, answer a question truthfully, or remove an article of clothing."

I laughed. "Are you serious?"

"I know you're concerned about losing to me, Ellie. But don't worry, I'll go easy on you." He winked and gave me a lop-sided grin that accentuated his dimple. God, he was handsome.

"Is that right? Well, we'll see about that. When I'm finished with you you'll be begging me for mercy."

"I certainly hope so," he said with a sly grin.

It took a few minutes to set everything up but once we were finished we stood at opposite ends of the island with six cups each in front of us. Mine held a small amount of wine in each, and his held a larger amount of beer. I'd reasoned that wine was stronger than beer and to be fair he'd have to consume more than me in each cup. He'd bought my argument and agreed. Since we didn't have a ping pong ball lying around we improvised and used a piece of tin foil we'd scrunched up into a ball.

Mason motioned to me with his hand. "Ladies first." He had a smug look and I couldn't wait to wipe it off his face.

I closed one eye, held the tinfoil ball in my hand and eyed up my targets on the other end of the island. I released the tinfoil and watched it sail toward Mason, where it landed in the cup closest to me.

"Woohoo!" I cheered, jumping up and down.

"Beginners luck."

"I don't think so. Now, I get to choose and I say you have to remove an article of clothing." I crossed my arms over my chest and cocked my hip out to one side, feeling confident in my ability to kick his ass.

"All right then." Mason grabbed his t-shirt behind his neck with one hand and pulled it over his head and let it slide down his arms and fall to the floor in front of him. He kicked it to the side with his foot.

I should've given more thought to my tactic. Having to see Mason's rippled six-pack every time I took a shot was going to be distracting as hell. He leaned forward to grab the tinfoil out of the cup and the muscles in his chest and abs flexed and tightened with the small effort. Yep, I definitely should've made him drink. Damn.

"I hope you're ready for me to return the favour." He lined up his shot, released it, and it almost went in one of my glasses but bounced off the rim. "Damn it."

"Now, now, don't be a spoiled sport," I said while shaking a finger at him. It was my turn again and I landed another shot. This time he could take a shot. Getting him tipsy might affect his throwing abilities and help me win. "Take a drink."

"I see, trying to get your opponent drunk are you?" He lifted the glass to his lips and swallowed the beer.

"There's nothing wrong with employing a strategy to ensure my victory."

"Strategize this." He let the tinfoil loose and it landed right in one of my cups. "Take it off," he said and cocked an eyebrow at me.

I blew out a breath and then lifted my tank top over my head and threw it on one of the stools. I was wearing a white lacy bra. I told myself it was no different than the two times he'd already seen me in a bikini but someone forgot to tell my nerves because my tummy got the swirly feeling in it again. I clamped down my self-consciousness and didn't wrap my arms around my chest the way I wanted to.

From the other side of the island Mason gazed at me through half-lidded eyes. All right, he wants to do this? Let's do it. I grabbed the piece of tinfoil out of the cup, threw it and it landed in another one of his. "Drink."

He said nothing, locked eyes with me while raising the cup to his lips and drank down the contents of the cup. He pulled the tinfoil ball from the bottom of the cup. "Game on."

We went back and forth for a while, each of us getting in more shots in than we missed. He now stood only in his Calvin Klein boxers. I was pretending not to notice the very noticeable lump underneath. When Mason sunk our makeshift ball in my cup and told me to remove an article of clothing I didn't find it as difficult as the first time. It's a teensy bit possible that was a side effect of the wine I'd been consuming. I started to undo the top button on my shorts.

"Wait," Mason said from the other side of the island. "Let me help you with those."

He didn't have to ask me twice. I'd been dying for him to kiss me for the last half hour but he'd been maddeningly well-behaved. He came to stand behind me and wrapped his hands around my midsection until he reached the button of my shorts. His hard chest pressed into my back and it was all I could do not to rub my ass across him like an animal in heat.

He slowly undid the button and lowered the zipper down inch by agonizing inch. My breathing had grown heavier and his breath tickled my ear every time he exhaled. I stood waiting for him to dip his hand into my shorts, instead he grabbed the bottom of them and pulled them slowly down my legs. When his hands couldn't pull them down any farther he crouched down until he was on his knees behind me. My shorts slid down to my ankles and I stepped out of them.

Thank God I'd ditched the idea of wearing the P.P.'s tonight. Instead, I'd worn the matching white thong to my bra. Mason ran each of his strong hands across my ass. My breathing hitched in anticipation of what was next. As he stroked my ass he planted a kiss on each side, then stood and walked back to his side of the island.

I was a little dumbstruck and a whole lot disappointed. Seriously? He was going to leave me hanging like that? He smirked at me from the other side of our battlefield. Hmmm...well, two could play that game.

I grabbed the tinfoil and leaned over the counter like I was gauging the distance to the cups, deciding which to aim for. The movement made my breasts almost spill out of my bra and it was clear that Mason had noticed. I mean the evidence was right there pointing in my direction if you catch my drift.

"Hmmm...which one should I aim for?" I shimmied a bit, causing my breasts to jiggle. Mason took a large gulp. Seemed my work here was done. I stood up straight, aimed for a cup and hit my target. "All right, you're getting truth."

Mason shook his head, his eyes still darting between my face and my chest.

I laughed a little to myself while trying to think of what I wanted to ask him. Our earlier questions had been tame to say the least: What's your favourite color? When was your first kiss? Did you ever have a crush on one of your teachers? To which I found out that Mason did in fact have a crush on his third-grade teacher Mrs. Henderson.

I didn't want to ask a tame question, though. I knew it was the slight buzz I had going, but I wanted to ask him something I probably wouldn't ask otherwise. I knew what I wanted to know most. Had this man ever given his heart to anyone? He was rich, successful and led a life of fame that I couldn't even begin to understand. I wanted to know if he had it in him to really love someone, or if everything was a good time to him. I'd never ask it in the context of what was going on between the two of us, but I could use this game to my advantage.

"Have you ever been in love?"

He blinked a few times and the expression on his face turned to one of hard plains. "Once."

Okay, that was good I guess. Wait. Was it? Did I want him to fall in love with me? It was way too early to be thinking of anything like that. But now I wanted to know more about who he was in love with and when.

"When was this?"

"It was a few years back."

"What happened?"

"The relationship crashed and burned."

"Do you still love her?"

"No."

A heavy silence fell between us. The mood had somehow gone from jovial to serious with my questions.

"Ellie, I really don't want to talk right now."

I swallowed past the lump in my throat. "What do you want to do?"

"Not what. Who."

He walked around the island toward me, never once breaking eye contact. When he reached me he put his hands around my waist and lifted me up to sit on the countertop. The granite was cold underneath me. He placed a hand on my inner thigh and exerted some pressure for me to part my legs. I did and he stepped in between. I put my hands around his neck. One of his hands trailed down my arm and when it reached my shoulder he brought it to the back of my head and scrunched my hair up in his hand. His other hand rested at my waist. He stood there looking at me with lust in his eyes for what felt like hours. The sweet torture of having him so near, but not having his lips on me was more than I could bear. I pulled on his neck and brought his face to mine.

The moment our lips touched it was like the starting gun had gone off at the beginning of a race. Our tongues met forcefully, each one looking for dominance over the other. I wrapped my legs around his hips and we ground ourselves into one another. His hands groped my body while my nails ran down his back.

I groaned into his mouth when his hardness met with a particularly sensitive spot on me.

He brought his hands to either side of my face and pushed them up into my hair. "Damn, Ellie. If you don't want this to lead anywhere that's cool. But we're gonna have to stop now. I don't know if I'll have the strength to end it if we keep this up much longer."

"I want to keep it up. I don't want to stop," I said.

A giant grin crept slowly onto his face. He picked me up by the waist. I was straddling him, his hands on my ass as we made our way to the master bedroom.

There was nothing slow and methodical about our approach with each other this evening. Tonight we were two people who'd denied themselves a physical manifestation of their lust and need for each other, who were now going to let all barriers drop. I knew we wouldn't be having sex, or making love—it'd be carnal and animalistic. And I loved it.

chapter eighteen

I walked through the great room with Ellie wrapped around me. I'd never needed someone physically so badly in my life. She was so goddamn beautiful, and I if I didn't bury myself in her soon, I'd go mad.

When I reached the bedroom I laid her on the white comforter. She unwrapped her legs from around me and shimmied herself up to the top of the mattress so her head rested on a pillow. She laid there wearing only a white lace bra and matching thong. If the sight of her perfect body hadn't already completely undone me, the expression on her face would have.

She looked at me as if I were the centre of her universe, like I was the only one who could provide her with what she needed right now. And I would. I wouldn't stop until she was screaming my name out in ecstasy, begging me to both stop and keep going at the same time.

I crawled toward her on my hands and knees and the pace of her breathing picked up the closer I got. I hovered above her, my knees and hands on either side of her mouth-watering curves, and trailed one finger along the lace edging of her bra. Her breathing hitched.

Lowering myself enough to reach her mouth, but so no

other part of our bodies were touching, I licked along the seam of her lips and her jawline until I made my way to her earlobe. I gave it the tiniest nibble and then sucked it into my mouth.

"Mmmm," she moaned beneath me. Her hands came around me and tried to force me down onto her body but I was stronger and I wasn't finished my slow torture yet. I wanted her begging me before I gave her what she wanted.

I moved my mouth away and brought my hands to the front clasp of her bra. When I released it and moved the cups to the side, her luscious tits spilled out, her nipples already erect. I laid down beside her, while Ellie tossed her bra to the floor beside the bed.

I bent my head and brought one nipple into my mouth, swirling my tongue around its taut peak and stretching it with my mouth as I backed away to give the same treatment to her other one. Ellie's fingers dug hard into my shoulders. I kneaded and tasted and sucked her tits until she was panting my name over and over again in between her moans.

I trailed kisses from her breasts up to her mouth; I needed to taste her again. I plunged my tongue into her mouth and moved my hand down to her warm centre, pulling her thong to the side and pushing a finger inside her. "You're so wet. So ready."

She moaned in response and squeezed my shoulders tighter.

I pushed in another finger and brought it out slowly. I repeated the action over and over until my fingers were coated in her desire and she was writhing underneath me. She arched her back every time I pushed into her. When she brought her hands up to her own tits and squeezed them I swear I almost came. Watching her come undone so completely was more than I could handle. I was desperate to get inside her.

I grabbed each side of her thong and pulled it down her long legs.

Ellie sat up slightly and reached for the waistband of my Calvin Klein's. I got up onto my knees so she could pull them down. When my cock sprang free it was only inches from her face and I couldn't help but fantasize about what her plump lips would feel like wrapped around my jutting cock. She pulled my boxers down until they were at my knees.

I hadn't been expecting her to fist the base of my dick, and I let out an audible hiss when she touched me.

"I want you in my mouth," she said in a low seductive voice.

Was there any better combination of words in the English language? Christ. I was so tuned up if I let her put her mouth on me this would be over before it even began. I'd been fantasizing about Ellie placing her lips around me, but it wouldn't be tonight.

I gently placed my hands on her shoulders. "No, Ellie."

She looked up at me with those big doe eyes full of hurt and confusion. "Why won't you let me do this for you? You stopped me last time too..."

I stroked her hair away from her face in what I hoped was a reassuring gesture. "Believe me. I've fantasized about you doing that to me more than you could imagine. But I want inside you, and you go there tonight," I said pointing to my junk, "there'll be none of that."

Her forehead creased in confusion.

"I feel like a fourteen year old boy saying this, but I'll finish. I won't be able to stop myself."

"Oh." She looked pleased with my answer and laid herself back down on the bed.

I got off the bed and pushed my boxers the rest of the way down my legs. Opening the nightstand drawer, I pulled out one of the condoms I'd put there. After the last time, I wasn't going to be caught without one again.

"Let me," Ellie said with her arm outstretched. I passed it over to her and moved back up onto the bed.

She ripped the package open with her teeth, pulled the condom out, and sat up. I moved in front of her and straddled her legs. She placed the condom at the tip of my cock and pinched the tip of the rubber then slowly slid the rest down the length of my shaft.

Seeing her hands work along the length of my cock was all I could take. As soon as she finished rolling the condom down I pushed her back onto the bed and covered my body with hers. She wrapped her legs around my waist and I positioned myself at her entrance.

I was finally going to claim what was mine.

I loved it when Mason took the reins. In my daily life I wanted control of my own destiny, but in the bedroom he could call the shots with no arguments from me. The look that came over his face was primitive and fierce. His green eyes filled with lust and determination. He was over top of me, and the muscles in his arms bunched.

He pushed into me slowly, inch by long inch, his abdominal muscles contracting and his eyes rolling back into his head.

"You feel so fucking good," he moaned.

I was so full with him inside of me that when he pulled himself out again slowly I whimpered at the loss. He pumped into me a few times at an agonizingly slow pace. I wanted to scream in frustration. He was so controlled. All I wanted was for him to take me.

Claim me.

To own me.

He pulled out so that only his tip was still in me. He paused before slamming back into me in one thrust.

I looked up at him as he worked himself in and out of me over and over again at a punishing pace. He was raw power. His muscles tensing and contracting with his movements. This was a man who knew what he wanted and he wanted me. A shiver ran up my spine that at this moment at least, this amazing man that was Mason Nash, was one hundred percent focused on me. It was a heady feeling.

The sound of my ass slapping into his hips only served to increase my desire. He bent down to take one of my nipples into his mouth, circling it with his tongue and playing with it between his teeth.

"Oh, yes, yes," I moaned into his mouth as he moved from my breasts to my lips. After he'd kissed me for a few minutes he raised himself up off of me so our chests were no longer touching.

"I want you to say my name when you come, Ellie. I want you looking at me and screaming my name."

I'd do anything he told me to right now if he just wouldn't stop. Heat pooled low in my belly and I knew my release was imminent. He circled his hips when he was deep inside and that heat turned to fire. I couldn't get enough of it. I tried to hold off my orgasm as long as I could because I didn't want the feeling to end.

When I couldn't deny it any longer I let the sensations wash over me and screamed Mason's name. My core spasmed and contracted around Mason's shaft. I opened my eyes to look into Mason's half-lidded green ones.

"Fuck, yeah. Ellie..." Mason moaned and I felt him twitch inside of me with his own release. Every muscle in his body tensed as he pumped into me a few more times before moving onto his back beside me. I tucked myself into his side and lay there catching my breath. He had one hand on my ass, the other was stroking lightly up and down my arm.

"That was...I don't even have the words," he said still breathing heavy.

"I know." He bent his head and kissed my forehead. Why did that one action threaten to open up a well of emotions I didn't want to deal with? I wouldn't ruin our time together by thinking about what would happen when it was time for him to leave. I wouldn't. *Enjoy it while you can.*

"Give me a second, babe, I gotta take care of this condom." I moved off him and he got out of bed and walked to the ensuite. I missed the hard warmth of his body instantly.

Moments later, he crawled back in bed and we positioned ourselves like we were before.

"Have you heard anything more from your manager about the pictures that got taken in Texas?" I asked.

"I haven't heard back from him yet. I don't want you to worry too much about it though. I'll do whatever it takes to protect you from the media, Ellie." His muscled arms wrapped around me and gave me a squeeze.

"You can't protect me, Mason. I wanted to know so I'd be prepared that's all. How did you deal with it when you first became famous?"

I felt Mason shrug his shoulder underneath me. "I didn't really. At first I basked in it. The attention, the money, the women. I won't lie and say I didn't like it. I was a poor kid from the trailer park who thought I'd be living pay cheque to pay cheque all my life...if I was lucky. I could never have conceived of any of this happening to me."

"When did it change?"

Mason sighed. "You asked me earlier if I'd ever been in love. I was once. Rebecca and I were together a while. I loved her. I thought the feeling was mutual. It wasn't. She betrayed me and that was the first time I really looked at the people I'd surrounded myself with. I realized everyone was there to get a piece of me. Take their share of my success. After the incident with Rebecca I took off the rose-coloured glasses. Got rid of the dead weight in my life."

"I don't know if I could deal with that. Is it worth it?"

"I get to do something I really enjoy. I get to see and do things I wouldn't be able to otherwise. There's a cost, sure, but Olivia and Justin have a better life because of it."

"Still, not feeling like you can trust anyone..."

"That's one of the reasons I like you so much. My fame actually works against me with you. I don't have to worry about you selling a story to the tabloids, or calling in a tip about where we might be so a picture of us together will show up in the media. I know you aren't going to leak any of the texts I send you."

"But you can't know that about me. How could you? We just met."

He bent his head and kissed my forehead while squeezing me with his arms. "I know."

With that declaration Mason Nash stole a sliver of my heart. I knew his trust wasn't given easily.

I didn't like how much I was growing to need him, how quickly. I didn't want to feel attached to him. I wasn't a novice at relationships but if I was honest I'd never *really* loved anyone. I always knew at the back of my mind that if things didn't work out I could cut and run and life would continue as I knew it.

I couldn't escape the feeling that when Mason left, my life wouldn't go on as it had before. I'd be altered in some way. I hoped against all hope that the piece of my heart he took with him wouldn't be too large.

We lay in silence for a long while. Our breathing became steadier and my eyes grew heavy as sleep took hold. I fell asleep on Mason's chest listening to his rhythmic heartbeat, hoping that when he left he wouldn't rip mine from my chest.

chapter nineteen

When I woke Ellie was draped across my chest, her dark hair spilled over top of me. The vanilla scent of her shampoo filled my nostrils and I inhaled deeply. I liked waking up with her near, especially if it meant I'd gotten to be deep inside her the night before.

The sex had been incredible. Beyond incredible—fucking fantastic. Best ever. Gold star. The. Absolute. Shit.

I couldn't wait to do it again.

And again.

And then again.

Speaking of which, time for Ellie to get up so we could make that happen. She didn't need any more beauty sleep. She was gorgeous. Another hour of sleep wasn't going to change that.

I rubbed my hand lightly up and down the bare expanse of her back, wishing she was lying face up so that I was rubbing her front. When she didn't so much as stir I applied a little more pressure. Still nothing. Apparently Sleeping Beauty was hard to rouse after a night of bedroom calisthenics.

"Ellie. Babe," I said in a hushed voice. No response. I really was going to start calling her Sleeping Beauty. If memory served the prince had had to wake her up with a kiss.

I could handle that, although I had a kiss of a different kind on my mind.

I gently eased myself out from underneath her. She stirred a little and mumbled something then repositioned herself on her back and fell still and silent again. Perfect. I moved down to her legs and separated them so that I could get myself in between them. Her head tossed to the side but she didn't stir.

My cock was as hard as a rock in anticipation of tasting her again. I bent my head down and licked her bottom to top. I couldn't see how I'd ever get enough of this. I stuck my tongue in and out of her like I was banging her with it and she began to moan in her sleep. I moved up and started vibrating my tongue on her clit, keeping my eyes on her face the entire time. When I exerted a little more pressure her eyes flew open and locked with mine.

"Oh God, Mason. What are you....ahhh."

Her hands came down on top of my head and she pushed my face into her as she rocked her hips. It was fucking hot how responsive she was. I knew she was close to coming when she cried out. I slipped a finger inside her and it was like flicking a switch. She came and when her hands tried to pull my head away I resisted until I'd wrung every last shiver and contraction out of her.

I loved doing that to her. I could do it all day every day just to see the look on her face after she came. The look she had right now. One of pure satisfaction and contentment. To know that I was the one who put that flush in her cheeks made me feel like a goddamn superhero.

Normally I'd be looking for her to return the favor so I could find my own release. I didn't seem to need that with her. Don't get me wrong; I was hard as a rock and my dick was aching for Ellie to touch it. But the satisfaction of giving that to Ellie more than made up for it.

I moved up beside her again. She was completely relaxed and let me mould her body to my own as I positioned her in the nook of my arm, her head tucked into my neck.

She spoke after a few minutes. "That was some way to wake up." Her voice was still gravelly.

"Good. That was what I was aiming for."

"You can wake me up like that anytime." She giggled. I loved her laugh. It was so joyful and melodic sounding. I could easily sample it in one of my tracks. Actually, that idea wasn't half bad...

"Mason?"

"Huh?"

"Where'd you go just now?"

"I was thinking about your laugh."

"What about it?" I could hear the confusion in her voice.

"Just how much I love hearing it."

She moved her head and kissed my neck then snuggled herself back into me. I know I sounded like a pussy but I swear my heart swelled in my chest. Knowing I said something that made her happy did that.

"Would you want to meet a couple of my friends? If not, I totally understand, it's not a big deal. I was going to get together with them tonight and I thought you might want to come."

I smiled thinking it was a good sign that she wanted me to meet her friends. "Sure. That sounds good."

"You don't need to worry about them telling anyone you're in town. They've both been sworn to secrecy."

"If you trust them, I'm not worried."

"My friend Katie is a big fan of your music."

"I like her already." I laughed and Ellie smacked me in the gut playfully. "Apparently you're not a fan though."

"Why do you say that?" She sat up and turned to look at me. The sheet had fallen around her waist and she hadn't seemed to notice. I sure had.

"The first night I drove you home...my song was playing on the radio and you made me change the station because you couldn't stand it."

Ellie's hand came to cover her mouth and her cheeks

turned bright pink. "That was your song? Oh my God. I'm so embarrassed. I had no idea."

I laughed again. She was cute when she was embarrassed. "It's not a big deal. My music's not for everyone."

"Don't take it personally. I don't know anything about hip-hop. I've never really listened to it before."

"Well, we'll have to rectify that, won't we? I can think of few ways you could make it up to me if you wanted." I reached for her and placed my hand behind her neck and pulled her to me. The minute our lips made contact my cell phone rang.

"Damn it," I murmured against her lips.

"It's okay. You answer it. I'm going to use the bathroom." She gave me a quick peck and got off the bed, taking the sheet with her, and walked to the bathroom, closing the door behind her. I don't know why she was being so modest when she had such a rockin' body. I'd never understand women.

I picked up my phone and saw that it was Troy. "Hey, man."

"Mason, I was able to get you a meeting with the E Network executives so we can plead your case as to why you're the better choice than Little Mac for the reality show."

"Good work. When's the meeting?" I asked.

"Tonight. Six o'clock. Can you fly to L.A. by then?"

Damn it. I'd just promised Ellie I'd meet her friends. I couldn't ditch this meeting with the executives though. It may be my only chance to schmooze them before a decision was made.

"Yeah, I'll be there."

"Great. Let me know when your plane is coming in and I'll meet you at the airport so we can discuss our approach beforehand."

"Will do. Listen, what happened with the story? You didn't get back to me." I heard the irritation in my tone.

"Relax. I was able to squash it. I told them there was a misunderstanding regarding your mother. As for that girl I gave them your story, said she was an addiction counselor for a rehab facility brought in to assist the guy your mom was with and that they needed to keep her identity private. They bought it for now but you're going to have the give the *Examiner* an exclusive first interview the next time we have any big news to share. It's the only way I could get them to agree not to pursue the story."

"Whatever."

"You sure this broad is worth the trouble?" My fists clenched at Troy's use of the derogatory term in reference to Ellie.

"Don't call her a broad."

He laughed but there was a bitter edge to it. "I'm sure that's probably what she is. I've seen enough of them float in and out of your life over the years. Always looking out for numero uno."

"She's not like that."

"Oh shit," he started laughing. "This girl has really got you pussy whipped. Don't forget to bring your balls to L.A. with you. You'll need them for this meeting." As was his way, Troy hung up without saying goodbye.

Ellie emerged from the bathroom, sheet wrapped around herself and sat beside me on the bed. "Everything okay?"

"I've got good news and bad news. Which do you want first?"

"Hmmm...good news."

"That's interesting."

"What?"

"That you picked good news. Most people do the reverse."

"I'd rather know the good news first. That way I can keep it in mind and be grateful for it when I hear the bad news."

"Good news it is. Troy was able to stop the *Examiner* from printing the pictures of the two of us in Texas."

"That is good news." Her face lit up. She was sitting with her legs tucked underneath her and she bounced excitedly on the mattress. I tried especially hard not to notice the way her tits bounced up and down underneath the thin sheet as she did it.

"The bad news is that I have to fly to L.A. so I won't be able to meet your friends tonight."

"Oh, well, that's okay." She put up a good front but I saw a flash of disappointment cross her face. I felt like an asshole. I didn't want to be the one to put that disappointed look on her face. Ever. "Troy's managed to get me an interview with the producers of the reality series so we can try to sell them on using me for the show."

"I understand."

"Today's the only time they could meet with me."

"Mason, I said it's fine. I get it." She was saying the right words but I could tell it bothered her anyway.

I leaned in to kiss her. "I'll only be gone the one night and then I'll be back and we can do more of this."

"Good because any more than one night and I might have to take matters into my own hands."

I pushed her back onto the mattress. "You always know just what to say."

As much as I wanted to rip the sheet away and bury myself inside her for the foreseeable future, I had travel arrangements to make and needed to get my ass in gear if I was going to be in L.A. by this afternoon.

I gave her a quick kiss and begrudgingly got into the shower.

I had a plane to catch.

chapter twenty

It was stupid of me to assume the fact that Mason and I had slept together meant something for our relationship, or whatever the hell it was we were doing. We'd only been together for the first time last night and he was already leaving. I was so sick of people always leaving me.

This was exactly why I couldn't allow myself to get in too deep with Mason. I knew he'd be gone in a few short weeks but it stung that immediately after sleeping with me he was taking off across the country.

Foolishly when he'd agreed to meet my friends I thought that meant something. That we were more than we were. What a chick thing to say. "I thought I meant more to him." Freaking shoot me. I refuse to be that girl.

I wasn't mad at Mason. It's not like he'd misled me or anything. In fact, I should be glad that I knew where we stood now. I needed to get back to my own life, not this fantasy world I'd been living in since we'd met, thinking I could have any type of future or real relationship with a celebrity like Mason.

I was hurt by his actions, but I liked spending time with him and the sex had been off the charts... I'd enjoy what our remaining weeks together had to offer and then get on with my life once he was gone.

I'd left when Mason got in the shower as I still had to go home and shower and change before I headed into work. My mom and Ralph were still sleeping, or doing whatever it is they do first thing in the morning, (I was still trying to get the image my mom had painted for me out of my head), so I didn't have to deal with her asking where I'd been last night.

I'd have to face Katie at work though. She knew I had headed over to Mason's last night and she'd want details but I wasn't sure I wanted to share them. I still hadn't decided how I felt about everything myself.

That afternoon I'd found myself with nothing to do but let my mind wander. I had the fleeting idea to Google Mason's name.

I knew I shouldn't, that it was self-sabotage. There's nothing Google was going to show me that was going to make me feel better.

I *knew* this. I knew it but I still found myself typing his name into the search field multiple times, then bitch-slapping myself mentally and backspacing until it disappeared. After an hour I finally caved, typed Mason Nash into Google and hit enter.

I was in no way prepared for the images and headlines that assaulted me. There were pictures of him with pop stars, actresses and—come on....seriously?—actual Victoria's Secret models. I thought he'd been joking. There were some candid shots of him kissing some of them...those ones made my stomach turn. It was stupid but jealousy seeped inside me through every pore. Logically I knew all these pictures of Mason with other women had happened before I even knew he existed. Apparently my brain didn't feel like doing logical at the moment.

I realized that this was the price of fame. Every moment of your life lived out in the public sphere was immortalized forever. It could all be brought back with the click of a mouse and some tapping on the keys.

A few of the headlines claimed he was cheating on someone, others that a woman in question was cheating on him. Apparently he'd been a part of a wild party in the penthouse suite at the Roosevelt in Hollywood and some known adult film stars were seen leaving the hotel the following morning.

I closed the search page. I didn't want to see any more. I already had the sight of Mason kissing other women now firmly embedded in my head. Besides, most of it was probably lies anyway. I knew better than anyone how good the media was at twisting things to suit their needs.

Still, I couldn't help but compare myself to some of the women. What could Mason possibly see in me when he was used to dating women like that? I hated how insecure I was. It wasn't a feeling I was used to but it seemed that being with Mason brought it out in me.

My phone vibrated in my purse so I pulled it out to see I had a new text from Mason.

Wish I was still there. I'm looking at the wrong ocean.

I smiled to myself thinking how sweet his words were, then reminded myself not to put too much stock in them.

Jeff's voice came from down the hall and was getting closer so I turned my phone off and threw it back in my purse.

The rest of the day passed in a blur since the reason for Jeff's visit to my desk had been to lay a shitload of work on my lap. I walked in my house after work and immediately went up to my room to lie down. I was bagged from my lack of sleep the night before. I expected to watch a half hour of TV or so to unwind. The next thing I knew I was wiping drool off my face and it was already dark outside.

I glanced at the clock. It was 9:30 p.m. I grabbed my purse from beside the bed to see if I'd missed any calls and realized I'd forgotten to turn my phone back on when I'd left work. I hit the power key and the text notifications started chiming.

There was one from Katie:

Don't think I didn't notice you avoided being alone with me at work today. That can only mean one thing...you hit it! I want details!!

I rolled my eyes. Typical Katie.
Skye had sent me a few messages, too:

How'd it go last night? How many screaming orgasms did you get? ;)

Hello? Why aren't you answering me? Are you still unconscious from all the mind-blowing sex?

We're here. Where R U?

If I don't hear from you soon I'm driving over there...

Dealing with my friends was like dealing with a bunch of horny teenaged guys, I swear. I quickly texted Skye to let her know I'd fallen asleep when I got home and wouldn't be making drinks with her and Katie tonight.

Bullshit. You're staying in to bang that hottie again. No worries. I'd do the same. Call me tomorrow!!!!!

Didn't I wish that was true.
I scrolled through my phone again. The last text I'd received had been from Mason. My breath hitched. I had equal parts excitement and trepidation running through my veins. I wanted to hear from him but my reaction made me remember that I needed to get a handle on my emotions before he had the ability to really hurt me.

Everything okay? Didn't hear back from you earlier.
XOXO (The Guy Whose World You Rocked Last Night)

I laughed to myself and pondered what to write back when my phone vibrated in my hand. It was another text from Mason.

Ellie...you there?

I typed a reply back.

I'm here. Sorry, fell asleep after work. Just woke up.

Seconds after I hit Send my phone rang.

"Hello?" I answered.

"Hey, babe. How are you?" Mason asked.

My heart fluttered at the term of endearment. He wasn't making keeping my distance easy. "I'm good. I didn't see your text earlier, sorry."

"I'm glad that's all it was. You were starting to give me a complex. I thought maybe I was the only one that enjoyed myself last night."

"I thought it was pretty obvious that I enjoyed myself," I said wryly.

"I would have thought that was true after a few orgasms...but you seemed to be in your head when you were leaving. Then when you didn't text me back I thought maybe you were having second thoughts about us again."

He couldn't really be worrying that I was going to reject him could he? This rich, famous, piece of male perfection that any woman would be glad to get her hands on?

"No, nothing like that. I've made my decision and I'm sticking by it. I'm going to enjoy our next few weeks together."

"The next few weeks. Right." There was something different about his voice but I couldn't put my finger on it. Looking for a change of subject I asked him how his meeting had gone. "It went well. I think we managed to convince the executives that I'm the right one for the show. They're making the decision in the next week or two."

"That's great news," I said, honestly happy for him. I may have been a little hurt that he'd left hours after we'd been together for the first time but the farther away I got from the situation, the sillier it seemed. He had a lot of responsibility on his shoulders and it wasn't like I could expect him to drop everything in his real life because he was spending his hiatus with me.

"I'm sorry I had to bail on meeting your friends tonight to come out here."

"I told you, it's no biggie."

"I'm gonna have to spend another couple nights in L.A."

My heart sunk which was further proof that I was letting my emotions get too involved. "Oh?"

"Have you heard of Amber Marshall?"

That was like asking if you'd ever heard of Santa Claus or the Easter Bunny. She was the hottest pop singer at the moment, at the top of the charts and the fodder of every gossip magazine. Not to mention beautiful. Even as a straight woman I knew she exuded sex; the barely there outfits she wore when she performed only helped.

"Of course I've heard of her."

"She heard I was in town and asked me to help her cut a single she's been playing around with. She wants me to do a little something in the middle of the track."

"What a great opportunity." The thought of him spending an entire day with a sex kitten like that did little to restore my fledging self-confidence where Mason was concerned.

"Definitely. Too good to pass up."

"When do you think you'll be back in town?" I asked.

"Probably not until Sunday night sometime."

"Oh, okay. Well, give me a call when you get back."

"About that..." He trailed off and took a deep breath. I steeled myself for what he was about to say. "I was wondering if you might want to head out here and spend the weekend with me."

"Really?"

"I'll be spending a lot of time in the studio but you can hang there if you want. I thought you might want to see how a song gets made."

I didn't know what to say. My earlier feelings melted away as I realized that he wanted to spend time with me enough that he'd invite me out to L.A. Did I want to go to Los Angeles? Dumb question. Yes, I wanted to see Mason. The real question was whether it was worth potentially getting outed and ending up in some gossip rag; the subject of public ridicule once again. "Umm..."

"Before you answer there's something you should know."

That sounded ominous. "Okay..."

"It's likely we'll be photographed. L.A. is a hotbed for the fucking paparazzi. They're like a swarm of killer bees almost anywhere you go in this town. We'll do our best to avoid them but there's no guarantees."

"Oh."

"I understand if you don't want to risk it. But I'm really hoping you will." The sincerity in his voice came through and I couldn't imagine how I'd ever thought I'd be able to keep my heart out of the equation with this guy. He was one in a million. The ache to see him outweighed my need to protect myself. I'd do what I could while I was there to stay out of the press but an entire weekend away with Mason was too good to resist. What could people say about me that they hadn't said already? It was time to just deal with the fallout, if there was any. I couldn't let my fear prevent me from enjoying what little time I would have with him.

"I'm coming."

"Not yet but you wait until you get here. I have plans."

"Oh, you do, do you?" My nipples beaded as my imagination ran wild wondering what those plans might involve.

"Like you wouldn't believe. If you were in my head right now you'd be blushing."

"Hmm. If you were in *my* head you just might be blushing,

too." Mason laughed. "I have to go see if any new job postings came up and get my résumé out tonight since I won't be around this weekend." If I let the conversation continue down the path it was headed I'd be beyond the point of sexual frustration when I hung up the phone. "I'll have to check the flights and see if I can get something to—"

"Jesus, Ellie. I'd hardly invite you out here and then expect you to book your own flight. I'll arrange a charter for you after work tomorrow and have a car meet you at the airport and bring you over to the studio."

"You don't have to do that. It's too much."

"I don't, but I am."

I wasn't comfortable accepting his offer but it was clear this was an argument I wouldn't win. "Well, thank you then. I appreciate it."

"Cool. I'll see you tomorrow night. Sweet dreams, Sleeping Beauty."

"You, too," I said and hung up the phone. I wasn't sure what the reference to Sleeping Beauty meant, but it was cute nonetheless.

Mason had asked me to L.A. because he didn't want to be away from me. I didn't have the first clue how to wrap my brain around that. It was becoming clear to me that preventing myself from feeling something for Mason was going to prove impossible. And really, what was the point? I was going to be hurt when he left anyway. I might as well enjoy the time together without worrying where my emotions were leading me.

For once in my life I'd decided to jump in head first and see where it led me. I was praying it wasn't to heartbreak.

chapter twenty-one

The flight to Los Angeles was uneventful, although it'd been awkward and uncomfortable traveling in a private plane by myself. It was safe to say it wasn't something I was accustomed to. Before I'd flown with Mason I'd never even seen a private plane except for on television.

By the time I reached the studio I was getting a little sleepy. It was still early in L.A. but my internal clock was still running on east coast time.

As we pulled into the parking lot of what honestly looked like a fairly old and decrepit building I texted Mason to let him know I'd arrived. He'd said the studio doors would be locked and he'd have to come let me in.

I stifled a yawn as I got out of the car and the driver handed me my bags. I wasn't sure how to handle this situation. Did I tip him? Had Mason already taken care of that when he'd hired the car? I stood there a little awkwardly for a moment and was reaching into my purse when Mason exited the building.

It'd only been a couple of days since I'd seen him but my eyes feasted on the sight of him. He wore a pair of worn jeans and a black t-shirt stretched across his muscular chest. I could stare at him all day he looked that good. I pushed all the other things I'd like to do to him out of my mind.

He tipped the driver and turned his gaze to me. Without a word he moved toward me until there was no space between our bodies, pushed his hands into my hair and crushed his lips to mine.

His mouth was savage, his tongue plunging in and out of my mouth in an attempt to consume me. I brought my hands around him and moved them over the muscular planes of his back. He pulled away and leaned his forehead down to mine.

"You're a sight for sore eyes," he said.

"Miss me, did you?" I sounded a little breathless even to myself.

"I've been watching the clock all day waiting for you to get here."

"Long day at the studio?"

"Going on twelve hours...we're just putting the final touches on everything so I shouldn't be too much longer."

"No problem. I'm excited to see how everything works."

He grabbed my suitcase with one hand and looped the other around my waist, leading me to the doors. "Well, let's give you the grand tour then. Amber's excited to meet you."

I stopped in my tracks. "Amber Marshall?"

"Yeah." Mason raised an eyebrow, a questioning look on his face.

"You mentioned me?"

"Of course. Why wouldn't I?"

I shook my head. "Nothing. No reason." In my excitement over Mason asking me to spend the weekend with him I'd totally blanked on the fact I'd be meeting Amber. She was a huge celebrity and I was suddenly nervous about how to act in front of her. It was different with Mason; I hadn't known who he was at first. By the time I did, I'd already gotten to know him a bit so it didn't feel as weird that he was a celebrity. But Amber Marshall was about as big as you could get in the music world.

Mason looked confused as I stood there frozen in my own thoughts but let the subject drop and led me into the building.

I'd pictured a sterile, modern studio with a grey-on-grey-on-black color scheme. Walking through the doors was only a warm, lived-in environment with worn beige tiles and a faux wood reception desk that looked like it'd probably been a high-end piece in the 1970's. The wall was littered with framed posters from various musicians with gold and platinum records underneath, some of whom I recognized, others I had never seen before. The building had its own energy and even knowing nothing about the place or sound engineering, I could sense that it had some deep history attached to it.

"It's not what I expected," I said.

"Really? What'd you think it'd be like?" Mason sounded amused at my reaction.

"I thought it would be more modern. More sterile."

"Some are. This place though...this place is special. Creative geniuses have worked here and made some of the biggest records in the past fifty years."

"I believe it. You can feel the energy as soon as you walk in. It's amazing." I was a little in awe. I'd always felt that people carried their own energy. Mason was a perfect case in point of how someone's energy could lure people to them like magnets. This was my first encounter with a place that had the same.

"Yes! That's exactly it. The studio itself is more modern since it houses all the equipment. Come, take a look."

Mason led me down a hallway by the hand and turned to look at me. "Not that I don't love looking at your legs, but if you have a sweater or pants in your bag you may want to put it on. The studio's always kept a little cooler."

I'd worn a pair of dark denim shorts and with a short-sleeve peasant shirt, but I had packed one sweater. "Oh, I was wondering why you were in jeans in the middle of the summer in California."

He smiled and then opened a door at the end of the

hallway. We walked in to find two men hovering over a board with a million dials on it, and Amber, who I recognized immediately, sprawled out on the couch with her arm over her eyes. The larger man of the two was sitting on a chair, his ebony skin a stark contrast to the white t-shirt he wore. A massive gold necklace with a diamond studded cross hung around his neck. He was probably a little older than Mason. The other man stood beside him in an expensive tailored suit. He looked to be in his early forties with brown hair cut short, and a stocky build.

Mason introduced the older man as his manager, Troy, and the other one as the producer, Deshawn. Deshawn gave me a warm smile and shook my hand. Troy on the other hand gave me the once over and, not looking at all impressed, said hello, but made no motion to take my hand and shake it.

"Um...hello? Still here," a female voice said.

I turned to see Amber had gotten off the couch and was making her way toward us. She was every bit as beautiful as she looked on TV. Her long auburn hair reached her waist and her large hazel eyes naturally turned up at the corners, giving her a bit of an impish look. She approached with a genuine smile on her face and reached her hand out to introduce herself.

"Hi, I'm Amber."

I took her hand in mine and did my best not to seem like the fangirl I was. "Ellie, nice to meet you."

She smirked. "Oh I know who you are. Mason's told me about you. I'm supposing you're the reason he's been watching the clock all day."

"Shut it," Mason said jokingly to her.

"All right. Break's over, boys. Let's get a few more takes and then put this puppy to bed until tomorrow." She looked at me again. "We've been here so long my manager has already taken off."

Mason gave me a lingering kiss on the lips and went through the door with Amber leading to the recording area.

"So, Ellie. First time in a recording studio?" Deshawn asked.

"Is it that obvious?" I laughed.

"Noooo. Of course not." He grinned. "Come on over while they're getting set up in there and I'll show you the basics."

"Thanks." I appreciated the fact he was trying to make me comfortable, when I was clearly out of my element. Troy went to sit on the couch and said nothing. I could feel his eyes studying me from behind when I took the chair next to Deshawn.

Deshawn explained most of the knobs, buttons and gauges to me but within minutes my head was swirling and I couldn't have told you one from the other. He pushed a button and spoke into a microphone. "You two about ready in there?"

"We're good," Amber said enthusiastically.

"Let's take it from the top." Deshawn let go of the button and pressed some more buttons and suddenly music poured through the speakers into the room. The music had a heavy bassline and a bit of a techno beat. It reminded me of something that thousands of people my age would dance to at a nightclub. Amber sang a bit of an intro of oh's and ah's and then Mason broke in rapping to the beat.

I found myself bopping along to the beat, my eyes glued to Mason. The building around me could have been burning to the ground and it wouldn't have mattered; the energy and confidence he exuded when he was rapping was hypnotic. It dared you to try to take your eyes off him. His voice was strong and forceful, saying each word with meaning. It was beyond anything I'd witnessed before. He was beyond anything I'd seen. Amber broke in again singing a few verses and a chorus. Her voice was fun, flirty and teasing, which seemed to suit her personality. By the middle of the song the sound level quieted a bit and Mason came in again. He performed with the same intensity he had earlier, but this time he moved his gaze to me when he said the lyric "...don't know what I'd do if I lost you."

It felt like he was singing to me, which was probably stupid. He was just reciting the lyrics the way he was supposed to. As he performed his body moved side to side and his hands were in front of him. The muscles in his arms flexed and hardened with his movements and had me wondering how much longer until we could head over to the hotel.

Amber sang for a couple more minutes and then the music ended. Both Amber and Mason looked up to Deshawn who said, "That was great, you guys. Let's do it again."

They both nodded. Mason winked at me then walked across the room to grab a bottle of water off a stool.

I turned to Deshawn. "Why do they have to do it again if it was great?"

He gave me an indulgent smile. "We need a bunch of different takes to choose from. We might choose to use the beginning few chords from one and the chorus from another. It all gets spliced and then pieced together into the perfect song you'll hear on the radio."

"I never knew that's how it was done."

"That's why it takes so long. To be honest Mason and Amber are such a pros we could've been done this morning. Sometimes we'll change it up, try some different lyrics out. This morning we had them performing it with a more laid back, island vibe. You can't ever really tell what's going to work best while they're in the booth. Sometimes it's only after it's all done and you're playing it back that you find the magic."

It was clear Deshawn was passionate about his work. He had a glimmer in his big brown eyes and a grin on his face when he spoke about it.

"We're ready," Amber said from the recording room.

Mason looked to me. "You wanna come in here for a bit? See what it's like on this side of the glass?"

Deshawn pointed to the button I should push to speak back to them. "Are you sure that's okay?" I said hesitantly, looking to Amber.

"Word to the wise. Your man invites you into the recording booth? You go. Now come on in," she said, smiling.

I got up from my seat and glanced at Troy, still on the couch, as I made my way to the door leading into the recording booth. He still didn't look very impressed with me. I shook it off as I made my way into the room.

Mason moved the stool at the back to the other side of him and patted it. He gave me a quick kiss on the lips after I sat and then gave Deshawn the thumbs-up.

The music started and he and Amber performed their parts. Again I was in awe of their talent and the attention they commanded, even in this small space with no audience. Mason had just started his part in middle of the song when Heart's "Barracuda" broke out in the studio. It took me a moment to clue in that my cell phone was vibrating in the back pocket of my shorts. Damn it. That was Katie's ringtone. It seemed appropriate when I'd set it but I cursed it now. I frantically pulled my phone out of my back pocket and hit the button canceling the call, then turned the damn thing off entirely.

"I'm so sorry." I was mortified. Deshawn had cut the track and everyone was looking at me. My face was on fire. I'd do anything to shrink down to nothingness.

Mason stroked my back up and down in an effort to make me feel better. "It's okay, babe. I should've told you to turn it to silent when you got here. My bad." He leaned in and kissed my cheek.

Troy's voice boomed through the speakers. "Any chance we can continue now. You wouldn't know this, Ellie, but time is money in these studios. Try not to waste anymore of either."

I tucked my head down and looked and my hands in my lap.

"Hey, ease up, man," Mason said to him with an aggravated tone.

It was nice of Mason to defend me but Troy was right. Anyone with common sense would've realized it wasn't a good idea to have your cell phone on while you were in a recording booth.

"No, he's right. I'll just go back into the other room and hang out on the couch until you guys are finished."

Mason pursed his lips but gave me a short nod. When I returned to the other room Troy was sitting beside Deshawn so I sat on the leather couch. I had a bit of chill so I got up and grabbed my sweater from my suitcase. I sat back down in the corner of the couch, tucked my legs up and positioned the sweater overtop of them. I stayed in the same position struggling to stay awake for the next two hours until the others decided to call it a night.

Mason sat beside me after he'd left the recording booth and put an arm around the back of me. "You ready to head to the hotel?" I nodded and a yawn escaped. Mason laughed and nudged me. "Come on. Let's go."

I said my goodbyes and followed Mason out into the parking lot. He approached a sleek black Mercedes CLS. Even I knew what that symbol was and it didn't hurt that Jeff drove a Benz, too. I thought this one was nicer than Jeff's as I took a seat inside.

When we were both inside Mason leaned across the car, plunged a hand into my hair and kissed me fiercely. His tongue darted in and out of my mouth. All the hairs on my body stood on end and I wondered how long it would take us to get to our room.

He pulled away and looked at me with half-lidded eyes. "I've been waiting hours to do that."

"How far to the hotel?" I asked a little breathlessly.

"Not far at all."

"Good."

Mason smiled and threw the car in reverse and peeled out of the parking lot. I realized it was well after one in the morning back home. No wonder I was tired. Mason rested his hand on my thigh as he drove. I leaned against the window of the car and my eyelids started to drift closed. I did my best to keep them open. I was losing the battle so I decided to give in for just a second. Just a second was all I'd need...

chapter twenty-two

I snuggled further into the covers, purposely not opening my eyes. My bed had never felt more comfortable and I had no inclination to get up and start my day. My pillowcase was super soft under my cheek, the mattress was the perfect firmness. I rolled over and stretched my hand out. Instead of mattress I hit a warm patch of skin.

My eyes shot open.

"Mason? Where am I?" I asked, still groggy and definitely confused.

"Well, Sleeping Beauty, we're in the penthouse suite at the Roosevelt Hotel."

I sat up a bit and took in my surroundings. Shiny dark wood floors ran throughout the suite and set-off the contemporary white leather furniture. It was old Hollywood meets modern day, which I guess was appropriate since we were in Beverly Hills.

"I forgot where I was for a second. I don't even remember coming up here last night." I looked at him questioningly.

"You fell asleep in the car on the way back from the studio. I didn't have the heart to wake you so I carried you up."

I rolled over and mashed my face into the pillow. "That's so embarrassing. I must have looked like an idiot with you carrying me through the lobby."

Mason chuckled. "There weren't that many people around, but I wouldn't be surprised if someone snapped a picture of us on their phone. Or if some paparazzi were hiding in the bushes." I lifted my head to look at Mason. "I did my best to avoid them but those fuckers are persistent."

"I'm trying to accept that there's nothing I can do about it."

"Be sure to let me know how if you ever figure it out." He leaned in and kissed my forehead. My heart warmed at the tender gesture.

I leaned over to Mason and pushed him down against the mattress with one hand, then straddled him. His big grin made an appearance complete with dimple.

"I see you're a frisky one in the morning," he chuckled.

"When I've gotten all my beauty sleep I am."

He brought his hand up to cup my cheek. "More beauty sleep is the last thing you need. You couldn't be more beautiful...inside or out." He said it with such sincerity, my heart about burst out of my chest.

I leaned in and brought my lips to his. Mason's arms came around me and his tongue sought entry into my mouth. I gladly gave it and groaned into his mouth as I felt the effect of our kissing growing beneath me.

His hand moved into my hair as the kiss went from slow and thorough to passionate and wild. After a while Mason pulled away and we sat staring at each other. The sound of our heavy breathing the only one in the room.

"I'd love nothing more than to continue this but I let you sleep late since you were so tired last night. We need to get up or I'm going to be late getting to the studio," he said.

Disappointed, I stuck my bottom lip out like a petulant four-year-old. Mason nipped it between his teeth then ran his tongue over it to sooth it.

"That's doing nothing for your cause," I said and pushed him back against the mattress.

He laughed and I got off his lap so he could get up. "I'm going to take a cold shower. Be back in a few."

"Want some company?" I asked.

"Are you trying to kill me?" He adjusted his nether regions and walked into the bathroom.

We arrived at the studio before everyone else. I was sitting on Mason's lap on the couch in the control room when Amber, Deshawn, and Troy arrived. I'd been a little disappointed to see them since Mason had been explaining all the things he could do to me while I was on his lap and wearing my sundress. I'd chosen a pale yellow dress for the day but had brought along my sweater in case. It'd look like a toddler had put my outfit together if I had to put it on but I didn't have any other options.

Mason was wearing a pair of black jeans with a dark grey t-shirt with some kind of designer emblem on it and a white hat. I'd secretly thrilled in the hotel room when I saw him grab it, remembering the way it'd looked on him the last time he wore it. It set-off his green eyes even more than usual.

Amber skipped into the room. "Hey, lovebirds."

I blushed and moved to sit beside Mason.

"Hey, Deshawn, can I talk to you about something real quick?" Mason asked.

"Sure, man. What's up?"

"Let's go into the hall." I was puzzled as to what that was about. Amber turned to look at me. "You able to get caught up on your sleep last night, or did Mason keep you up all night doing unspeakable things?" She grinned ear to ear.

"Uh, no. I got my rest."

"Glad to hear it because we'll be finished here today and we're all going out to celebrate tonight." It was difficult not to catch her enthusiasm. She always appeared chipper and full of life. "I'm going to go into the recording booth and warm up my voice," Amber said.

That left me alone with Troy who'd leveled me with a steely gaze. Stellar.

"So, Ellie. How did you and Mason meet?" he asked from across the room. He stood with his legs spread wide and his arms crossed in front of his white button-down shirt.

"I work for the real estate company he rented the beach house from in Virginia Beach." I hoped he couldn't sense my discomfiture. I wasn't about to let this asshole make me feel bad.

"Hmm. You go to school?"

"No, I've already graduated."

"Where from? What did you take?"

What was this, twenty questions? "I went to school in Miami and graduated with a degree in Comparative Media Studies. Why?"

"It just seems curious, that's all."

I raised an eyebrow wondering what he was referring to. "Curious?"

"That you just *happen* to work for the rental company that Mason used, and that you just *happen* to have a degree in Media Studies."

Now I got where he was going with this and his barely contained hostility toward me made sense. "I can assure you I have no designs on using Mason to launch any type of career in entertainment. Believe me, there's nothing more I'd like than to stay out of the spotlight."

"You have to realize that's never going to happen if you're dating Mason."

"Of course I do. But let's be clear that I'm under no fantasy that this thing between us is going anywhere permanent. I know that when his time in Virginia is done I'll only be a distant memory."

That seemed to appease him a little, if the fact that his jaw had stopped twitching was any indication. "As long as you know where you stand," he said curtly and turned to look at the control panel so that his back was to me.

I almost respected the guy for looking out for Mason but it still irked me that he'd called my integrity into question. But then who was I to him? I'm sure he'd seen his fair share of wannabe actresses and singers make their way in and out of Mason's life. Mason had alluded to the fact that he'd dated people who only wanted something from him.

Mason and Deshawn returned before I could respond to Troy. He must have been able to sense the ominous air in the room because he asked if everything was okay.

"Of course," I responded.

Deshawn clapped his hands and rubbed them together. "Let's get this show on the road."

Hours later Deshawn declared it a wrap as we all listened to the tracks in the engineering room. "Great job, you two. This is gonna be a hit. I'm tellin' you right now."

Amber turned to Mason. "Thanks so much for agreeing to do it on such short notice."

"No worries. We've been talking about working together for a while now. I'm glad we finally found the right project to make it happen."

Amber turned to the group. "Okay, so to celebrate we're all meeting at Boulevard3 tonight. I don't want any arguments."

Holy shit. I didn't make a habit of following celebrity gossip much but even I'd heard of Boulevard3 before. I knew all the top celebrities frequented it when they were out on the town.

"We'll be there," Mason said.

"Great. I gotta run. I have an appointment with my trainer. This body will not stay fit on its own." She leaned in to give me a hug. "Ellie, it was great to see you again."

"Same here," I said. It felt strange that this huge superstar was being so nice and so normal with me. I'd seen her on the cover of so many magazines and the fact that she made an effort to not only acknowledge my existence, but to be nice to me was more than I would have expected.

"Boys," she said and nodded at the rest of them and then left. I noticed that Deshawn watched her until she was completely out of sight. Interesting.

"Deshawn, think we can take care of that thing we talked about earlier?" Mason asked.

"For sure, man. Give me a minute to get set up."

Mason put his arm around my shoulders and pulled me in to him. The contact with his muscular frame instantly sent the message to my lower half to be on high alert. I really needed to get a grip on my physical reaction to this guy.

"Come in the recording booth with me," he said.

After yesterday's embarrassment I really didn't want to be back in there but I'd made sure to leave my phone back at the hotel so there could be no more accidental interruptions. "Why?" I asked warily.

"You'll see."

"Mason, I'm not singing anything."

"I know. I don't want you to. Just come with me."

"Okay." I acquiesced and walked with him into the recording booth. He motioned for me to sit on the stool while he stood in front of me. "So, what is this about?"

"You. Your laugh more specifically."

Was he on something? This was making no sense. "I don't understand."

"When I heard your laugh the other day I knew I wanted to record it and sample it in a song. It's something that happens sometimes. I hear something and I see how I can incorporate it into a song."

"I hardly think my laugh in a song is going to be a good thing."

"Are you kidding me? You're laugh is so rich and full of joy...how could it not be?" He brushed his thumb along my cheek as he looked down at me.

"All right. What do you want me to do? Just sit here and laugh?"

"I don't think that will work. Have you ever tried to laugh? It almost always sounds forced. No, I had another idea."

"Such as—"

Before the words were fully out of my mouth he started tickling my under arms. I bucked up off of the stool and laugh uncontrollably. I begged him to stop with what little breath I could muster but he paid me no attention, continuing his assault for another torturous minute.

He finally stopped and wrapped his arms around me. I was still trying to catch my breath when he leaned in to kiss me. "Thank you for that."

I smacked him on the arm. "No problem, although I don't know what you're going to do with that. I'm sure I sounded like a cackling hyena."

He chuckled. "You'll see."

chapter twenty-three

I watched as Ellie stood in the hotel room gaping at the rack of clothing hanging in front of her. "This is too much," she said, clearly overwhelmed.

I came up behind her and pulled her into my chest. Her warm flesh and her vanilla scent sent my mind spiraling into the abyss where all I could think about was getting inside her.

"Stop it. Just go try some on," I said.

After leaving the studio Ellie had confessed she hadn't packed anything suitable to wear to a nightclub, so I'd called up my stylist and asked her to have some outfits sent over to the hotel room for Ellie to go through.

"I'm looking at the names on these tags, Mason... They must have cost a small fortune."

"Well, no worries then. I'm only paying for the one you *do* decide to wear tonight." I gave her a squeeze. God, her body was so soft.

"Still." She shook her head and looked at the rack in disbelief.

"Think of it this way. You really have no choice. You need something to wear and there's no way we can leave Amber hanging and not show up tonight."

Ellie turned to face me with her arms crossed over her chest. "Nice use of guilt."

"Thanks. I thought it was pretty clever myself."

She smiled that smile that was meant to capture a man's heart with one look, grabbed some dresses off the rack and headed into the bathroom in a huff.

"I expect you to model each and every one for me," I called after her.

"Dream on," she yelled from behind the closed door.

I laughed. Oh, Ellie. She had no idea the dreams I had for the two of us.

I ended up settling on a shimmery bandage dress. It had a dark grey hue at the bottom and gradually got lighter until it was cream at the top. It was like a second skin, holding in all the right places, had straps, and ended above my knee. I matched it with a pair of nude and silver hooker heels the stylist had left for me.

I purposely didn't look at the tag; if I knew how much it cost, the price would be running through my head all night. I was out of my element. I'd never worn anything so expensive and I was pretty sure I'd never worn anything quite so sexy either. It wasn't revealing but it didn't leave much to the imagination.

I finished curling my hair and styled it down in loose waves. I purposely hadn't let Mason in the bathroom when I was getting ready, for two reasons. One: I wanted it to be a surprise since he'd never seen me this dolled up. Two: I was pretty sure if we were in close proximity for any amount of time, we'd have a hard time getting out the door tonight. I didn't want to disappoint Amber by being a no-show after she'd gone out of her way to be so nice to me.

I studied myself in the mirror. I looked pretty good. I felt sexy and desirable and I was ready to have fun with Mason outside the bedroom. He'd already warned me there was a good chance we'd be photographed at some point during my visit. Truthfully, I was over it. It was time to just deal with the fallout, if there was any. I took a big breath and walked into the main room ready for my big reveal.

Mason was sitting on one of the white leather chairs facing away from me. When he heard the bathroom door open he turned in my direction.

His jaw slackened and his eyes went wide as he slowly got up from the chair.

I'd thought a sexy reveal would be fun but now I was feeling awkward with Mason just staring at me not saying anything. "Ta da," I said throwing my hands out to my sides. Okay, now I felt like an even bigger freak.

Mason scrubbed a hand over his head. "Ellie. You're...exquisite. And sexy as hell."

That's the reaction I was looking for. I beamed. "You like?" I spun around to give him the full three-sixty view.

"Understatement of the year. You'll be lucky if I let you out of this room tonight looking like that." He walked toward me with purposeful strides, the look on his face telling me he was about to devour me. The phone rang and he stopped in front of me, ignoring it. Instead he stood there looking into my eyes, breathing heavily. Not taking his gaze from mine, he slowly ran a finger along the seam of my dress, from my shoulder down across the top of my breasts. When he reached my cleavage he stopped and dipped a finger in between. He closed his eyes tightly.

I pressed my thighs together as my nipples puckered. "Shouldn't you get the phone?" I whispered, swallowing the lump that had formed in my throat.

He turned on his heel and walked back to pick up the receiver. He said nothing for a moment and then, "We'll be right down." He placed the phone back down on the receiver.

"Our car is here. It's time to go."

I nodded, unable to form a coherent thought to manage

the words. I walked in a sexual haze to the hotel room door. When I placed my hand on the door knob I felt Mason's presence behind me. He leaned in and his breath brushed across my ear.

"We'll go make an appearance for Amber's sake. But remember this...every time you see me watching you from across the room, know that I'm envisioning all the ways I'm going to take you when we get back here tonight. Remember I'm counting the minutes until I'm deep inside you again, until I'm tasting your sweetness on my tongue." He patted my ass and then grabbed the handle from me and opened the door, motioning for me to go ahead of him.

A shiver raced up my spine and my knees trembled. Actually trembled. I'd always thought that weak-kneed stuff was bull. I knew now that it only took a once-in-a-lifetime person to make it happen. I knew Mason was that once-in-a-lifetime person and I'd enjoy being with him while I could. In the end, it'd never last. No one had ever stuck around in my life. I could count on only myself.

I pushed the thought to the back of my mind and walked ahead of Mason down the hallway.

Enjoy it while it lasts.

I couldn't forget my mantra.

We rolled up to Boulevard3 and my first impression was that it looked unlike any club I'd ever seen. There were large iron gates that opened into a courtyard with a rectangular pool in the centre and canopied open-air rooms running along either side. A few photographers with cameras looked at our car with interest. We'd stopped in front of the club on Sunset Boulevard briefly, but the driver continued past the club and pulled into a parking lot.

I looked out the back window to see the photographers had tried to follow our vehicle into the lot but were being stopped by a security guard.

"Don't worry. They can't follow us back here. Amber rented the entire balcony so we can go in the back entrance," he said, grabbing my hand and giving it a squeeze.

The driver stopped the car near a staircase at the back of the building. Mason helped me out of the car. We walked up the stairway hand in hand. When we reached the top the door opened and I was assaulted with the driving bass from music pumping inside.

Mason shook hands with the bouncer and stopped to have a conversation with him. I couldn't hear what they were saying over the music but it appeared they knew each other.

The balcony we walked into was really a massive room perched above what I would later learn was the ballroom, where the main dance floor was. I stepped a little closer to the railing between one of the arches to see thousands of bodies pulsing and gyrating to the beat of the music. Blue lights from various points within the massive room washed over everything, but I could tell that without them the room would be primarily white.

The balcony had wood floors and cream couches nestled between various marble coffee tables scattered around the area. There was a bar at one end of the room. The balcony was recessed—probably so the rich who could afford to be up here could maintain some level of privacy.

There were a good number of people in the room. I didn't recognize most of them but a few stood out as people I'd seen in movies or on TV, which made me uncomfortable. I had no business being in a place like this, with people like this.

My thoughts were interrupted when I was almost bulldozed down by a set of arms that locked around me and squeezed.

"Ellie!" Amber screamed over the music. "I'm so glad you guys came."

I laughed and gave her an awkward hug back. "Thanks."

She pulled back, taking in my dress. "You look smokin' tonight. I'm lucky Mason let you out of his room." She laughed and I did, too, thinking of the comment he'd made to me as we were leaving. "What can I get you to drink?" she asked.

"Maybe a wine spritzer?"

"Come on. You're not having a spritzer. That's for ladies who lunch, and you my friend are definitely not a lady who lunches in that dress."

"Okay then, surprise me."

"That I can do." She scurried away before I could respond and made her way through the crowd of people toward the bar at the far end. She had on a strapless red dress and stood out in the crowd.

She was such a laid back girl it barely registered she was a celebrity when I was around her. Now that I was left alone though the feeling of not belonging was returning. I didn't know anyone so I wasn't sure what to do. I'd decided to go back to the door in search of Mason when a set of familiar arms came around my waist.

"You okay?" he asked, nuzzling into my neck.

I nodded. "Who are all these people?"

"People from the industry. Friends of friends." A girl my age who'd clearly had her chest surgically enhanced to epic proportions walked by in a barely there gold dress. "Gold diggers."

I chuckled at first because I was sure it was an apt description, then sighed, feeling once again like I didn't belong.

Mason seemed to be able to read my mind. "Ellie, you're more exquisite than any of the women in here. Never doubt that."

I turned in his arms. "I'm not, but I appreciate you saying it anyway." I got up on my tippy toes to give him a peck and he brought his hand to the back of my neck and pulled me in to deepen the kiss. Our tongues tangled and my lips started to tingle.

"Jeez, you two. Get a room," Amber shouted as she approached. "I could see your tongue down her throat from the other side of the bar, Mason." She was carrying a silver tray with an assortment of drinks and shooters on it.

Panic flared at the realization that we were in public. It wasn't something I was used to thinking about when I was dating someone.

Amber must have seen the alarm on my face. "You don't have to worry about anyone seeing you up here. I know everyone and anyone I thought would try to sell a picture or give a quote to the damn press wouldn't be up here. Besides, they can't see you from below unless you go right up to the edge of the railing so you guys are covered."

"Thanks, Amber," I said.

She turned to set the tray down on a nearby table and plucked a couple of shots off it, handing one to both Mason and me before she grabbed one for herself.

"Cheers," she said clinking both our glasses.

"What is it?" I asked.

Amber rolled her eyes.

"Best just do what she wants, El. She can be relentless," Mason said with a laugh. That was the first time he'd called me El. The only other person who called me that was Skye. I liked hearing him use it.

I swallowed the shooter, and the liquor burned down into the pit of my belly. Amber and Mason had both taken their shots, too, but apparently I was the only one unaccustomed to liquid fire being poured down my esophagus because they'd had no reaction. Amber grabbed my empty shot glass and set it down on the tray, stifling a laugh.

She picked up a pair of drinks and handed one to Mason and one to me. "Don't worry, this won't burn as much." She gave me her sweetest smile and batted her eyes at me.

"You're trouble," I teased her.

"Very perceptive," Mason added.

She threw her head back and laughed. "All right, I'm going to go mingle for a while before I go out on stage. I'll see you two later."

"You're performing tonight?" Mason asked.

"Yeah, the owner is a friend and he asked, so I said I would."

"Good luck," Mason said as she walked away into the crowd.

I took a sip of my drink. Mmmm. This one was good.

"So, do you wanna dance or would you prefer to sit for a bit?" he asked.

"Let's sit for a bit." I still wasn't overly confident around all these celebrities. I normally really enjoyed dancing, but I'd be needing some liquid courage to get out on the dance floor.

Mason led me to an unoccupied loveseat in front of a marble table, a matching loveseat directly across from it. The majority of the room was laid out in front of us from where we sat side-by-side.

We talked and sipped our drinks for a while. I was comfortable when it was only the two of us—when I talked to him I tended to tune out the rest of the room.

An older gentleman in a pair of dark slacks and a button-up shirt approached and leaned down to say something to Mason. He must have known him because he smiled and said something back. I looked around the room while they talked and spotted Amber talking to Deshawn in the far corner. They seemed like they were having an intense conversation but when I caught her eye she smiled easily and raised her drink to me. I returned the smile.

There were a couple of girls dressed scantily not too far from our table. They were obviously checking Mason out; whispering and giggling to each other. The dark-haired girl looked amused but the blonde had predatory eyes on Mason. She flicked her gaze to me and smirked, raising an eyebrow. What the hell was that about? As I studied the rest of the room it was apparent to me just how much female attention Mason commanded. Even women there with a partner would let their gazes wander over to him from time to time, if only to admire the view. Mason seemed oblivious, continuing his conversation with the older gentleman. I did my best to do the same but I imagined the room full of people wondering why Mason was here with me and not some Hollywood starlet.

I sipped my drink and flagged a server down, signaling that I'd like another. The man Mason had been talking to left without being introduced. My insecurities didn't get to run too wild with that one before Mason leaned over to speak into my ear.

"Sorry for not introducing you. That guy drives me crazy but he's from my label so I have to talk to him. If I'd introduced you he would have parked himself here for the night...which would have been a shame because then I couldn't do this."

He brushed my hair behind my shoulder and ran his tongue lightly along my collarbone. I closed my eyes basking in the sensation. Placing his hand on my cheek he turned my head and kissed me. His lips barely touched mine at first, their smooth surface grazing softly over my own. I wanted more though so I moved to deepen the kiss when I sensed a presence to my left. I opened my eyes while still kissing Mason to find Deshawn sitting on the table in front of us grinning wide. I pulled back from Mason and giggled. Thank God it was dark in the club, maybe my embarrassment wasn't too obvious.

"Don't let me stop you," Deshawn yelled over the music with a smirk.

"Hey, man," Mason said and leaned forward and did that thing guys do that's sort-of a hand shake and a hug in one.

"You guys having a good time?" Deshawn asked.

"We were before you interrupted," Mason said.

"Ignore him," I said, gripping Mason's biceps and pushing him sideways playfully.

"That's what I usually do," Deshawn said in return. The server came by and dropped my drink off at which point Deshawn grabbed it out of my hand, placed it on the table and replaced it with a shooter he'd brought over. What was it with these people and shooters?

Mason got one next and finally Deshawn picked up his and raised it to make a toast over the loud music. "To getting what we want." It seemed an odd toast and I looked over to Mason, unsure what to make of it. Apparently what he wanted was some lovin' because his eyes were heated under half-drawn lids. I gave him a small smile and clinked my shot glass with Deshawn's and then Mason's. I swallowed the liquid; thankfully this shot hadn't been as bad as Amber's pick.

I was feeling good when I decided to take a trip to the ladies room. "I'll be right back," I told the guys.

I wandered off in search of the restroom and found it at the back of the balcony. A pair of girls were giggling as I entered. The room was floor to ceiling marble with wood vanities and granite counters. When I looked at the girls and saw them bent over the counter I stopped short.

They each had rolled bills in their hands and were taking turns snorting white powder off the counter. The bathroom attendant was quite literally looking the other way. I wasn't a complete angel; I'd been to lots of college parties where people had smoked pot, although I'd never partaken myself, but I'd never seen what I assumed to be cocaine before.

I was shocked that these girls were doing it so openly. Weren't they worried about being caught? I backed up to leave when one of the girls noticed me and held the rolled bill out to me. "You want to join us?"

"Uh, no thanks." She shrugged and I bolted. My bathroom trip would have to wait. I hurriedly made my way back to the couch where I'd left Deshawn and Mason. Deshawn still sat on the coffee table. Mason however was engaged in conversation with the blond I'd noticed earlier. She was facing him, draped across the arm of the couch and leaning in toward him.

I checked my irritation. I'm sure this kind of thing happened frequently. I just happened to have a front row seat this time. I stopped my approach a few feet from the couch to see how Mason planned to deal with the situation. I was unable to hear their conversation but when she placed her hand behind his head and began running her fingers along the base of his skull he firmly grabbed her hand and removed it. She was clearly put out by whatever he said after that and I took it as my cue to rejoin the group.

Deshawn saw me approach first and smirked. I took my seat beside Mason and he immediately placed a hand on my thigh.

She huffed and glared at Mason. "I see how it is."

"Yeah, exactly how I've been telling you it is for the past five minutes. Now take the hint."

She turned to me. "Enjoy it while it lasts," she said and stormed off into the crowd.

L.A. was beginning to feel like a viper's nest.

"Sorry, Ellie. I tried to get her to back off." He squeezed my leg.

"I could see she was persistent."

"That's an understatement."

The three of us sat for a while longer, but I decided it was time to hit the dance floor when one of my favourite Rhianna songs came blaring through the speakers. I turned to Mason. "Would you mind if we danced? I love this song."

He gave me an indulgent smile. "Of course. Come on." He stood up and put his hand out for me to take. I did and we made our way slowly through the crush of the crowd to the dance floor. We made a little spot for ourselves near the edge.

I began dancing and Mason came up behind me with his hands on my waist. Deshawn had joined us and as Amber flitted by the dance floor he grabbed her by the waist and forced her in front of him in a similar position to what Mason and I were in. She looked startled at first, but then relaxed into Deshawn, seemingly having as much fun as I was.

As the Rhianna song ended another one took its place. This one had a slightly slower beat and more sensual feel. Mason's heat penetrated through the thin fabric at my back. His hand moved from my hip to wrap around me and he palmed my waist and pushed me harder into him. I felt the evidence of his arousal on my lower back and it served to feed my own fire.

I leaned back into him and moved an arm up to wrap around his neck and pulled his head down. His heated breath was warm on the side of my face. His teeth lightly bit down on my earlobe and I groaned and closed my eyes, concentrating only on the sensation. I had no idea if he could hear me or not over the music. Probably not, but he seemed to be able to tell how he affected me because he did it again.

Our hips swiveled back and forth to the music coursing around us and I became less and less aware of our surroundings. People were all around us but I couldn't have cared less. It might as well have been only the two of us alone in an empty club. Mason kissed my neck slowly. Small kisses at first that deepened to swipes of his tongue and gentle bites. I groaned and ground myself against him. His hands moved along the sides of my body and across my rib cage, brushing the undersides of my breasts to continue down the centre of my stomach.

My breathing was fast and shallow; my body was humming and Mason was the maestro. I turned in his arms and our lips met with fire and passion. He devoured me right there on the dance floor for all to see. It might have been the alcohol, but more likely it was just the effect being in Mason's presence had on me because my self-consciousness had disappeared.

I was feeling like a temptress for the first time in my life. It was powerful knowing the effect I had on Mason. It felt like forever since Mason and I had first been together in Virginia and I was ready for it to happen again. I wanted to be the aggressor tonight. I had my opportunity moments later when I felt a tap on my shoulder.

It was Amber. "I'm headed downstairs to perform. By the looks of you two I'm not sure how long you'll be sticking around so I wanted to say goodbye."

She leaned in and gave me a hug, which I warmly

reciprocated. She'd been nothing like I'd thought she'd be. I'd pictured a pampered prima donna but I couldn't have met anyone sweeter or more down-to-earth.

"Thanks for everything, Amber."

"Don't mention it." She looked from me to Mason. "You take care of this one. I'm pretty sure they don't come around too often. Especially in our line of work."

Mason smiled and winked at her before she flitted off toward the stairs.

I looked around and Deshawn was nowhere in sight so I turned back to face Mason and pressed my body to his, wrapping my arms around his neck. "So, what do you think? You ready to head back to the hotel?" I said into his ear and flicked it with my tongue for good measure.

He gave me a quick deep kiss and then pulled back. "Don't have to ask me twice."

I took his hand and led him to where I remembered the stairs to be. As I walked in front of him I may have sashayed my hips a little more than normal because of the sexual abandon I was feeling, but who's to say?

We were halfway down the staircase when I was blinded by the flashbulbs.

chapter twenty-four

It was like rapid fire lightning with no break in between. I stumbled on the stair a bit when I brought my hands up to cover my eyes from the assault. Mason grabbed my upper arm from behind and steadied me.

"For fuck's sake. Where are the security guards?" He kept his hand wrapped around my arm and led me the rest of the way down the stairs. He must have spotted our car; when we got off the stairs he headed right for it at as fast a pace we could muster with a crowd of paparazzi swarming us like piranhas feasting on prey.

The photographers all shouted out at the same time. It was difficult to hear exactly what they were saying but I was able to make out a few "is this your new girlfriend?" and "how long do you think she'll stick around?" directed at Mason.

"Just ignore the leeches," Mason said into my ear. "You're doing great."

Thank God he was taller than most of them; I hadn't the faintest idea of where we needed to go. Finally they parted in front of us and we came to the black limo. Mason reached in front of me and opened the door, helping me quickly inside. He followed me in and slammed the door shut just as one of the photographers attempted to put his camera in through the door to snap a shot off.

"Get us out of here," Mason yelled up to the driver. He closed the privacy wall then angled his body to face mine.

"Are you okay?" There was deep concern etched over all his features. His eyebrows were drawn, his normally bright and sparkling eyes were clouded.

I looked at him unable to speak. Was I okay? I'd gone from a sexual high to complete shock in a matter of seconds. It was overwhelming to have a mass of people converge on you out of nowhere, but right then all I wanted was to continue the amazing night I was having with him—not worry what might have been and what was to come. Especially since I had no control over either.

"I'm sorry, Ellie. I don't know where the bouncer—"

I pressed my lips to his to cut him off. It was avoidance, and I was normally a person that liked to deal with things head on but at that moment it suited me fine.

Mason followed my lead, placing both hands on either side of my face as our tongues tangled. I let out a small moan as the adrenaline in my system dissipated in favor of lust. My skin tingled, hungry for the feel of Mason's touch all over my body.

He moved a hand to my lower back and pushed against me to get me to lie down on the seat but I still wanted control. I wanted to do what I'd been I'd aching for since the night we'd gotten back from Texas—make him lose his mind the way he made me lose mine on the edge of the pool. I wanted no barriers between us. No celebrity and average girl. No rich and middle class. No man and woman. Just two bodies, two souls delighting in each other above all else.

I pulled my lips away from his and pushed his shoulders back against the seat while I slipped down on to my knees in front of him. Desire-laden green eyes stared down at me while I loosened his belt and pulled the zipper down.

He scrubbed his face with his hands and reached up to press a button beside the window.

A voice came through the speaker. "Yes, sir."

"Keep driving until I tell you to head back to the hotel."

"Yes, sir."

Mason brought his hand to my cheek and stroked it, saying nothing.

I reached my hand in through the hole in his boxers to release him. His shaft was rigid in my hand and sprang out of his pants at the first opportunity. That thing knew how to make an entrance. I licked my lips and began stroking up and down his length slowly. I planned to draw this out.

"Jesus," he said on a large exhale of breath and closed his eyes.

I leaned down and put him in my mouth, running my tongue in slow circles around the tip of him, then sucked him further in. He placed one hand on top of my head and gripped my hair, the other gripped the edge of the black leather seat.

I moved my mouth back up the length of him sucking in still and circled his tip again when I reached the top. I repeated this process over and over, sucking him fully into me until he breached the back of my throat and then up again, hollowing my cheeks and sucking in. His hand on my head began guiding my ministrations exerting slight pressure. I increased my pace until I was wildly bobbing up and down on his shaft. Mason's panting was shallow. He moaned and cursed under his breath.

I felt his cock twitch in my mouth and harden further, which I hadn't thought was possible. I groaned myself when he was at the back of my throat, knowing the vibrations might send him over the edge when suddenly his hands were latched around my arms pulling me up from his lap.

"Christ, Ellie. You're going to be the death of me...you're too much."

I tried to move back down but his arms held me in place. "What are you doing?" I asked huskily.

"I want inside you. Now."

He'd get no argument from me. I was as worked up as he

was. I shimmied my skirt up my thighs, which wasn't easy given how snug it was.

"Damn. You weren't wearing underwear all night?" Mason asked and rubbed his hand along the top of his head. Underwear hadn't been an option with how fitted the dress had been. No girl wants panty lines. "If I'd known that we *wouldn't* have left the hotel room."

He pushed himself off the seat a bit and reached into his back pocket for his wallet, pulling out a condom. I grabbed it from him, opened and rolled it down his thick length.

I straddled his lap and our eyes locked but I couldn't keep mine open as I settled myself fully on top of him. I was still for a moment, reveling in the feel of him. Finally I began moving up and down, my movements slow and languid at first. Mason's hands came to rest on my body; one at the nape of my neck, the other gripping my waist. I moved faster and with more force, pushing him deep inside as I came down on top of him with full force. Eventually both hands gripped my waist and the only sound that filled the limo was our heavy breathing, intermittent moaning, and the sound of my ass hitting his pelvis.

I could tell he was close. I wanted to watch him climax, wanted to see the look in his eyes when I took it from him. He brought a hand to my core and circled my clit with his thumb. It was all I needed to bring me flailing over the edge. I called out his name as he did the same, finishing with a few last jerks of his pelvis.

I brought my forehead to his. I'm not sure how long we sat there, trying to catch our breath, but it felt like an eternity. Eventually our breathing returned to normal and I moved onto the seat beside him. Mason helped get my dress back down, then disposed of the condom in the garbage.

He brought me into an embrace, squeezing me tight. "You're incredible." It was muffled since he was speaking into my neck but I could make it out. He leaned away and instructed the driver to return us to the hotel.

I wrapped myself around him and struggled to stay awake in my post-coital bliss. I must have dozed off because Mason was shaking me gently, trying to get me to wake up. I yawned and smiled up at him thinking it didn't get much better than this. No matter what happened I would never regret our time together. It was something I'd hold dear in my heart always.

As it turns out, the old adage "never say never" exists for a reason.

chapter twenty-five

I awoke in bed naked with covers wrapped around half my body and Mason wrapped around the other half. We'd continued our adult wrestling match in the hotel room after we'd arrived.

"Good morning," Mason murmured into my hair as he snuggled me from behind.

"Mmm." My body was sore and achy from the night before but in the best way. I'd missed this since he'd had to leave Virginia Beach.

"You know we're going to have to talk about what happened last night," he said in serious tone.

"I rocked your world, that's what happened," I said cheekily.

"I meant the bad part, not the best part."

"I don't know what you're talking about," I said as innocently as I could muster. Mason turned me around to face him as we lay in the bed, his green eyes boring into mine.

"The paparazzi took our photos," he said in a quiet voice.

I didn't want to talk about this. I'd managed to avoid the conversation the night before but I wasn't going to be able to avoid it any longer. I didn't want things to change. I wanted the two of us to exist in the little bubble we'd created for ourselves in Virginia Beach without the interference of fans, photographers and public opinion. I let out a heavy sigh. "I know."

"Those photos are going to get out. I'm not gonna be able to stop it from happening again." I nodded my head. "Say something. Tell me how you're feeling."

I sat up and pulled the bed sheet up around me. "I don't really know what I'm feeling. I knew it was going to happen eventually if we kept spending time together."

"Knowing it and living it are going to be two different things."

I looked down and fiddled with the sheet, not knowing what to say to that. "It's just..."

"What, Ellie? It's just what?" I could tell he was getting frustrated that I wasn't being forthcoming but his hand came to my cheek and stroked it delicately anyway.

"After having such a great time with you this weekend it's hard to be upset about it. It seems worth it if I get to be with you." I said the last part quietly. This was the first time we'd come close to discussing our feelings for each other. I knew mine had grown stronger for him. I also knew there was nowhere for this to go. He'd be traveling the world again soon and I'd be stuck in Virginia Beach.

He tilted my head so I was looking down at him. "I'm glad you feel that way," he said. I leaned in to brush my lips with his. I wasn't sure what to make of that comment but when I pulled away from him he smiled.

I motioned to the nightstand on his side of the bed. "Pass me my phone and we'll see if anything has been posted online yet." If I was going to have to deal with this I might as well get it over with. Mason rolled to his other side, grabbed my phone and passed it over.

"Sure you want to do this?" he asked.

"No sense in delaying the inevitable."

"Sometimes it's better not to even read what they say."

I laughed and looked down at my phone, realizing it was

turned off. Crap. I guess I hadn't remembered to turn it back on after I'd had that embarrassing moment in the studio. I pressed the button and waited for it to power up while Mason's hand rubbed my upper thigh.

Hmm. I had a message. Probably Skye or Katie just calling to see how my trip was going. I hit the voicemail button and put the phone to my ear.

"This message is for Ellie Wagner. Ellie, this is Tasha Stevens from Mediacon. I'm calling because you sent us a résumé this week for the position of Assistant Manager of Account Relations. It's a bit of an unusual situation in that we'd already conducted the interviews and decided on a hire when we received your résumé, but your schooling is exactly what we'd been hoping to find when we posted the job. I wanted to see if you were available to come in for a quick interview sometime today. I'm sorry for the short notice but we need someone to start on Monday and if you aren't going to be a good fit I need to call the other candidate this evening to offer her the position. If you could give me a call back as soon as possible I'd appreciate it. If I don't hear from you today I'll have to offer the other candidate the position but I wish you the best of luck with your search. You can reach me at—" I hit End on the message and looked at my screen. She'd called early yesterday morning. I let the phone slide through my fingers to land with a soft "thunk" on the bed while I stared straight ahead.

"Ellie. Ellie, is everything okay?"

While I'd been out here chasing after Mason and having a good time partying it up at a nightclub I'd let my opportunity at independence slip away. God, I was so mad at myself. I knew better than to put everything I had into a guy. I'd watched my mom do it for years and had seen it backfire on her time and time again.

Mason sat up and grabbed both my shoulders. "What's going on?"

I picked up the phone and started the voicemail message

again and handed the phone to Mason. He listened intently and put the phone down when the message finished.

"She called yesterday morning," I said.

"This is all my fault. If I hadn't asked you to come out here..."

"It's not your fault, Mason. It's mine. If I'd remembered to turn my phone back on I probably would have gotten her call." I could've kicked myself. If I hadn't been so wrapped up in lusting after Mason I would've checked my phone for e-mails and messages. Would've remembered there was a world outside of him.

"I can make some phone calls. I'm sure one of my contacts knows someone somewhere who's looking for someone with your qualifications.

"No!" I'd said it louder and more abruptly than I'd intended judging from the look of surprise on Mason's face. "I don't want you to do that."

"Ellie, I—"

"It's not up for negotiation. I don't need you to find me a job."

Mason put both his hands up in front of him. "Okay. Consider the subject closed."

I shouldn't have snapped at him but under no circumstances did I want him pulling any strings to get me a job. I wanted to earn it. I was educated and bright and I could find a job on my own. Unlike my mother, I could make my way in the world without the help of the guy in my life.

"I need to get in the shower before we catch the plane," I said and rose from the bed with the sheet still wrapped around me. I needed a minute to clear my head and I hoped Mason wouldn't follow me.

When I reached the doorway to the ensuite I looked back to find Mason lying on his back with his palms pressed to his forehead. I guess we both needed a minute.

chapter twenty-six

Ellie had been quiet on the plane ride back to Virginia Beach but over the past few days we fell into a regular routine. She'd go to work during the day and then come by the beach house and spend the night with me.

Neither of us had brought up what was going to happen when my time in Virginia was over. I knew we could make promises to each other about how we'd keep in touch and try to see each other when we could... I also knew being on the road wasn't conducive to a relationship. She deserved someone who could be there for her. She should have a relationship that didn't have to put up with the near constant rumour mill of speculation as to whether we were making up, breaking up, or making babies.

The pictures of us together in Los Angeles still hadn't surfaced anywhere. I had a bad feeling about that. Experience had taught me the longer they took to make it in print the more salacious the story that accompanied them; true or not. They were probably up for auction between a bunch of the tabloids or someone was still trying to put a name to Ellie.

I walked out on to the deck to deliver Ellie's glass of wine. She was sitting at one of the tables with my laptop checking to see if any new job postings had come up. Since she'd missed the interview while she was in L.A. she'd been diligent about checking the postings every night.

I placed the wine to the side of the computer as I walked by. "Here you go." She nodded her head absently. She was concentrating deeply, her eyes darting from left to right on the screen while she read. I took a seat across from her.

Her natural beauty still struck me every time I saw her. Her face held such openness but there was a fiercely independent spirit inside her I'd only gotten a glimpse of in L.A. It was a unique combination. I kept most people at arm's length—it was easy to do after you'd been burned by some opportunistic asshole or a gold-digging bitch. Somehow Ellie had managed to sneak past my defences without me really noticing, or her really trying.

I didn't worry she was going to call and tip off someone about our whereabouts or try to bat her eyelashes to get me to buy something for her. She didn't ask me to introduce her to someone so she could get a leg up. No, in fact Ellie was the exact opposite. When I'd mentioned helping her find a job she'd about bit my head off.

She let out a sigh and leaned back in her chair.

"Anything new posted today?" I asked.

"Nothing." She grabbed the wine glass off the table and took a sip. "What's your web address? I've been meaning to check your site out."

"Should I be worried?" I laughed.

"You tell me," she said as her fingers raced across the keyboard. "Found it." She scrolled through for a few minutes. When she was done all she said was "Huh" and looked up at me. Her forehead wrinkled in what I guessed to be confusion.

"That can't be good," I said good-naturedly. But seriously, what the hell was that about?

"It's just...I don't know. That site doesn't really do much for you. It's basically just a bunch of links to your music on iTunes and press coverage you've gotten. It's really more a sales page than a fan-building page. You don't even have anywhere for your fans to sign-up for a newsletter. Are you on social media at all?"

So. She really didn't like it. "I have no interest in doing that shit. I don't have time for it."

"You need to make time. I can't believe your manager and PR people haven't told you this already."

"Oh, they have. I've ignored it."

"Mason, you could gain so many new fans by exposing them to your music. People will follow you who've never listened to anything you've done because it's easy to just click 'follow' or 'like' on social media. There's no commitment. If they don't like what you have to say they'll just unfollow you."

"I have no interest in letting people into my private life. I have a hard enough time keeping things private as it is."

She reached her hand across the table and placed it over mine. "It could help you land the reality show."

She definitely knew how to pique my interest and not just by leaning over the table and revealing her cleavage.

"I'm listening."

"Let me tweak some stuff on the back end of your site and show you the kind of things you can do on the social media sites. If you don't like it you don't have to move forward with it and you can leave everything as is." She reminded me of a kid at Christmas waiting for permission to open the presents. Her eyes were wide and she bounced up and down on the edge of her seat waiting for my answer. She must really miss using her skills. As much as I didn't want to have to open myself up to social media I found it near impossible to say no to those big doe eyes of hers.

"All right."

"Really?" When I nodded my head she came around the table and plopped herself on my lap, giving me a big hug. I felt her tits pressing against my chest I knew I'd said yes for a reason.

"You won't regret it." She pulled back and brought her plump lips down on mine for a brief kiss. Much too brief for my liking so I pulled her back in. As the kiss started to deepen she pulled away. "I'll need to know your passwords and your web host."

I pulled her back to my mouth. "I'll have everything sent to you. Let's not worry about that now."

I didn't hear anything else about my website or social media after that. In fact, we didn't talk much at all the rest of the night.

I'd decided to come home after my day at Beachside Realty. I had spent every night that week at Mason's. I'd used the excuse that I needed to get caught up on my laundry but in actual fact I needed to put some space between us. I was becoming too dependent on him and I needed to prove to myself I could survive one lousy night without mooning over him the whole time. Besides, I only had a bit more work to do on his website and I'd wanted to finish up so I could have a big unveiling for him after our plans tomorrow.

Mason was visiting a woman's shelter the next day and had asked if I wanted to accompany him. I had Saturdays off so I'd agreed but I was nervous. I had no idea what to expect. Apparently this was part of what Mason had to do to keep his mother from serving jail time. Originally they'd wanted him to travel to Texas to make the rounds at some local community charities there, but Mason had insisted he wasn't leaving Virginia Beach. They'd agreed and now as he toured the country he'd have to make some charitable stops along the way. He could pick the charities. I'd wanted to ask why he'd chosen this one but I suspected I already knew the answer, given some of the history he'd shared about his mom's past.

My phone buzzed. I grabbed my purse off the end of my bed, pulled out the romance novel I was reading, pushed past my hair brush and found it sitting at the bottom. A picture of

Skye smiling wide with hair whipping around her face was displayed on the screen.

"Hey, chica."

"Are you sitting down?" she asked.

My stomach dropped. Something was wrong. I could tell by the sound of her voice that whatever she had to tell me, it wasn't good. I'd already been sitting on my bed but I moved to lean back against the headrest for extra support. "What is it?" I asked, my voice breaking at the end.

"I was online checking my e-mails, Facebook, Twitter, then I decided to go into my Pinterest account—"

"Skye, get to the point." She had a habit of rambling on when she was nervous.

"I went on to some celebrity gossip sites and I saw something...something about you."

I blew out a relieved breath. The pictures of Mason and I leaving the nightclub must have surfaced. I'd steeled myself for the talk about who I was and what the nature of our relationship was. "It's okay. I know about it." I felt some of the nervous energy I'd been holding in the pit of my stomach dissipate.

"Wait? You're okay with this?"

"I knew they got a picture of us when we were in Los Angeles."

"Sure, a picture of you together is one thing, but this..."

I chuckled. "What? Are they saying we're engaged, or that I'm pregnant?" I laughed.

"Ellie, have you read the story?"

Something in the way she asked the question made the hairs on my arms stand like soldiers at attention. "No..."

"I think you should take a look."

My heart beat wildly in my chest and a giant lump formed in my throat. "Hang on." I grabbed my laptop off the dresser. Skye said nothing as I waited for my computer to boot-up; the silence between us was thick and full of tension.

I pulled up a gossip blog, typed Mason's name in the

search field and hit enter. Those seconds between hitting enter and the image appearing on the screen seemed endless. I'm not sure what I was expecting but when I saw what was staring at me from the screen my jaw dropped.

"What the hell?" I yelled.

It was a picture of Mason and me leaving the club all right, but instead of me looking as sexy as I'd felt I was coming down the stairs in front of Mason with his hand on my upper arm. My eyes were somewhere between open and shut, my leg was at a weird angle that made it look like I was in danger of tumbling down the stairs. I looked like I was drunk as hell and could barely stand up straight. The picture must've been taken when I stumbled and Mason had prevented me from falling. The headline underneath read, "Why Can't Nash Keep the Addicts Away?"

"So you didn't know about this?" Skye asked me.

"No, I didn't know about this! I knew they got a picture of us outside of the club. I thought at worst they'd be speculating who I was and maybe at some point tie me to that video."

"What are—"

"Shhh. Give me sec to read this."

I skimmed through the article briefly and my horror turned to outrage. How could it be legal for people to make shit like this up? The article alleged that I'd been hired as Mason's mom's addiction counsellor after her run-in with the law. Where had they come up with that? They even had a smaller picture of Mason and me leaving the Texas police station further down the page. How lucky for me. Apparently while treating Mason's mother he and I had begun a hot and heavy affair. Unbeknownst to him I was secretly hiding my own addiction and that terrible night at the club I couldn't help but give in to the temptation of booze around me. They even had quotes from people who'd supposedly been at the club that night who witnessed us arguing after he confronted me about my lying, scheming ways, and accused me of only being with him to try and break my way into Hollywood.

What a load of crap! Where did they get this stuff? These people should be career novelists for fuck's sake.

"None of that is true."

"I know that. What are you going to do?" Skye asked.

"What can I do? It's already out there and that stupid picture makes it look like what they're saying is true."

"Are you going to tell Mason?"

"I don't think I'll have to. I'm sure he has people on his payroll to do that."

"I can't believe they can just print whatever they want," she said.

"I'm so sick of not being in control. People keep saying these horrible things about me and no one seems to care if they're true or not, while I just have to sit here and take it."

"Anyone who knows you will know all of this isn't true."

"But what about everyone else?" Tears burned hot behind my eyes but I refused to let them fall. I was sick of feeling sorry for myself. There had to be something I could do. "I feel awful for Mason. He's going to be upset that his mom's situation has been dragged into the spotlight. I can't even call him. When I told him I wouldn't be coming over tonight he made plans to work from some small recording studio in Richmond. I guess it'll have to wait until I see him tomorrow."

I wasn't sure how Mason was going to take the news that his mother's story was all over the press. I worried that it would bring him to that dark place I'd seen a glimpse of on our way to Texas.

The next morning I logged onto my Facebook account and sure enough I'd been tagged several times with links to the bullshit article. My page was full of posts about Mason and me. Those who knew me pretty well knew the article was a lie, but were more interested in knowing about Mason, while the rest of the posts came from people expressing their extreme disgust that I could go to such lengths to try and trick Mason and hurt his ill mother.

I was beginning to understand why Mason didn't want to be on social media. This'd only be a glimpse of what he'd have to deal with. I logged out and closed my laptop and was taking a final glimpse in the mirror when my mother barged in through the closed door.

"I saw the article that's making the rounds this time," she said in a concerned voice.

"None of it's true." I turned away from my reflection and faced her.

"I know that, Ellie."

"How'd you find out about it?" I asked.

"Reporters started calling the house phone early this morning."

My eyes might have bugged right out of my head. "Are you serious?"

She nodded. "Don't worry. I told every one of them that called the same thing. The entire article is a lie and my daughter is a bright, college-educated girl who is most certainly not an alcoholic and not trying to trap some man into something."

"It might be better not to say anything at all."

"If that's what you prefer. I'll ignore the phone when it rings for the next few days."

"Thanks for defending me, Mom."

"Would you ever doubt it?" She looked a hurt by my comment. She placed her hands on my shoulders, looking me in the eyes.

It was silly because I saw her every day, but I suddenly realized how much older she was. Crow's feet had started to form at the corner of her eyes. She had some wrinkles set into her forehead, and her skin no longer had the same glow I remembered from my youth. For some reason it made me sad. Sometimes you have a picture in your head of a person and then they change so slowly you don't notice it until one day it slaps you in the face and you wonder how you could have missed it.

"I realize I didn't set the best example for you growing up—"

"Mom..."

"No, let me finish...we've never talked about this. I know I clung to men and had them provide for us instead of providing for myself. I know you're probably ashamed of me, but you're not me. I'm not strong like you are. When I read that article I didn't think for one second there was any truth to the fact that you were trying to trick this Mason boy into something for your own gain. That's not who you are. I'm proud of who you've grown up to be, Ellie. You may not have the job you want or deserve right now, and I know you've had a hard time dealing with public opinion lately, but you *will* be okay."

"You can't know that, Mom."

"I do know that. Sweetie, you have always had an independent spirit. Even when you were a toddler you wanted to do everything yourself. Nothing's changed. People like you aren't down and out for long. If something doesn't happen for you soon I know you'll make your own luck and land on your feet."

To my utter embarrassment a tear slipped down my cheek. My mom and I didn't do emotional. We locked everything in the vault never to be spoken of again. This was the first time she'd ever mentioned the way she acted around men, and I wasn't sure how to react so I pulled her in for a hug. She gripped me back tightly.

"I've never been ashamed of you. I know you were just doing your best."

She nodded her head against me but didn't say anything. When she pulled away I saw that she'd been crying, too. I suppose we'd both been overdue for that talk.

"So," she said, wiping the tear from her cheek and composing herself. "When do I get to meet this Mason you've been spending all your time with?"

I smiled at the mention of his name. "He'll be here to pick me up soon. You could meet him then if you want."

"I believe I will. I want to ask something though." I gave her a questioning look. "Is he worth all of this trouble you've found yourself in?"

I hadn't been sure what she was going to ask me but that was an easy one. "I think so."

She seemed to accept that. She said nothing, just headed to the front door to wait for Mason.

chapter twenty-seven

Ellie slipped into the car after we'd said goodbye to her mom on the driveway. I saw now where she got her looks from. She'd been a nice enough lady; not quite what I'd expected given how Ellie had described her. I'd pictured a women with teased hair, lots of make-up, sporting leopard print leggings and too much plastic surgery. What I'd found was an attractive woman with warm eyes, not that unlike Ellie's, and a modest wardrobe.

I leaned across the seat to kiss Ellie on the lips. "Hi." She kissed me back and gave me that smile that made me feel what fifty thousand screaming fans couldn't. I hated it, but I was going to have to wipe that smile off her face. "I need to talk to you about something."

"I already know about the picture and the article, Mason."

"Why didn't you call me last night?" My question had an accusatory ring that I hadn't intended.

"Because I knew you were busy working. I was too angry anyway."

My stomach clenched. Since day one I'd been waiting for Ellie to say all the bullshit that came with seeing me wasn't worth it. Here it was. "I didn't find out until this morning. I'm sorry."

She spun in her seat to face me while I drove. "You're sorry? Why would you be sorry?"

"It's my fault you're being dragged into this. When the Texas pictures were taken I suggested to Troy that we say you were an addiction counsellor." I punched the steering wheel with my hand.

"Even so. You didn't take the pictures and pick the one you could twist into some juicy gossip, and you're not the one saying nasty things about me on social media."

"If it wasn't for me none of that would've happened in the first place."

"People make their choices, Mason. The people who've chosen to work at the tabloids know what they're doing. They have to realize they're destroying people's lives. They *choose* not to care."

"What do you want to do about it? I spoke with Troy this morning and he wasn't happy but he had a few ideas—"

"I don't want you or Troy to do anything. I'm worried about you. You know they mentioned the trouble your mom had with the law right?"

My grip on the steering wheel tightened. "I know. Assholes."

"Are you okay?"

"It's not me I'm worried about. If Olivia and Justin see the article I'll have to deal with it. I know that if my mom continues to drink I won't be able to protect them forever. I've just been doing it so long the thought of them finding out exactly what their mother is makes me sick."

Ellie's hand came to rest on my leg. "Even if that happens they'll be okay because they have you."

"We'll see."

"How is your mom doing?"

"I spoke with her and her sober companion this morning to give them the heads-up about everything in the press. Seems she's been going to her meetings, following the program. I wish I could trust her but she's just let me down too many times."

"It'll all work out."

I took my eyes off the road to look at her for a second. "We can't not respond to the allegations against you."

"I didn't say there wouldn't be a response. I said it wouldn't be coming from you."

Her reaction wasn't what I'd expected. I'd expected her anger, sure, but I'd assumed it'd be directed at me. Instead she seemed resigned to the fact that she'd been dragged over the coals again. "What do you have in mind?" I asked.

"You'll see. They've got me good and mad now and I intend to do something about it."

I laughed. "Remind me not to piss you off."

She chuckled for a moment and from the corner of my eye I saw her looking at me thoughtfully before she spoke again, her voice quieter. "I wanted to ask why you chose to visit a woman's shelter."

"You're smart. I'm sure you realize it has to do with my mother. Growing up I saw her get into more than one abusive relationship. A couple of them weren't so bad...they just shoved my mom around. I heard them yell at her. The worst of them would hit her right in front of me."

"I can't imagine." She shook her head in disbelief.

"I always felt so ashamed I couldn't do more to stop them. I was the only guy in the house. I should've been able to do something."

Ellie's hand came to rest on my khaki coloured shorts. "You can't blame yourself...you were a kid."

"I know."

"Isn't it unusual for them to let a man in one of these places? I've never been to one but I'd think they didn't see too many men around there."

"You're right, they don't. When the director heard that this was where I was hoping to volunteer she spoke to all the women staying there and they were okay with it. I guess some of the older kids are fans of mine."

"That's great." She squeezed my thigh for emphasis.

I pulled the Range Rover up in front of a nondescript building and got out of the car. We were in a residential area with some small sixplexes and corner stores dotting the block. This property looked more a mix between a commercial building and a small apartment building. A set of cameras mounted on top of the building tracked our movements as we made our way to the front entrance. We waited as an older woman with short greying hair and a long floral dress walked through a set of double doors. She locked them behind her and came to unlock the outer door we stood in front of. She smiled and opened the door wide.

"You must be Mason," she said. She reminded me of the type of woman you saw on TV playing someone's grandmother. She was warm and friendly and instantly put us at ease.

I reached my hand out to shake her hand. "Mason Nash, pleased to meet you, ma'am."

She waved a hand in front of her at that. "Please call me Lorna. I'm the Director here. And who do we have here?"

"This is my friend, Ellie."

They shook hands. "Pleasure to meet you, Ellie."

"Likewise," she responded.

"Well, everyone here is very excited to meet you. As you can imagine they haven't had a lot of happy occasions in their lives lately."

"I'm happy to come and spend some time with them, really," I said.

"Terrific. Well let's get you out there. I can't wait to see everyone's reaction!"

Lorna led us inside and down a hallway with threadbare carpet. We went through a door and exited into a courtyard. The building was a large square and in the middle was the courtyard. It was covered in grass and well-protected from the street. It was perfect to keep the residents of the women's shelter free from the prying eyes of anyone outside the building. Some women were sitting at picnic tables dotted throughout the yard. Others sat with little ones on blankets. A group of teenagers crowded in one corner keeping to themselves.

Lorna put her hands to either side of her mouth. "Can I get everyone's attention please?" All conversations ceased and everyone turned to look in our direction. Some of the women blushed, the teenagers eyes bugged out of their heads, and the little ones couldn't have cared less. "This is Mason Nash...I know you're all familiar with who he is, but he's here to spend some time with us this afternoon. This is his friend, Ellie." We both gave small waves to the crowd. Lorna turned to face Ellie and me. "Please make yourselves at home. If you need anything at all let me know."

Ellie leaned in to say something to me. "What do we do now?" she whispered.

I turned and winked at her. "We mingle."

We walked to the group of women closest to us and I introduced myself and Ellie again. They made room for us at their table and we sat down. So it went. We'd talk with one group for a while and move on to another. Eventually Ellie and I split up and visited with different groups.

I watched her talking with a woman and bouncing a baby on her knee. There was absolutely no judgment at all on her face as she took in the horrific stories of the women around her. I'd been sent here to use my celebrity stature for the greater good, but these women would've taken or left me. After speaking with Ellie it was clear they were enamoured with her.

I'd felt it when I met her the first time and clearly they had, too. There was something about her that made you want to open up and spill your soul. She reminded me of news footage I'd seen as a kid of Princess Di as she moved through a room, providing comfort to others.

Ellie looked up briefly and I caught her eye. She smiled wide and winked at me. That small gesture and a thousand like it before cemented her into my heart.

I was still staring at her across the courtyard with an idiotic grin on my face when the guy with the gun stormed in.

chapter twenty-eight

This poor woman's story was breaking my heart. As I bounced her baby boy on my lap, I sensed a pair of eyes on me and I glanced up. Mason was looking at me from the other side of the courtyard. He had an amused smile on his face and his green eyes sparkled. I winked and smiled back.

A commotion across the yard had me turning to see what was going on.

Time stopped and everyone seemed to move in slow motion. I guess that wasn't something that only happened in the movies. A middle-aged blond man wearing a Hawaiian shirt was yelling and waving a gun around. I remember thinking he'd been out in the sun too long because his face looked burnt. What a strange and innocuous thing to think at a time like that.

He was yelling the name Trina over and over. The baby on my lap started fussing and crying. That was enough to draw the man's attention to us.

"Shut that fucking kid up! Now!" He came closer, pointing his gun at us. Blood thrummed through my ears; it was all I could do to hear him over the sound. I handed the baby back to his mom and he quieted once he was in those familiar arms.

"*Trina! Trina!* Where are you? I know you're here, you

stupid bitch!" He moved in circles frantically looking around the yard. I had no idea how he'd gotten in but I hoped he hadn't hurt anyone to gain access.

Some of the staff members were trying to herd the women and children to the door leading out of the courtyard. The gunman spun in their direction shaking his gun at them. "Don't fuckin' move. You all stay where you are."

I couldn't sit and do nothing when there were so many women and children that'd already been exposed to so much violence. Despite legs that felt like Jell-o I stood up with my hands in front of me in what I hoped was a placating gesture. "Please don't hurt anyone."

He whirled to face me, his plump red cheeks full of fury. "Who the hell are you?"

"I'm nobody. I just don't want to see anyone get hurt."

"You find me Trina and no one gets hurt."

Lorna came forward from my right. "Trina isn't here anymore. She left two days ago."

"Bullshit! Where would she go? She has nowhere to go! She has nothing!" His eyes bugged out of his head, his pupils so dilated I couldn't tell you what color his eyes were. This guy was hopped up on something.

I saw Mason slowly and cautiously making his way behind the guy. It took everything in me not to make eye contact with him and will him to sit back down.

"It's true. She's gone to a different facility," Lorna said in a calm voice. She looked so at ease, as if there wasn't a crazy man waving a gun around a few feet from us.

Me on the other hand? Sweat pooled underneath my shorts and t-shirt. My mouth was as dry as the Sahara and I felt light-headed like I might pass out. I needed to keep my shit together though. The best thing I could do for Mason was to keep this guy talking and hope Mason knew what the hell he was doing.

"Is Trina your wife?" I asked.

"She's my girlfriend! What's it to you?" he yelled, spittle flying out of his mouth.

"When was the last time you saw her?" I asked, barely able to get it out.

"A month ago before she fucking left me in the middle of the night after a misunderstanding."

"What happened?" I asked.

Wrong question.

He pointed the gun at me, square in the chest. Mason was getting closer, almost there. I took a deep breath and, looking him in the eyes, tried to use my calmest voice. "You love her a lot." I said it as a statement of fact, not a question.

"Yes, yes. I love her so much. It was all a mistake." Tears streamed down his cheeks.

"I know...I know. You probably feel so terrible about everything that happened."

He shook his head and when he went to rub the tears from his face with the hand holding the gun, Mason sprung from behind, grabbing his hand. My feet were locked in place watching the exchange and fearing what would happen to Mason. Lorna forced me behind the picnic table where the woman with the baby was already hiding. In retrospect the picnic table wasn't going to do much to stop a bullet but it was better than nothing.

I watched in horror as Mason and the guy struggled for control of the gun. Mason had age and condition on his side, but this guy was pretty beefy, not to mention he was so high on drugs he was feeling no pain. They struggled until Mason managed to smash the guy in the nose with his elbow. He grabbed at his face with both his hands, dropping the gun. Mason kicked the gun over in our direction and tackled the guy to the ground.

I swear I'd kick his ass later for that stunt but in the moment all I wanted was to launch myself on top of him and never let go. If anything had happened to him I knew I'd never get the image out of my head.

Sirens blared in the distance, but were getting louder. Someone must have called 911.

Mason held the guy until the police arrived. We all had to keep our hands in the air until after the police were able to sort-out what had happened. They finally took the guy from Mason, cuffed him and led him away. Women and children were scattered across the lawn; some sobbing, some yelling, and all of them holding their loved ones close as the officers attempted to take statements from everyone.

I ran over to Mason and threw my arms around him. "What were you thinking? Are you okay?" I gripped him tight, not willing to let him pull away from me. Eventually I leaned back to look at him. He brought his thumbs up to brush the tears I hadn't realized I'd shed, off my cheeks.

"I'm fine. Are you okay?" he asked.

I smacked him on the chest. Now that I knew he was in no danger anger filled me. "What the hell, Mason? Were you trying to get yourself killed?"

"Me? Are you crazy? You're the one who put herself in harm's way!"

"I had no choice after the baby started crying," I said, even more agitated now.

"Ellie, I couldn't sit there and do nothing while some lunatic pointed a gun at you. Do you have any idea the horrible images that flashed through my mind? What could have happened to you? I'd never let anyone hurt you like that."

That explanation took away some of my anger. He was right. If he hadn't stepped up something much, much worse could have happened. I looked down at my hands and realized they were shaking. Mason pulled me in for another hug and I felt better just being surrounded by his strong arms.

"How do you think he got in?" I asked.

"I don't know. I'm sure they'll figure it out and make sure nothing like that can happen again."

I nodded against his chest. Mason held me, without complaint, for a long time. He seemed to realize I needed him close, needed to be connected to him physically.

Eventually we had to split up to give our statements to the police and then we were free to go. As we were making our way, hand in hand, to the exit women and children kept coming up to us to thank us for what we'd done. Mason brushed it off as no big deal, but it was a big deal.

This was supposed to be a casual thing with Mason, no future in it, but if something had gone wrong? I couldn't even force my brain to go there. That was how anyone would feel though, right?

Lorna was the last one to approach and she took us both into an embrace. "Thank you, both of you, for everything."

I spoke first. "We didn't do it alone, Lorna. You were so calm...you didn't even seem nervous."

"Oh, I was nervous. Believe me. The only difference is that I've been trained to deal with a situation like that. You two though...I can't tell you enough what it means to everyone here that you did what you did."

"Thanks," Mason said. "I'd like to do something to help. I know it'll be tough for them coming back outside as the days go on. I was thinking maybe I could send over a jungle gym for the kids to play in and maybe get some patio sets and stuff for the women, so they don't have to sit on the blankets and picnic tables anymore. If it's okay with you."

Tears formed in the corner of Lorna's eyes at Mason's thoughtful gesture. "That would be wonderful. Thank you."

"Consider it done then." Lorna nodded.

We waved to them as we left the building. The parking lot was still teeming with police officers as we made our way to Mason's Range Rover.

I wanted nothing more than to be back at Mason's with him holding me in his arms, where I knew I'd feel safe. Where it felt more like home than my actual one.

chapter twenty-nine

When we got back to the beach house, Ellie and I had lain on the couch for hours. She seemed content to be in my arms. I was pretty sure we were both replaying what had happened at the shelter over and over in our minds, thinking how if one thing had changed it could have ended very differently.

We hadn't spoken much since the car, where Ellie had insisted she was okay. I didn't see how she could be. Yet again another situation she wouldn't have found herself in if not for me.

When I'd seen the guy pointing the gun in Ellie's direction there was no question I was going to step in. I may not have been able to help my mom when I was younger, but I was no kid now, and there was no way in hell I was gonna let some abusive asshole harm another person I cared about.

My stomach growled, and Ellie looked up at me. I guess nature still called even in the aftermath of near-death experiences. "Are you getting hungry?"

"There's no rush." I gave her a squeeze.

She pushed up off of my chest. "I could go for something. Want to order a pizza?"

"Pizza sounds good, sure." She began to get up off the

couch, but I caught her arm before she got that far. "Are you sure you're okay?"

She said nothing for a beat, looking into my eyes as if she was deciding what she wanted to say. "I'm still a little freaked...I mean...I'm not sure it's really set in yet."

"I knew it. Come here—" I reached out to pull her in but she put her hand out in front of me.

"Wait, let me finish. It's also made me realize something."

"What's that?"

"It's cliché, but life's short. If things had gone bad there today it could have been all over. And here I've been worrying about what a bunch of people I don't know think about me, what they're saying about me. You know what? Who cares? Who are they to me? No one. If they choose to believe the lies and think the worst of me than so be it. I don't care anymore. I'm going to live my life and do my best to carry on without worrying what a bunch of strangers think of me."

I felt my grin split my face in two. "I think that's a good way to look at it." She'd learned in a few short weeks what it took me years to figure out.

"And I know what I'm gonna do about it, too." The excitement on her face was palpable.

"Do tell."

"I'll do better than that. I'll show you."

"Mmm. Does you showing me involve all or part of you being naked?"

She laughed. "Sorry to disappoint, but no." I stuck my bottom lip out and she giggled again. After today I was glad to see her smile. "I'm not going to tell you what it is...I'm just going to do it before I lose my nerve, but I'll definitely show it to you."

"So mysterious, Miss Wagner."

"So curious, Mr. Nash." She planted a chaste kiss on my lips and got up to order the pizza.

After we'd eaten Ellie turned to me with an excited look on her face. "Where's your lap top?"

"On the nightstand...why?" Something was up. I could tell by the look of mischief on her face.

"I want to show you something." She bounded into the bedroom and came back a second later holding my laptop. She sat beside me on the couch, put the laptop on the coffee table and waited for it to boot up.

"What are you up to?" I asked her as I fingered the nape of her neck.

"You'll see," she said in a sing-song voice.

I grinned. Her enthusiasm made me decide to try patience on for size.

"I know you said you didn't want to participate in social media because it's a pain in the butt. But I think it's important for you to be on there. You don't need to spend every waking minute on there but you need some kind of presence. No, no. Before you say anything just look at what I've come up with. I revamped your website and moved some things around. None of this is live so if you don't like it, it's nothing for me to get rid of it. Take a look and let me know what you think. I think it's much more...you."

She shifted the laptop to face me and I saw a website I didn't recognize. It was mine. My name was there, as was my image. But this one was cooler looking, more streamlined.

"Let me point a few things out to you. Before, when you landed on your page you'd be met with one of your songs blaring full blast and a whole lot of graphics all over the page. The eye didn't know where to go—there was so much happening. Studies show people don't like music playing on a site when they land there. Who knows what level the volume is at and if they're at work or somewhere they aren't supposed to be surfing the web that poses a problem."

"Good point. I'd never really thought about it. Not that I visited my site much."

"Well, now the first thing people see is the option as to whether they want your music to play or not. If they pick yes, then they can narrow down their choices by album, who else is performing in the song with you, or even random. I also had the idea that when the song was playing you could have a story scrolling underneath the player explaining how you came up with the lyrics for that song, or some kind of inside scoop on the making of the song. Fans love anything that makes them feel closer to a star, like they really know you as a person, understand the motivations behind your creations."

"That's a really great idea."

"I'm not done yet." She flashed me a big smile. "You can see here I've streamlined your page, too. I've broken it down into basic tabs rather than all the scrolling graphics and stuff that was flying around before."

"What's this tab here for F.A.N. Club?"

"Ah, that my friend is the Fanatic About Nash Club, or your F.A.N. Club. I know you already have one but from everything I could dig up it was pretty much a glorified e-mail list. With this people will be able to buy merchandise only available to people in the F.A.N. Club, they'll get a section of tickets blocked off for first purchase at all the shows you headline, and they'll get a bunch of extras like a video message from you at the holidays, maybe you can give them access to a new song before it's released to the radio and stuff like that. I even thought that maybe the cost to join could go directly to a charity of your choice."

I clicked around the site she'd developed. Half of me was blown away she'd accomplished so much so quickly and the other half was a little pissed that the people I paid for shit like this hadn't already thought of it.

"Ellie, this is amazing stuff. I mean, I never would have thought a website could give the actual feel of a person, but you've managed to do it."

"Well, your last site screamed gangster rap and I know that's not you."

"So what about the social media stuff? Am I going to have to tweet semi-naked pictures of you to stay relevant?" I grinned devilishly.

"I've had enough media attention this year, thank you." She leaned in to kiss me and when I tried to deepen the kiss she pulled away with a grin on her face. "Behave for minute. I had some ideas about that. I know you don't want your personal business everywhere...I was thinking you could use your social media in another way."

"How?"

"Instead of telling the world you're about to eat Fruit Loops for breakfast you could do things to involve your fans. Like contests or having them vote for two different album covers, or maybe pick what song you open your next show with...stuff like that. When you have a contest you make sure that everyone has to give their e-mail address for your newsletter. That way when you have a new album, tour, or video releasing you can send an e-mail to all your fans. The newsletter is key. It's a money maker and it's the kind of thing that's going to drive people to buy your album when it first comes out and get you to the top of the charts faster."

"You seem to have thought of everything." I pushed the laptop away and pulled her on to my lap.

"I don't know about that."

I kissed down one side of her neck and up the other. "Mmm. I do. Did you think of how I'm going to repay you for all your hard work?" I nipped at her neck and Ellie squirmed, letting out a soft moan.

"I'm sure we could come to some type of arrangement we'd both find satisfactory."

My hand brushed up her waist and grazed the side of her plump breast. "I have a few ideas. Maybe I can show them to you and see what you think?"

"You most definitely can." I brought my hands to the hem of her shirt to raise it over her head when she stopped me. "After."

"After. After what?" I sounded like I a whiny kid but damn. This girl's mind was as much of a turn-on as her damn body. A man could only take so much.

She slid off my lap. "After I do that thing I mentioned before."

That might have been the only thing that would've gotten my one-track mind off the track it had already been barreling down. Whatever it was it had seemed important to her after what happened earlier. "Are you going to tell me what it is now?"

"No. But I'll show you once I'm done."

"That's very cryptic."

"Hand over your laptop, buddy."

"Or what?"

"Or you won't be getting me naked later like your banking on."

"What makes you think I'll be trying to get you naked later, huh? Maybe I won't be in the mood anymore."

"This," she said and grabbed the hard-on I'd been hoping hadn't been too noticeable. Guess not.

"Touché."

She stood up and I smacked her ass since the fine thing was dangling right in front of me. She yelped but continued to the spare bedroom and closed the door.

My mind ran wild thinking of all the things she could be doing in there. Laptop, webcam...the possibilities were endless. I knew she wasn't. But hell, it was way more fun to think of her in there making me some kind of sex tape than thinking of her typing up a letter or something.

My mind drifted to thoughts of what had happened at the women's shelter. We'd gotten lucky, real lucky that no one was hurt. The thought of something happening to her was more than I could bear. Ellie had fast become important to me and even though we'd both been avoiding the topic, we only had one more week together in Virginia Beach.

What would happen once I got back to my regular life? What did she want to happen? Hell, what did I? When we'd started this thing we'd both agreed it wasn't going to go anywhere. That was before I knew what an intelligent, straight-to-the-point, compassionate woman she was. I'd never met anyone like her before and it didn't escape me that I probably never would again.

Time was running out. We'd have to talk about it soon. I planned on making the case that we should try and make something work between us. Screw that. I was going to prove to her we could make it work. She'd just have to get used to the idea of me spending money on her and doing things for her because that's how it was going to be if we were together.

I sounded like fucking caveman. I needed to chill. I'd worked myself right up. I wasn't sure if that was because of the day's events or the fact Ellie was running through my system like a hard-core drug, but it was all clear to me. And important.

I'd figure out some way to make Ellie realize we were good for each other. I wasn't giving up until I did.

A while later Ellie returned, laptop in hand. Her lips were pursed and her forehead crinkled. She'd gone in there like a raging bull full of confidence, now she looked more like a lamb being led to slaughter.

"All done?" I asked.

She took a deep breath in. "Yes, but I wanted to show you first before I hit the upload key. I'm not sure it's a good idea now."

"I saw your ideas in action earlier tonight. I'm sure it's brilliant."

"Thanks for the vote of confidence but I don't know. Here take a look."

She set the laptop down in front of me at the breakfast bar where I'd been having a beer waiting for her to finish. After she pressed a button, a video of her came on the screen. She was sitting cross-legged on the bed.

As the video started, Ellie stepped back, chewing on a fingernail, clearly nervous.

"Some of you may know who I am. For those of you who don't my name is Ellie Wagner. I graduated from the University of Miami with a degree in Comparative Media Studies. I'm like a lot of other twenty-one year-old college graduates. I'm a boomerang kid, back at home with Mom and I'm still looking for that elusive first job in my field, but lately I've been best known for this..."

A brief clip of the video of Ellie shoving food down her date's throat played for a few seconds. I suppressed a chuckle because I didn't think she'd appreciate it.

"And this..."

A picture of the two of us outside the nightclub flashed on the screen followed by the article scrolling slowly by. This time I didn't chuckle but clenched my fists in my lap. Images of various newspaper articles about bullying and kids who had taken their lives as a result followed. Ellie's voice spoke over them.

"You never know what someone else is going through until you've walked in their shoes. After the video of me went viral I received all kinds of hurtful messages. I didn't know anyone who sent me these messages but they caused me pain regardless. I was wrong for throwing my date's dinner in his face. What none of you know is that I was upfront with him. He knew I wasn't going to sleep with him and chose to keep seeing me. He thought maybe his charm would work himself into my pants, and when I assured him it wouldn't, he dumped me, called me every vulgar name in the book and told me I was a worthless whore. I didn't take too kindly to that, which is when the food and foul language went flying.

"I only tell you this to show you that when you say nasty things to people you may or not know the whole story. But you WILL hurt them. Words can cause as much damage as fists, if not more. The only difference is that the damage is on the inside where no one can see it and it accumulates over time. Please, the next time you find yourself ganging up with others to make fun of someone think of this. And think of all

the faces that you've seen on the screen while I've been talking. Every single one of these kids could still be with us if the people tormenting them had stopped to consider the repercussions of their actions.

"I decided to speak out because something happened earlier today that put everything in perspective for me. I've decided to stop worrying about things I can't control and continue to do what it takes for me to succeed. I know who I am and it doesn't matter what a bunch of strangers think of me. I'm an honest, intelligent, forthright person. I know this and for the first time in a while I believe it in my own heart.

"I want to say to anyone else struggling out there whether it's because someone you know is bullying you, you have low self-esteem, or maybe you're just going through a hard time...it will pass and you'll be okay. You ARE good enough. It doesn't matter what anyone else says or thinks of you, as long as you know your worth in your own heart. So stay strong because life really is too short and it can all be taken from you like that.

The video ended and the screen went blank. I turned to Ellie who was now pacing the floor behind me.

"Well?" she said quietly.

"That rocks."

A smile crept on to her face. "Are you sure?"

"You have to put that up. It's like a big F.U. to everyone who talked shit about you. Besides, it has a great message for other people to hear."

"I wanted to take control. I figured I could tell my side of the story and people could either choose to believe me or not. If not, then there's nothing else I can do about it. I'm going to move on."

I hopped off the bar stool and gave Ellie a fierce hug. "I'm so proud of you."

"Why?" she mumbled against my chest as I rocked her back and forth.

"Because. You've been through a lot the past couple of

months and instead of wallowing in the fetal position, you're grabbing life by the balls."

She laughed into my chest because I hadn't yet let her go. It felt right for her to be there. She belonged there.

"I hadn't really thought of it like that...but okay. So you really think I should do it? What if a potential employer sees it?"

"If they see it and they don't realize all the reasons they should hire you, it's their loss." I let her pull away. Finally.

She nodded. "You're right. Let's do it." She leaned down to the laptop, pressed a few buttons and straightened. "Done."

"How do you feel?" I asked.

"Like a weight has been lifted. Now that I'm done wishing I could change it or control what people think of me I feel better about it."

"I'm glad. How long until I can get all the changes for my website working?"

A huge grin split her face. "Really?"

"Yeah. You've got so many great ideas. I want to get started on them right away. The sooner the better since I think they'll help with my pitch to the show producers."

"I can have everything going in a day or two tops. All the stuff on the site is pretty much done I just have to bring it live. But I'd want to get your social media set up beforehand so we can announce it via those channels."

"Let's make it happen."

"Shouldn't you talk to your manager or record company or something first?"

"Last time I checked it was my face and my name on the music. I don't need their permission."

"Okay, if you're sure."

"I am. Make it happen. Let me know if you need anything from me."

"You've already given me best thing," she said as she threw her arms around my neck.

"Oh, what's that?"

"Your confidence. Having someone believe in me. It means so much. I won't let you down."

"I know you won't." I grabbed the hem of her shirt and pulled it over her head in one motion, leaving her in a white lace bra. "Now I have to figure out how I'm going to show you how grateful I am."

Ellie's eyes heated and she reached around to unclasp her bra. She slid it slowly down both arms until it dropped on the floor in front of her.

"Oh, Mr. Nash...I'm sure you'll think of something."

I actually thought of a few somethings that night and showed her every single one.

chapter thirty

The next few days went by in a blur between work at Beachside Realty during the day and getting everything up and going for Mason's social media platform at night. I think he may have started to regret letting me do it because he spent a couple of nights sulking on the couch when I wasn't paying him any attention. It was adorable.

A few days later everything was online and live. Some time would have to pass before we knew how the public was going to react to the changes I'd made. While I'd enjoyed using my skill set again, before I knew it, it was the end of the week and we only had one more day together.

I'd been putting this day out of my mind. Any time it slipped into my consciousness I'd push it back and refuse to acknowledge the impending doom I felt. Mason hadn't brought it up either. I took it as a sign that he was okay sticking to the original plan of moving on once our time together was done.

Skye and Katie had been blowing up my phone all week. First about the video I'd posted and how proud they were of me. The response online had been overwhelmingly positive. I'd graduated to people calling me 'c' words of a different variety now, like compassionate, caring, and considerate.

Then they'd try to see if Mason and I had broached the subject of him leaving yet. I finally got so sick of telling them we hadn't that I'd been doing my best to avoid them for a couple of days now.

It was the day before Mason was to leave and we were lounging around the pool, having a few drinks before we went inside to make dinner. I was sitting on a lounger watching the water flow in and out of Mason's six pack as he floated on his back in the water.

There was something so damn sexy about that man in his swim trunks slung low on his hips. The perfect 'V' leading from his hips to his groin was positively X-rated. At least it made *my* brain travel to X-rated thoughts.

I took a sip of my beer and closed my eyes, relaxing under the warmth of the summer sun heating my skin. Just as I was drifting off to sleep the bottom of my lounger dipped down and water dripped onto my legs. Without opening my eyes I said, "I'm going to get you for that."

Mason chuckled a bit from where he sat by my feet. He started drawing patterns on my leg with his wet hands, his touch slowly inched up higher and higher toward the apex of my thighs and my girly parts all roared to life.

"You'd better not start something you're not going to finish," I said with a grin and finally opened my eyes. His face was serious. Not what I had expected. I was immediately on alert. "What's going on?" I asked warily.

"We need to talk." His voice was low and much softer than usual.

This was it. The Dear John speech. The it-was-fun-while-it-lasted talk. I thought I'd at least have until tomorrow. I gulped and braced myself. I felt like a little kid waiting for the bandage to be ripped off. I knew it was coming, knew it would hurt but there was nothing I could do about it except wait for the pain that was sure to come.

I nodded and with that one small gesture felt like I'd set the guillotine in motion. It would be hard. I'd probably cry for weeks but I'd get over it. I knew better than to let him become important to me, knew it would only lead to heartbreak when he left. They always left. Whether they were your daddy, your stepdaddy or your lover. I had no one to blame but myself.

His hand rubbed up and down my calf in what I'm sure was supposed to be a soothing motion. It only put me more on edge. "When I came here I was looking forward to being by myself, relaxing before my next tour began, and one other reason."

"Which was..."

"I'd wanted to do some soul-searching and figure out what was missing in my life. I was successful in a career I enjoyed, I had money but there was still something missing. Some piece of me that wasn't satisfied with everything I had and all I'd accomplished. I thought being away from all the demands of my daily life might give me some perspective. I didn't expect I'd meet anyone like you, let alone find you sprawled half-naked on the bathroom floor." I gave a sad smile at the memory. "When this first started we agreed it'd be casual, that neither of us wanted anything more." *Here it comes...* "Things have changed for me."

Wait—what?

"How have things changed?" Hope bloomed inside of me.

"I don't want tomorrow to be the last time I see you. Since I met you I haven't once felt like something is missing in my life. I'm not sitting around thinking about why I'm unfulfilled because when I'm with you that's not how I feel. That has to mean something. I enjoy spending time with you and I want to do more of it. I want to try to work something out even though I'm on the road most of the time."

My heart leapt at his words, but then did a nosedive back to earth. As much as I wanted to be with him I knew it would never work out in the long run. He'd be surrounded once again by starlets, get sucked into the demands of his world and I'd end up a distant memory. I was taking charge of my life now. It was better to sever our ties at this point rather than after I'd fallen in love with him. And there was no doubt that if I gave my emotions free rein, I would. I'd fall hard and fast. I couldn't deal with anyone else choosing to leave me behind.

I knew walking away was the right thing to do but I couldn't make myself say the words. I wanted to make one more memory with him to hold onto when I was drowning in the depths of the murky ocean I'd be left in with no glimmer of light from above.

"Mason..." I slid down the lounger and placed my hand on his cheek, staring deep into his extraordinary green eyes. We stayed like that, just breathing and looking at one another, each with our own unsaid thoughts.

I leaned slowly toward him and our lips pressed against each other softly until finally our tongues met. His hands pushed into my hair. We kissed, content to go no further for longer than we ever had before. It was like we were telling the universe to back off. We had all the time in the world and we'd take as long as we wanted. When Mason finally pulled away from me those green eyes were heated embers and could have seared my flesh.

He stood up, then bent down to pick me up so he could carry me inside. He said nothing but never broke eye contact once as we made our way through the house to his bedroom where he gently laid me on top of his bed.

Mason stood at the end of the bed in all his perfection, his swim trunks still wet and clinging to his muscular thighs. He undid them, slid them to the floor, and crawled on top of me.

He kissed me again and languidly trailed more kisses down my neck. Eventually he got around to removing my bathing suit, which he did slowly and with intention. He laved my breasts, my stomach, my arms, my legs...there wasn't an inch of my skin that he didn't worship with his tongue.

When he arranged himself at my centre I was more than ready. He gazed straight into my eyes and slowly slid himself, inch by glorious inch, into me until he was seated to the hilt, filling me completely—mind, body, and spirit.

He pumped in and out of me at an easy pace, his forehead against mine, both our eyes open to the other. I'd never felt so connected to anyone before, the intimacy we shared in that moment would have brought me to my knees had I been standing.

Mason began to increase the pace and our breathing became more laboured. Tension curled in my belly and I arched my back. He rocked his hips into me, circling my core. The tension snapped, filling me with light and love. It poured out of me as I watched Mason rock into me and achieve his own release.

We lay there panting and Mason kissed both my eyelids. I was so overwhelmed with emotions that a lone tear rolled down my cheek. That had been the purist, most beautiful moment of my life and now I had to say goodbye to this man.

"Hey...Ellie. What's with the tear?" Mason whispered.

I couldn't speak past the painful lump that had formed in my throat. It felt as if I had swallowed a hot coal. I shook my head. Another tear escaped, despite my best effort to stop crying. When I finally managed the words I spoke quietly. "It'll never work."

Mason looked confused. "What won't work? Us?" I nodded. "How can you say that when we already do?" He brushed my tears away with his warm fingers. I resisted the urge to lean into his hand.

"That's different. This isn't your real life."

"I'm not saying it's gonna be easy. I know I'm traveling most of the time but you can come visit me on tour. I have some small breaks where I can come visit you. We can talk every day. We'll figure something out."

I didn't dare believe what he was saying. My heart had been broken before but this man held the power to completely annihilate it, the likes of which it would never recover.

"I don't see how it's possible."

"Don't do this, Ellie. You're the first woman in so long that I've let myself trust. We're good together. Don't throw it all away because you're scared. Don't let your fear control you. You didn't let fear control you at the women's shelter, don't let it now. Please. Fight. For Us." He dropped his forehead back down onto mine.

Those words changed everything. With that one statement I realized he was right; fear *was* controlling me. I'd managed to take control of my situation in the press. It was time to risk a piece of my heart. This man was worth it.

With trepidation and shaking lips I nodded against Mason. "Okay," I said softly.

"Okay? You'll try?"

"We can try."

Mason squeezed me tight against him and kissed my cheek. "Don't you ever do that to me again. You just took ten years off my life." I squeezed him back. Inside I hoped I wouldn't have to hold on to him this tight, in order to keep him near.

Monday morning at work I was wallowing by myself in the lunchroom when Katie came in and plopped herself down in the seat beside me.

"What's shakin', bacon?"

"Really?" I asked.

"What? It's a saying. People say it."

"If you say so."

"How you doing? Talked to Mason yet since he left?"

"We talked on the phone briefly last night and he texted me this morning."

"That's good." She looked at me intently. "Why don't you sound like that's good?"

"It's hard. I'm happy to be able to talk to him still, but being away from him sucks."

"Put so eloquently."

"Leave me alone. I'm wallowing."

"By all means. Don't let me interrupt a good wallow. After

all, if anyone deserves a good wallow it's definitely the woman with one of the hottest men on the planet practically begging her to continue seeing him."

"All right, now I feel stupid."

"That was never my intention." Katie batted her eyelashes innocently. "When do you get to see him next?"

"I'm flying out Friday night to Atlanta. He's performing at a music festival this weekend."

"See, that's not so long."

I sighed. "You're right. Thanks for making me see what a baby I'm being about the whole thing."

"I have a gift for making others see the error of their ways, what can I say?"

"I'll have to remember that."

"Now, let's talk about your latest viral sensation. Holy crap, girl. No one knows how to make a splash like you do."

"I was tired of letting everyone else control what was out there about me. It was time to set the record straight."

"Good on you. I thought your video kicked ass. Has Jeff said anything about it to you yet?"

"No, I've been dreading that." Dealing with my boss' reaction had been the repercussion I'd feared most. I didn't want to lose my job, but really if I did it wouldn't be hard to replace. My problem had been finding a career in the field I'd studied in, not finding a minimum wage entry level position somewhere.

"Be sure to let me know when he does. On second thought, I have a feeling the entire office will be able to overhear *that* conversation."

"Gee. Thanks."

Katie stood to leave but clamped her hand on my shoulder. "Seriously though, I'm proud of you. I didn't think you had it in you." She left the room humming under her breath, not at all aware her last comment could be construed as a backhanded compliment.

I smiled to myself, happy that I had such a great friend.

chapter thirty-one

My body was humming when the car pulled up outside the security gates Friday night. I'd been looking forward to seeing Mason all week. Thankfully the flight from Virginia to Atlanta wasn't a long one so it was still early when I arrived. Mason had said to text him and he'd come meet me after I'd made it through the security check.

The beefy guy who stopped us checked his clipboard, seemed satisfied with what he saw and pulled up the metal barrier that'd been blocking the way. The car crawled down the makeshift road past enormous trailers and miles of electrical cables until we came to the end.

Immediately the car door opened and sex on a stick slid in beside me. He was wearing khaki cargo shorts, a fitted black t-shirt and a black baseball cap on backward. He was absolutely edible.

"I couldn't wait for you to get out." Mason's lips came down on top of mine in a crushing kiss, as his hands ran up and down my back. I'd missed this. I relaxed into his kiss and wound my hands around his neck. Eventually we came up for air. "I also didn't want everyone to think I was a pussy because I couldn't wait two seconds after seeing you to get my hands all over you."

"We can't have anyone thinking that about you now can we?" I giggled and Mason led me from the car by the hand. The driver was standing beside the car by this point and Mason asked him to put my bags in his trailer. Mason placed a lanyard over my head. It held all my credentials, allowing me backstage.

"You hungry?" Mason asked.

"I could eat." I hadn't eaten any dinner yet but I'd barely noticed on the flight. I'd been nervous about seeing Mason again. Worried that somehow things might have changed, that the dynamic between us would be different. I felt silly now since it was clear nothing had changed.

"I've just been hanging in the trailer working on some new material but I've heard they have a pretty good spread. Wanna check it out?"

"That sounds great. Are you performing tonight?"

"No, I'm up tomorrow evening. I figured you'd want to see some of the acts since most of them tend to lean toward your rock."

"I never said I didn't like your music...I just hadn't heard it before." Mason enjoyed giving me the gears when he could about my love for rock and roll and lack of knowledge about hip-hop. The festival this weekend had a little something for everyone. There was rock, hip-hop, electronica, pop, and even some folk bands on the bill.

He brought our linked hands to his face and kissed the back of my hand. We walked past row after row of trailers until we came to an open area that'd been set up between two rows of trailers, with event tenting overhead. There were living room sets here and there, a bar in the one corner and a dozen tables overflowing with food. Music was piped in from the stage and all kinds of people were milling about. I didn't recognize anyone but I was doing my best not to stare so I didn't look like a total newbie.

"What is this place?" I asked.

"People hang here when they aren't performing...

sometimes reporters do interviews back here."

"Wow, that's cool."

"I don't spend too much time at these places anymore. I'm usually in my trailer doing my own thing."

"How come?" I asked.

Before he could answer a rough-looking man in his fifties, wearing a black leather vest over a t-shirt and a black bandana on his head approached. He had a cigarette poking out of the corner of his mouth.

"Mason, got a sec? I need to run something by you."

"Sure. Brawley this is Ellie. Ellie, Brawley. He's handles the sound for my tour." I shook the man's hand and smiled.

"Nice to meet you."

"Same. Been a while since Mason's invited anyone backstage," he said.

Mason turned to me. "Ellie, why don't you go grab some food while I talk shop with Brawley. I'll be right there."

"Okay, sure." I made my way over to the table. I'd been nervous about looking like I didn't belong but no one was paying me much attention. Suited me fine.

I walked over to the closest food table and stood behind the guy who had gotten there right before me. He must have heard me approach because he turned, and seeing me passed me the plate he just picked up.

Oh. My. God. I was about to go all fangirl because the lead singer of my favourite band had just handed me a freaking plate and was standing no more than two feet away.

"Ladies first," he said smiling and motioned for me to go ahead of him. He tucked a piece of his long brown hair behind his ear.

"Th-thanks." What a time for my tongue to take a vacation. I was doing my best to get my shit together and not make a complete ass out of myself. I walked around him and began perusing the table.

My eyes were open. I was looking at the table, but nothing on it was registering. It was a blur of undefined color. He stood beside me waiting for me to grab something and move on. I saw the feather tattoo on his forearm out of the corner of my eye. Not knowing what to do I just started reaching down, putting unknown items on my plate.

"You should try the king crab. I heard it's the best," he said to me. He was actually saying words directly to me. Unbelievable.

"Thanks," was my über-intelligent response. He was going to think that was the only word I knew in the English language. I reached the end of the table, grabbed a napkin and turned to see Mason approaching.

The object of my fangirling finished with his plate, walked by me and said, "Have a good time at the festival."

I refused to say thanks again so I smiled and nodded as Mason reached me.

"Did you get everything you wanted?" he asked and glanced down at my plate with a confused look. I followed his gaze to see that I'd filled my plate with some lunch meat, no bun, beets, couscous and cookies. Terrific. "What's with that?" he said and raised a questioning brow.

I ignored the question. "Did you see who that was?"

"Who, Dave? Yeah, he's cool."

"Cool? That hardly covers it."

"He's one of the best lyricists in the business if that's what you mean."

"Damn straight. I can't believe I just stood beside him. This is crazy."

"Easy there. How come I don't earn this kind of reaction from you?" he said as he took the plate from my hands, put it on the table behind me, and slipped his hands around my waist.

"Hmm...you earn plenty of other reactions from me." I kissed him and ran my tongue along his bottom lip. He let out a small growl. God, I loved that growl. That growl did funny things to my insides.

Mason picked my plate up and passed it to me. "Here.

Let's get you fed so you don't pass out from malnourishment. Then I'll show you what the inside of my trailer looks like."

"Oh really, I've never seen the inside of a celebrity's trailer before."

"Allow me to give you a guided tour..."

We never did end up making it out of Mason's trailer that night. He'd been a great tour guide and I now had intimate knowledge of the couch, kitchen table and bedroom. In the end when we were done with the "tour" we'd decided to go to his hotel for the night since he was performing the next day.

We arrived back at Piedmont Park, where the festival was taking place around one the next day. I'd opted to wear a pair of cut-off shorts, gladiator sandals, and a double-layered sheer white tank top. Atlanta was humid in the summer and today was no exception so I'd pulled my hair up into a messy bun.

"Troy's going to meet us here in a bit. We have some business to discuss."

"Did you want me to give you guys some privacy?" I'd only been in the company of Mason's manager the one time, and even though Mason spoke highly of him, something about the guy had rubbed me the wrong way. I didn't think he'd cared too much for me either but I told myself it was probably because he was looking out for his client. I'm sure he'd seen some real succubus types make the rounds a time or two.

"No, we're not discussing anything you can't hear."

A few minutes later there was a knock at the door and Troy walked into the trailer. The room suddenly felt entirely too small. He eyed me briefly but said hello. "I didn't realize you'd be here, Ellie. Mason fly you in?"

I didn't like how the statement rolled off his tongue—more of an accusation than anything else. "Yes, Mason asked if I would come." I wanted it clear to him I hadn't had to beg Mason to include me this weekend.

Troy walked past me and sat on one of the chairs. "So,

Mason when can we talk?" His eyes darted to me briefly when he finished speaking.

"Now's as good a time as any."

"Are you sure you wouldn't be more comfortable talking...in private?"

"Troy, anything you have to say you can say in front of Ellie. She's not running to the press with anything."

Troy cleared his throat. "All right then, we have a few things to go over. I have it on good authority that you'll be getting a nomination at this year's music awards."

"Really? I didn't think there was any chance that was happening. The competition was fierce," Mason said.

I couldn't contain my excitement. "That's terrific!" I got up and hugged him where he stood.

"Thanks, babe." Mason leaned down to kiss my forehead. As usual, goner.

I heard Troy pipe up behind me, seemingly unable to let us have this moment. "You do realize, Ellie, that information can't leave this room. The announcements won't be made for another few weeks."

I removed myself from Mason's embrace and returned to my seat. "Of course I realize that, Troy." I kept the agitation from my voice as best I could but it was probably obvious anyway.

Troy continued like I hadn't spoken. "That being the case, the TV producers are even more interested in looking at you for the reality series now. They want to shoot a pilot so they can test it with target audiences and get some feedback."

"Finally we're getting somewhere with them. I bet all Ellie's hard work on my site and social media presence helped, too."

"Gaining millions of followers in the span of a week certainly didn't hurt things. Case in point as to why I've been telling you to get on there for years."

"I didn't like anyone's approach to it until I heard Ellie's."

Troy looked like he'd swallowed glass, but Mason didn't

seem to notice. "They'd like to start shooting as early as next week."

"That works. They can get some footage of us backstage on tour. People love that shit. Make it happen. Anything else?"

"Nothing that can't wait. We have a few details about the tour to hammer out but we should wait until someone representing the promoter can be here, too. Tomorrow maybe."

"Cool. I'm gonna chill for a bit before makeup gets here and insists on covering every inch of my body with pressed powder."

"I'll see you out by the stage." Troy got up, nodded at me as he passed, and left the trailer.

I wasn't going to waste the short amount of time I had with Mason worrying about that guy. Mason had just gotten some amazing news and it deserved a celebration. I got up, grabbed his hand and forced him to sit where I'd been seconds before. When I straddled him his eyes became pools of lust.

"That was a lot of good news, Mr. Nash. I think it calls for a celebration of some kind." I leaned in to nibble on his ear and his head fell back against the couch. He let out a small groan.

"You do, do you? What did you have in mind?"

"Well I thought a little of this..." I trailed kisses down his neck. "...And this..." This time I bit down on his shoulder. "And maybe even some of this..." I moved my hand between us and cupped his groin.

"Hey, Mason, I figured we'd get started and—"A female voice behind us startled me. I jumped off Mason like I was fourteen year old who'd just got caught making out with her boyfriend. My cheeks flamed. "I'm so sorry. I didn't know there'd be anyone else in here. Oh my god. I'm so embarrassed."

Mason laughed. "Don't worry about it, Jas. No need to be embarrassed, looks like Ellie's got that covered for you." He slumped over, laughing hysterically.

I smacked his back, which was the only part I could reach otherwise it might have been a more delicate area of his anatomy. When he was finished he sat up and wiped tears from under his eyes. Seriously? I mean, come on. My embarrassment was not *that* funny.

"Jasmine, this is Ellie. Ellie, Jas." She walked over and shook my hand a little timidly. She was a pretty girl with straight light brown hair and almond-colored eyes. A few freckles dotted her nose, giving her a fresh-faced look. I wondered if she'd ever been with Mason. He'd made it clear he'd pretty much banged anyone willing his first few years of fame. She could well have been collateral damage. "Jas does makeup."

"Nice to meet you, Jasmine."

"Same, but sorry I barged in. I'm not used to Mason having company in his trailer these days...I didn't even think to knock."

I could tell she felt bad and then I felt bad that she felt bad. "It's not your fault. If we were looking for privacy we should have locked the door."

"Let's forget it ever happened," she said.

"Deal."

"Down to business then. Mason you know the drill. Park it so I can get to work. I have a bunch of dancers to do after this and you know how they get if there isn't enough time to get everything perfect."

"Aye, aye, captain." Mason gave a mock salute and made his way over to the makeup chair.

"Shirt off, buddy," Jasmine said.

"You have to get makeup on your chest?" I asked a little confused.

"Sure does. If pretty boy here could manage to keep his shirt on his whole set he wouldn't have to, but it seems to be a particular problem of his."

Mason and I both laughed at her quip while she got her makeup ready. It seemed there really wasn't much to putting makeup on a guy. Pretty much just powder for the most part.

The three of us chatted while Jasmine was hard at work on Mason. She was a nice girl who seemed to be very genuine.

"Okay, pretty boy. Stand up so I can do your chest." Mason did as he was told and she started brush powder over his abs.

"Tough gig, eh?" I joked.

"It's certainly not the toughest job in the world, that's for sure," Jasmine replied.

"I hear you'll be gracing us with your presence for the rest of my tour. Can I expect more of the same torment from you two when you're together?" Mason asked jokingly.

"That's right. It was either take your tour or get stuck on the road with the latest pop princess and even I'm not patient or tolerant enough to work for her."

"You're going on Mason's tour?" I asked.

"Sure am."

I was glad to know that I'd at least have one other girl around when I was with Mason. And a girl I liked at that.

"Okay, you're done. You two try to keep your hands off each other so I don't have to come back here and touch him up, okay?"

"Yes, Mom," Mason said.

"Ellie, it was great to meet you. I'm glad to see Mason finally found himself a normal girl."

"Thanks, I think."

"It's a compliment. Believe me," Jas said.

"In that case it was nice to meet you, too. I'm sure I'll see you around."

Jasmine grabbed her case and made her way to the trailer door. "I hope so. I could use some more estrogen on the tour. See you later, Mason."

"Later, Jas."

I laughed after her. I imagine it would be difficult being stuck traveling with all these men all the time.

"We should probably head backstage now," Mason said.

"Let's do it."

"Before we do there's something I wanted to ask you. You mentioned you had some holidays to use up. What do you think of taking a week and joining me on tour?"

"I think there's no other way I'd rather spend my time off." Excitement zipped through me.

He leaned in to kiss me but cut it short before it could escalate further. "I was hoping you'd say that. Come on, let's go."

I stood just off stage with Mason and Troy, waiting for Mason's intro so he could take the stage. This was the first view I'd gotten of the festival grounds and I was a little awestruck. There was a sea of people as far as the eye could see. We were in the bottom of a bowl and the parkland spread up a hill that surrounded the stage area. Fans closest to the stage jockeyed for position in front of metal railings. Some held signs, others had girls up on their shoulders and, oh yep, those were breasts. I guess tops were optional. With the heat and the crushing crowds I didn't much blame them.

The atmosphere was electrifying, the anticipation of the crowd palpable. A steady hum rose from the crowd as they waited for Mason to take the stage.

"I'm so excited to see you perform," I yelled over the noise.

Mason placed an arm over my shoulders. "I'm glad you're here, babe."

We stood there while the concert promoter pumped up the crowd and sang Mason's praises. When it was evident Mason would be taking the stage any second he started bouncing up and down in place. He reminded me of a boxer before a fight.

After his name was announced he leaned in to give me a quick peck on the cheek and ran out on stage to the roar of the crowd. They went crazy waving their hands, screaming and jumping up and down. It was like a wall of energy had been released from them and was hurling toward the stage. I swear I could feel it coursing through my veins. To be the target of all that adoration must be addicting on some level. I'd always assumed performers must have nerves of steel to get up in front of tens of thousands of people. I was starting to think they probably just ran on the adrenaline rush the crowd gave them.

Music started up and a few seconds later Mason started in with lyrics about how it was time to get the party started and it would last all weekend long. This was one of my favorite songs of his. He thought I didn't know anything about hip-hop and while that was still true I'd downloaded all his albums to check them out shortly after we started dating. I didn't let him know that, though, didn't want it going to his head.

The audience's hands were up in the air moving to the beat. It was an awesome sight. They sung back during certain sections of the song when Mason would turn the microphone in their direction. He had them eating out of the palm of his hand. I snapped a picture of Mason on-stage with my phone thinking it'd be a great pic for him to post on social media afterward.

A few songs into Mason's set and Troy turned to me as I was bopping away. "Mason told me about the little video you made," he said loudly into my ear.

Why was he bugging me about this stuff now? I wanted to watch Mason perform and besides, I didn't feel comfortable engaging him in conversation anyway. Maybe it was rude but I just nodded, hoping he'd take the hint.

No such luck.

"It seems to be getting quite a bit of attention from what I've heard."

All right. Let's get this over with. "That was kind of the point." I turned to look at him. He was nodding his head slowly, deep in thought.

"You made a lot of changes to Mason's website...you've come up with some interesting ideas."

I wish this guy would come out and say whatever it was he wanted to say already so I could get back to the show. "You're welcome. The changes were needed."

"I can't believe you managed to get him on social media. I've been trying for years...he's been very resistant to the idea."

I shrugged. I was over this conversation if he wasn't going to get to the point. Normally I'd just ask him what his problem was but it was clear Mason respected the man. I didn't think Mason would appreciate me getting into it with him so I kept my thoughts to myself. We watched the rest of the show in silence. I tried to put Troy out of my mind so I could enjoy the show but couldn't. I felt like prey around the guy for some reason.

Mason ran off stage when his set was finished. His muscled chest and abdomen were on display, his tattoos covered with a sheen of sweat. He'd taken off his shirt during the middle of his performance just as Jasmine had predicted. His hat was on backward and his shorts hung low on his hips. If we weren't in public I'd be pushing him down on the ground and having my way with him.

"So what'd you think?" he asked loudly when he got close to Troy and me.

"You were phenomenal. So talented." I wrapped my arms around him and kissed him, not caring that he was hot and sweaty. He kissed me back with just as much enthusiasm. From the look on his face, our display of affection hadn't impressed Troy.

"Great job," Troy said.

"Thanks, man. All right we're going to the trailer. I need a shower and I'm thinking Ellie might need one now, too." He pointed at my shirt, which was now damp with his sweat.

I grinned, my cheeks flaming a little but took his hand and began to lead him off stage. I was looking forward to the shower Mason had mentioned but my biggest impetus was to get away from Troy.

chapter thirty-two

The next week away from Mason was a long one. Much to my displeasure it seemed that my happiness was increasingly tied to him. Whenever that fact would dawn on me I'd push it to the back of my mind, not wanting to examine it too much.

Surprisingly Jeff had agreed to give me the following week off. I had a hunch it had more to do with my latest video. Although he hadn't fired me he'd made it clear that if any attention I got from it affected my duties at the brokerage I'd be on the unemployment line. He was probably glad to have me out of there in case any press came knocking.

I was in flight to meet Mason in New York City where he had two shows that weekend. I'd get to spend an entire nine days straight with him and I couldn't have been more excited.

The only thing I might have been more thrilled about was that I had to fly to L.A. on Wednesday for an interview I'd landed at *Session Magazine* the following morning. I'd be flying back east to meet-up with Mason after my interview. Someone at *Session Magazine* had come across my video and looked up my résumé on Monster before they'd contacted me. Landing a job at a place like *Session* would be more than I'd hoped for. It was a well-respected magazine focusing on the music and entertainment industry and they had a huge

231

online presence. I felt good about the interview since they were already aware of the media attention I'd gotten in the past.

Mason didn't perform until Saturday night so I met him at the hotel instead of at the venue. He'd texted me to say he'd instructed the driver to take me around to the back entrance because there were a number of fans lolling around the lobby hoping to sneak a peek at him. Somehow they'd figured out what hotel he was staying at.

The car pulled down a narrow alley. Mason stood beside an open door waiting. When the car stopped he slid into the car and kissed me hello. I really liked his new custom.

"How was your flight?" he asked.

"Uneventful."

"Glad to hear it. Come on. Let's get you up to the room and then I have to talk to you about something."

I nodded. His words gave me an ominous feeling. When people said you "had to talk" it wasn't usually followed by good news. I scolded myself mentally for always jumping to the worst conclusion.

Mason asked the driver to be sure my bags got up to the room and led me in the open door, which turned out to be the kitchen. Cooks and other kitchen staff worked to plate meals, barking orders at one another. It looked like complete chaos to my untrained eye but they all appeared unflustered, although they were clearly busy. They'd paid no attention to us as we walked through, trying to stay out of the way.

When we reached Mason's hotel suite he led me directly to the bathroom. "I thought you might want to relax in the tub when you got here."

An enormous bathtub sat in the middle of the room with steam rising out of it. Bubbles almost reached the top but weren't quite falling over the sides. He'd placed candles sporadically around the room. They emitted a light vanilla scent.

"I didn't know you were such a romantic." Warmth spread

throughout my chest. This was the sweetest thing anyone had ever done for me.

"It wasn't entirely unselfish. I *do* get to see you naked and if I'm lucky I'll get an invite into the tub, too."

I laughed. "Of course you're invited. I would never dream of denying a man access to a hot bubble bath."

Mason nuzzled into my neck from behind. "Mmm...perfect."

"Last one in has to wash the other one's back!" I said and grabbed the hem of my sundress and lifted it over my head. My sandals were next, followed by my bra and underwear. Less than a minute later I was easing myself down into the warm water while Mason had only gotten so far as removing his shirt and shoes.

"That was hardly fair," he complained. "But since washing your back isn't that much of a hardship, I'll let it go." Once he'd removed the rest of his clothes I tried not to gawk at what a piece of male perfection he was as he made his way to the tub. He slid himself in behind me and I settled myself between his legs. The mixture of his hard chest behind me and the warm water and soft bubbles was heaven.

"So...what did you want to talk to me about?" Mason's muscles stiffened beneath me, which further added to the feeling that I wasn't going to like what he had to say.

"Troy got a call from the producers of the reality show today. They want to shoot a week's worth of footage. They'll edit it together and show it to some test audiences to get some reactions."

"That's great news. Why was I getting the feeling I wouldn't like what you had to say?"

"They're going to start filming on Sunday."

"Oh." That meant they'd be around the week I was spending with Mason.

"I need this show to bring me into the mainstream, Ellie. I know the timing couldn't be worse but I tried and it can't be changed."

"I'll get out of your hair Sunday morning then."

His arms cinched me tighter. "I don't want you to go anywhere. Will you stay?"

I didn't know what to say. Part of me was relieved he didn't care if I appeared on camera with him, and another part of me had no interest in displaying any of our personal relationship to the public. Then there was a whole other part of me that was a little ticked he'd even ask me to take time off when he knew there was a possibility of this happening. I called him on that.

"Why did you ask me to come if you knew there was a chance you'd have to be filming?" I tried to keep the irritation from my voice but failed—it was evident I wasn't pleased.

"I wasn't exactly sure when they'd be filming."

"Well, I wish you'd thought to maybe ask. Now I've taken the week off to spend time with you and you'll be working the entire time."

"I was always working this week, Ellie. That hasn't changed."

I moved away from his chest and turned to my side so that I could see his face. "Yes, but that doesn't usually involve having cameras filming us. It doesn't mean we have to watch everything that comes out of our mouths, and that we can't be...intimate with each other when we want to." I sounded spoiled but I couldn't help it. I'd played out what our week together would be in my head, and this wasn't it.

"It's a reality show. We can do whatever we'd normally do. That's the point."

"I'm not an idiot, Mason. I know it's a reality show."

"I never said you were an idiot...we're getting way off topic here."

He was right. I knew what this meant to him. "I'm sorry. I'm disappointed is all."

He brought his hands up to either shoulder and rubbed up and down my arms with his strong hands. "No, I'm sorry we're going to be followed around by camera crews while you're here."

What did I think it was going to be like if he got the show? They'd be around—a lot. If I was going to continue seeing Mason it was something I'd have to get used to. I'd just make myself scarce. They couldn't possibly be filming twenty-four/seven, could they?

"Will you...stay?" he asked.

"Yes," I said softly. I had to keep the mindset that it didn't matter what anyone else out there thought. I knew who I was.

"Thank you." He leaned forward and kissed my forehead. The bloody man knew how to use those things on me and they were lethal. "So, excited for your interview this week?"

"You have no idea. Excited but nervous."

"No worries. You'll ace it."

"It's a great opportunity."

"Absolutely. My dealings with them have all been good. Their staff always seem professional."

"I'm really hoping it works out but let's not mention it on camera in case it doesn't, okay?"

"How about we make good use of the time we do have together before the cameras arrive then."

"I like how you think," he said, looking at me with heated eyes.

We certainly made good use of the bathtub that night and I sure as hell wouldn't have wanted any camera crew around to witness it.

We hadn't had as much time together the next day as I would have liked. Since this was Mason's tour alone it was different than the music festival. This involved sound checks every day, all kinds of interviews with the press, meeting fans who'd won contests before the shows. I'd had visions of us sneaking around the city incognito seeing some of the sights during the day. As it turned out the only sights I saw were our hotel room and the inside of Madison Square Gardens.

My vacation wasn't turning out exactly as planned.

chapter thirty-three

The producer and cameramen arrived at the hotel suite bright and early on Sunday morning. I was glad Ellie had decided to stick around but I knew she wouldn't be comfortable in front of the cameras. I was used to having them shoved in my face by now but I could remember what a pain in the ass and invasion it'd felt like when I'd first gotten in the business.

The producer had introduced himself as Vincent and the cameramen as Trace and Dom. They miked us up and told us to do whatever it was we'd normally be doing.

"I don't think we can do that. This is a PG show right?" I joked.

Ellie smacked my arm as color crept into her face. She was so damn cute when she was embarrassed it was worth doing just to see her reaction.

"I'm going to get ready," she said and walked toward the bathroom. Dom followed her with his camera. Ellie stopped in her tracks. "What are you doing?"

"I'm coming to shoot you getting ready," Dom said with the tone of voice that implied she was an idiot for even asking the question.

Ellie looked over to me with a beseeching look on her face.

"Is that really necessary?" I asked and turned to the producer, Vincent. "The show isn't about her. I'm sure America doesn't care if they see her put her mascara on or not."

"I'm not changing in front of a camera."

"It's all right, Dom. Let her get ready on her own," Vincent said.

"Thank you," she said and stalked off.

"We'll need to sit down with both of you later on to do some Q and A in front of the cameras," Vincent said.

"Sure, no problem."

That afternoon we were still at the arena after sound checks. I was scheduled to meet some fans who'd won a radio contest. Those were usually pretty quick...say hello, sign something, get a few pictures, and say goodbye.

Ellie was hanging out with Jasmine somewhere so it was just Troy and me in the makeshift green room. Security came in with a teenage girl around sixteen or so. She had a huge smile on her face and was holding some t-shirts and CD's in her hands.

"Oh my God, it's really you!" she practically shouted.

I chuckled. You could never be sure what a fan's reaction would be. Some, like this girl, were excitable, others stood like statues barely able to utter a word, and some acted like it was no big deal. "What's your name?" I asked her.

"Jessie," she said with a bit of a squeal on the end.

"Well, Jessie, it looks like you've brought a few things for me to sign. Should I make them all out to you?"

"Yes, that would be awesome!"

"All right, don't be shy then. Come take a seat beside me and let's see what you've got there."

She practically skipped over to where I was and took a seat on the couch beside me. We went through her stuff and I signed it all. After chatting for a couple minutes, we took some pictures and it was time for her to leave.

We were saying our good-byes when Vincent spoke up. "All right, that was great but can we do it one more time? We want to try it shooting it from another angle. Jessie, maybe you could add something about how this is the best moment of your life."

"Okay, sure!" she said.

She had no problem being asked to replay the moment but I did. Wasn't this supposed to be a reality show? Why were we re-enacting scenes and feeding lines to people? I felt like I was on a damn video shoot.

We said our goodbyes again re-enacting as best we could what had happened before. It seemed wrong to me. Like we took an honest moment between two people and turned it into something it wasn't. I brushed it off and continued with the rest of my day—cameras following me the entire time.

A couple of days later Ellie and I lay in bed enjoying breakfast before the camera crew arrived. We'd had to steal moments together like this all week. It was nothing specific but we were different with one another when the cameras were rolling. I didn't like it. I wanted to be the us I was used to.

"Everything okay?" Ellie asked interrupting my thoughts.

"Just thinking about this reality show. Yesterday the producer asked me if we could re-enact our original meeting."

"I hope you told them no. There's not a chance I'm letting someone tape me lying sprawled on the floor with only my underwear on."

"Yeah, not happening. That's for my eyes alone. That's not the first time they've wanted to re-shoot something either. A few times they've even fed lines to people and told them what to say."

"I take it you weren't expecting that kind of thing?"

"Maybe I did...I don't know. It feels like I'm being dishonest and misrepresenting myself when I do it."

"Could you tell them you don't want to do it?"

"I'm not in a position to ask. I haven't landed the job yet."

"Do you think you could if you got the show?"

"Maybe, but it makes me wonder what else they're gonna want me to do. I mean, if the show is a success are they gonna want to create storylines about shit that doesn't even exist?"

"No sense worrying about it yet. Why don't you wait to see if you get the show and then maybe you can negotiate something with them then?"

"You're right. I'm not going to borrow trouble." I picked her hand up and kissed her palm.

I had no way of knowing the cost to do the show would be even higher.

chapter thirty-four

I walked into the *Session Magazine* offices. The building was approximately twenty stories of dark glass and chrome and reeked of success—I wanted to be a part of it. I approached the large desk set in the middle of the sparse lobby but the chair behind the desk was empty.

It was a few minutes before I started to get nervous that the receptionist's absence might make me late for my interview. I had no choice but to wait since I didn't know where to go. Another minute passed and I was beginning to get really antsy when a pair of heels clicked across the floor behind me. I turned to see a girl about my age with shoulder length strawberry-blond hair wearing a black A-line dress approaching.

"I'm so sorry, have you been waiting long?" she asked.

"Not too long."

She sat down. "I spilled my coffee all over myself and had to run to the bathroom to try and get it out. Then I had to dry my dress underneath the dryer. How embarrassing."

I wasn't someone to whom embarrassing situations were a foreign concept so I decided I'd forgive her for almost making me late for my dream job. "I hope you got it all out."

"I did a good enough job. Now, what can I help you with?"

"I have a job interview with Steve Parsins. My name is Ellie Wagner."

She clicked away on her keyboard and satisfied with what she saw said, "You're all set. You need to take the elevator up to the seventeenth floor, turn left when you get off and go all the way down the hall. His receptionist is seated at the end."

"Thanks for your help," I said and walked away.

"Good luck with your interview," she called after me.

When the elevator doors opened up on the seventeenth floor I followed receptionist number one's instructions to arrive at receptionist number two's desk. This woman was middle-aged with short greying hair and an ample bosom.

"Hi, dear, can I help you?"

"I'm here to see Steve Parsins. I have an interview."

"Oh please, go on in. He's expecting you."

"Thank you."

I followed the direction of her hand to a set of wood double doors. They'd been left slightly ajar so I knocked lightly and poked my head in.

"Mr. Parsins?"

"Ellie, come on in. I recognize you from your video."

He was a slick-looking man of about forty or so and wore dark grey suit pants with a lavender button-down shirt. I stuck my hand out to shake his. "Pleasure to meet you."

"Likewise. Have a seat." He directed me to a couch and chair set away from his desk. I took a seat in the middle of the couch while he sat on the chair. "So, I know a bit about you from your résumé and your video but why don't you tell me what type of hands-on experience you got at school."

The interview proceeded well from there. We had easy conversation and he seemed to like my answers and was interested to know more. He explained that the job entailed handling a new division they were launching online. If it did well it would extend into the print version of the magazine. It involved discovering new talent online via YouTube, doing features on them, and running competitions for indie artists.

Listening to him talk about the position got me even more enthusiastic about it. I could picture myself doing the job, and my mind immediately started drifting into ways I could expand on the concept.

As I sat there I knew in my gut that all the other dead ends and crappy interviews were leading me here. This was the job I was supposed to get. So I couldn't have been happier when he said at the end of our meeting, "I think that's all the questions I have for you, Ellie. I'm really pleased with everything you had to say. When do you think you could start?"

My stomach pitched and my pulse sped up as I tried to control my reaction. "I need to give my current job a couple weeks notice and I'll need a week to find a place to live out here. So...three weeks?" I tried to remain professional and stoic but I could feel the corners of my mouth edging up.

"Excellent. There's only one thing we haven't discussed yet."

"Okay." I'd assumed he meant salary or benefits since I'd basically already accepted the position without even asking for any of those details. I wasn't exactly negotiating from a position of power though.

"You're in a relationship with Mason Nash, correct?"

"We're dating..." Was that considered some kind of conflict of interest?

"I'd like to know more about that."

"I'm not following."

"Let me be more specific. I'd like to do an exposé on the real Mason Nash. The one only those close to him see. The behind-the-scenes guy. Tell us what no one else knows. He's a pretty private guy...we want the inside scoop."

"You want me to see if he'll do an interview with you guys?"

"No. Ellie, we want *you* to write the piece. Use your inside knowledge to give us a picture of Mason no one is familiar with."

He wanted me to sell-out Mason. "So what you're saying is you want me to do this behind his back?"

"I wouldn't put it that way exactly but I'm sure you've been privileged to information no one else has."

"And if I say no?"

"Then I'll understand. Unfortunately I may have to re-think our need for a new employee, but hey—no hard feelings." I sat there in stunned silence for a moment. He used the opportunity to continue his line of bullshit. "Let's be honest...how long do you think this fling with him is going to last? Celebrities like him move through women like a model changes outfits. Think of yourself, what will you have after he's done with you? If you do this at least you'll have a promising career."

If I was a man I would've punched him. He obviously took me for some gold-digging whore out to take what I could get from Mason. He had the wrong woman. I grabbed my purse from beside me and stood up. "This meeting is over."

"Don't be so quick to dismiss this opportunity, Ellie. I'll give you a few days to think about it."

"I don't need a few days. I already know what kind of person I am and it's not the kind who would do something like that." I stormed out of his office with fire in my gut and the sound of my own blood rushing through my ears. I didn't recall making my way out of the building or hailing a cab but the next thing I knew I was pulling up to LAX.

Unlike my last interview this time I was confident my not getting the job was more a reflection of him than me. I wouldn't allow a jackass like Steve Parsins to reduce me to feeling ashamed. I had nothing to be ashamed of.

I had to wonder if it would always be this way. Was being with Mason going to affect my prospects in my chosen field? Would every potential employer want me to give them the inside track because I was with Mason? Even if they weren't as blatant as Steve had been, would I be free to come in and talk about my time with Mason the way a normal twenty-something with a boyfriend would? Or would I have to worry about being quoted in some magazine or gossip site somewhere?

My flight to Boston didn't leave for a few hours. Since I had time to kill and a lot on my mind I went to the airport gift shop in search of some light, frivolous reading material to get my mind off the interview.

I was perusing the magazine shelf when one of the covers caught my eye. There between *People* and *In Style* was a cover with a picture of Mason kissing a pretty blond that most definitely was *not* me.

chapter thirty-five

The headline screamed "Nash Rekindles Old Flame." Mason and the attractive woman were pictured walking down the street. She wore a blue floral dress fitted perfectly over top of her voluptuous body and Mason wore a grey t-shirt and jeans. His arm was slung around her shoulder and he'd pulled her into him and was kissing the top of her head. She was smiling. It was an intimate gesture, one that Mason had done to me many times before.

I had to swallow back the bile I felt rising in my throat. I grabbed a copy, stalked to the register, almost bowling over some guy browsing in the business section, and threw the magazine on the counter.

"Will this be everything?" the girl asked. I nodded and threw a ten dollar bill down. She looked at the front of the magazine. "Don't you love him? He's so hot. I'm loving that he and got back together with Rebecca Stark. Didn't they make the best couple?" She passed me my change.

I threw it in my purse without looking and stormed off.

I sat in the first open seat I saw and flipped through the magazine until I reached the article about Mason. More pictures of him and Rebecca Stark were plastered over the pages. I didn't know who she was but she looked vaguely familiar so she must be in the business. Her blond hair and stacked figure told me she probably spent her time in front of the camera, not behind it.

I scanned the article. The only mention of me in the story was a quick reference that Mason must have found it too difficult to deal with my "issues" and let me go. Either that, they speculated, or he was playing the both of us. Apparently he and Rebecca had dated up until a couple of years ago but had recently stepped out together in New Jersey where he'd played a couple shows before heading to New York.

I told myself not to put too much faith into the article, knowing full well what kind of bullshit they'd make up to sell magazines. It was much easier to tell myself that than it was for me to believe it. The visual proof was difficult to ignore. There was no mistaking the fact that they were holding hands in some pictures and kissing in others. I told myself it could all be lies several times but I couldn't shake the sick feeling of dread in my stomach. I paced the airport from one end to the other before I finally decided to call Skye and get her take on it.

When she picked up I filled her in on what I held in my hands. She immediately went into best friend mode, telling me all the reasons why I shouldn't be worried.

"You know first-hand the lies the press will put out there. You can't jump to any conclusions until you've spoken to Mason," she said.

"I know but what am I supposed to think when I'm staring at photo after photo of him with his tongue down her throat?" I don't care who you are. No girl wants to see pictures of her man being intimate with another woman, past or present.

"You think you don't know the whole story. You remember how they twisted around that photo of you and Mason and something like that could be exactly what's happening here."

"I'm trying. I really am."

"You need to call him," she said.

"I'd rather wait until I see him. That way I can see his reaction when I show it to him."

"Make sure you call me or text me as soon as you've talked to him."

"Will do. I'm going to turn my phone off until I get to Boston in case he tries to call. If I talk to him he'll be able to tell something is wrong."

"Okay, hang in there."

"I'll try. Thanks." I appreciated Skye doing her job as my bff and trying to cheer me up. My mindset was mildly better when I got off the phone but I couldn't seem to stop torturing myself by pulling out that damn article to look at it again and again. I probably could've recited the stupid thing word for word by the time I boarded my plane.

If this was the girl he'd once been in love with who's to say he hadn't met up with her in Jersey. Maybe he felt bad I'd already taken the time off work and was waiting to end things until the week was over. Or maybe he was trying to get away with playing the both of us. My imagination ran wild as I flew across the country. It was the longest flight of my life. I was antsy and nervous about seeing Mason and the possibility of hearing things I didn't want to.

By the time I landed I knew Mason was already at the arena for sound check so I took a cab to the hotel. Since I'd left my phone off I didn't know if he'd sent a car or not. I felt bad about it but I didn't want to chance a phone call with him right before his show. I knew myself well enough to know I'd bring up the magazine cover; regardless of what the truth was, it wasn't fair to him or his fans for me to spring something like that on him right before a show. Thankfully he'd left my name with the front desk and I had no trouble getting a key to the room after showing identification.

I took a long soak in the bath to relax and changed into a pair of yoga pants and tank top, throwing my hair up into a messy bun. I ordered some comfort food from room service and got comfortable on the bed. I forced myself not to look at the magazine article again. Not that I needed to—the images were permanently burned into my retinas. It was after midnight and I was a few episodes deep into a *Law and Order SVU* marathon when Mason returned to the room.

One look at him and it was evident he hadn't taken the time to shower after his show. He wore a pair of tearaway pants and white tank he'd probably thrown on after getting off stage. His hands were fisted at his sides, accentuating his muscled arms underneath his tattooed skin. He leveled me with his stare from across the room.

"Why'd you have your phone off? Did the battery die or something?"

"No, I turned it off. I *was* flying."

He clenched his jaw. "You had it off well before you got on your flight." I said nothing, not sure how to start this conversation. I didn't want it to come off accusatory, although I wasn't quite sure how to avoid that.

Mason saved me the trouble. "You saw the magazine." It wasn't a question, but a statement of fact.

I nodded my head slowly, not breaking eye contact.

"I tried to call you as soon as I heard about it but you had your phone off. You have to know that's all bullshit. Tell me you know it's bullshit, Ellie."

"Is that your ex-girlfriend in the picture?"

Mason swallowed hard. "Yes, but—"

"When I asked you in Virginia if you'd ever been in love and you said yes, was that the girl you were in love with?"

He hesitated this time and I knew it was. "Yes," he answered quietly.

"If it's bullshit how did they get a picture of the two of you together?" I kept my voice even through sheer force of will.

"I don't know. All I can tell you is that I was not with her when I was in New Jersey." He scrubbed a hand over his shaved head.

"So what...they photoshopped you into the picture or something?"

"I just said I don't know where the picture came from. I was not with her! You don't believe me?" He sounded angry now.

"I don't know what to believe, Mason. I know how the press can turn things around and make them seem one way when they're the complete opposite. But I don't know what to think when I see those pictures. I've had images of the two of you together cavorting through my head all day. I can't turn them off." I brought my knees up to my chest and sunk my head down. Frustration brought tears to the corner of my eyes but I refused to let them fall. I wanted so badly to believe him.

"I know how it looks. You gotta believe me…I would never do that to you."

I bounded off the bed to my purse. I grabbed the magazine from it, flipped to the pages with pictures of him and Rebecca and held it up into his face.

"What do you expect me to think when I see something like this?" Mason's eyes darted over the page, taking in the pictures. "I don't care what the article says about me, I know that's all bullshit. But what about these pictures?"

He grabbed the magazine from me and walked past, concentrating on the pictures. "These are old." He let out a long sigh and sat on the end of the bed. "Come here, I'll prove it."

A seed of hope formed in me at the confidence and calmness in his last statement. I moved to sit beside him on the bed and he passed me the magazine.

He pointed to his left wrist in the picture. "See this here?"

"Yeah, what about it?" All I saw was his sleeve of tattoos on the length of his exposed arm. I wasn't sure what he was getting at.

"Look at the difference." He pointed to his left wrist and I saw that he had Latin words tattooed across his wrist that weren't in the photograph. "I got this long after we broke up. This picture was taken when we were together, but years ago. How else can you explain the tattoo missing in the picture?"

I glanced from his wrist to the picture and back again as relief washed through me, followed soon by mortification. "This isn't me." Mason remained silent. "I'm not some insecure girl who freaks out at everything."

He wrapped an arm around my waist and pulled me close. "Don't worry about it. I know how it looked. But you've got to understand that this won't be the last time something like this happens."

"Why didn't I take one look at that picture, know it was a lie and put it out of my mind?"

"Because you're human, Ellie."

"I don't like feeling this way. I've never been the girl who needs constant reassurance from the guy she's seeing."

"It's a lot to take. I was new to it once, too, so I understand. It means a lot that you're willing to go through it for me."

His words gave me a warm feeling in my chest but I was still preoccupied with the despicable actions of the press and this needy, unconfident girl I was becoming. "How can they print pictures that are years old and make up a story about them? Look how easy it was for you to prove it's not true. They have to know the truth will come out."

"They don't care if someone can disprove it. They'll blame it on the anonymous individual who sold them the pictures." He made air quotes around the word anonymous. "It doesn't matter whether it's true—not if it sells magazines."

I'd considered believing the worst of Mason when he'd done nothing but treat me well the entire time we'd been seeing one another. "Can you forgive me?" I asked softly.

"There's nothing to forgive. I *want* you to talk to me if something is bothering you. But know this, Ellie." He turned to me and took my face in his hands. "I'll never lie to you. I may tell you things you don't want to hear from time to time, but I will never be dishonest." He leaned in and kissed my forehead and I melted into him.

"Thank you," I said. He was letting me off too easy but I'd take it.

"Now, tell me. How did the interview go?" I groaned. "That doesn't sound good."

I explained what happened and how I stormed out of the

office. It must've angered him as a muscle twitched along his jaw while I told the story. Instead of addressing his anger once I'd finished, he took me into a tender embrace.

"I can't tell you what it means to me that you didn't do what they asked. I know how much that job meant to you. You could have easily sold me out. The fact that you didn't shows me how right I was to trust you. I already knew it, but this is further proof. Trust is the single most important thing to me, Ellie. It's something I don't give many people."

"It was never a consideration," I whispered.

He kissed me thoroughly and I went to take his shirt off but he stopped me. "I have to have a quick shower first. I didn't have one after the show because I wanted to get back here."

I rubbed my hand across his pecs. "Or you and I could take a long shower together."

"Your ideas are always so much better than mine," he said and smiled.

We made slow and sensual love in the shower full of all the unspoken emotions neither of us dared say aloud. When it was over we moved to the bed where he tucked me into his side. I fell into a blissful sleep and dreamt about the two of us and a world where tabloids, paparazzi, and doubt didn't exist.

chapter thirty-six

Ellie and I spent the day playing tourist in Boston and managed to stay under the radar. We looked pretty damn ridiculous in our baseball hats, sunglasses, and oversized clothing but they did the trick. No one seemed to recognize us. She'd been tired and had opted to stay back at the hotel instead of joining me at the venue.

I was relaxing backstage and Jas was doing my make-up when Troy joined us.

"Hey, man, how's it going?" I'd worked with Troy long enough to know the expression on his face was smug so he must've had good news.

"Couldn't be better. Got a call from the producers of the reality show. They've made a decision."

"And?" I swear he always liked to drag things out for dramatic effect.

"And...you're in."

"Fuckin' right, man. Thanks for your help pulling our chances out of the shitter after my mom's incident."

"That's why I make you pay me what you do."

"Don't I know it," I said.

"That's great news, Mason. Congratulations," Jasmine said while she dabbed some type of cream under my eyes.

"I have to call Ellie and tell her." I reached for my phone on the table in front of me.

"There's one thing," Troy said. I didn't like his tone. I looked at him in the mirror, standing behind me. "Ellie's out."

"What do you mean, Ellie's out?"

"Market research showed overwhelmingly that their core audience didn't want to see you with a girlfriend. There can be females coming in and out of your life but anything serious and long term is a problem. Apparently young girls can't imagine they have a chance with you if you're seriously involved."

I glanced to Jas who dropped her gaze, looking like she'd rather be anywhere but here. "They *don't* have a chance," I said.

"That doesn't matter. They need to fantasize that they do and they can't do that with Ellie hanging around."

"I hope you told them where they could put their stipulation."

"I told them it wouldn't be a problem." His gaze was firm and unblinking.

"Then you need to call them up and tell them it is a problem and to figure something else out."

"It's a deal breaker, Mason. Ellie goes or you don't get the show."

This was unbelievable. I finally got Ellie to put a little trust in our relationship and give us a chance despite all her hangups about being under public scrutiny and now this.

"I think I'll let you two finish your conversation in private and come back in a little bit," Jas said.

"Thanks, Jas," I said.

"No worries. I'll come back in twenty or so." She left and closed the door behind her. I turned in my seat to face Troy.

"I hope you didn't make any promises I can't keep, Troy."

"I said I'd discuss it with you and get back to them in a couple of days, but that it likely wouldn't be an issue. Come on, Mason. You're not seriously going to let an opportunity like this pass you by because of some girl you met, what...a little more than a month ago?"

"What's your problem with her anyway?" I asked, real anger seeping into my voice.

"What do you mean?"

"I can tell you're not her biggest fan. I figured at first you were worried she was another Becca, but you've been around her enough to see that's not the case."

"I don't have a problem with her, but if you're asking if I'm looking out for your best interests then yes, I am. That's what I get paid to do."

"Ellie's not bad for my career."

"You're sitting here considering giving up an opportunity anyone would kill for, all for her. I'd say that's not a great career move. At least think about it. Consider all the possibilities."

He had a point. This was too big an opportunity to just squander without giving it due consideration. I hadn't gotten this far in the business by acting impulsively every time there was a decision to be made. "Tell them I need time to consider it and I'll get back to them in a day or two."

He sighed. "I'll support whatever decision you make, Mason. I want to be sure you're considering all the facts, that's all."

"I know you will. It's not the first time we've had a difference of opinion on things. Won't be the last."

"Of that I'm sure," he said, shook my hand and patted my shoulder before leaving the room.

Jas came back in to finish my makeup a few minutes later but didn't mention my talk with Troy. It was just as well; I had a show to do. I didn't need any distractions running through my head while I was on stage. I needed to bring my A game— that's what I got the big bucks for after all.

The next day we flew to Chicago to head to another music festival. Ellie commented a few times on how distracted I seemed but I brushed it off, telling her it was nothing.

I felt guilty as hell for not telling her what was on my mind but I couldn't. How did you tell the girl you cared for you were deciding whether you'd pick her or the career you'd spent years building? I racked my brain for some way to make both the reality show and my relationship with Ellie work but came up empty.

I did get a small piece of good news in a text from Deshawn as Ellie and I were cuddling on the couch in the hotel watching a movie. It was something I'd been working on for a couple of weeks and I was excited to share it with her. I hit pause on the TV controller.

"What are you doing?" she asked.

"I have something I wanted to show you."

She creased her forehead. "Okay...what's this about?"

"Deshawn and I have been working with a track to go on my next album. I'd already recorded it but we both felt it was missing something. We've been tinkering with it the past couple of weeks and came up with something I think works really well. I want you to listen."

She shrugged nonchalantly. "Okay."

I pulled the file up on my phone and started it. The bassline kicked in immediately and then the sample of Ellie's laugh worked itself into the song. I watched Ellie's face for recognition but saw nothing until a few seconds later when her eyes darted to mine.

"Is that...?"

"I told you I'd make it work."

Her hands came up to cover her mouth in disbelief. "Oh my God. I can't believe that's me."

"Believe it, babe. And that song is going to be at the top of the charts so everyone is going to hear it."

"I don't know what to say."

"I could've written you a song and thrown poetic words your way but I wanted to create something that had some of me and some of you in it. Something we could put out into the world. Something that'd always be there. It's our secret, the only people that'll know will be us, and Deshawn I suppose. If you decide to tell anyone that's your decision. While everyone else is trying to tear us down, this song will live on."

Ellie brought me into a fierce hug. When she pulled away I saw she had unshed tears in her eyes. "This means so much to me, Mason."

"There's something else."

"What else could there possibly be?"

"Because technically you're performing on the track you're going to get royalties for any sales."

"I don't need your money, Mason. I can't accept it."

I put my hand up in front of me. "It's already done."

"I just...this is so unexpected. I wouldn't feel right about taking the money. I mean, I didn't really do anything for it. Would you be angry if I donated it to a charity? Maybe I could give it to the women's shelter we visited. I'm not well off but the women and children staying there have it so much harder than I ever will."

"It's not even a fraction of what I want to give you, but the money's yours to do what you want with. I've never had anyone in my life like you. For five years all I've done is live and breathe the music industry. You've made me believe there are good people in this world. People still untarnished. You make me a better person by just being with me. You force me to open up to you and leave myself bare. I want to give you the world, Ellie. I want to give you every piece of me, every piece of my soul until we're so intertwined there's no beginning to you or end to me, we're just one."

A single tear traced down Ellie's cheek but she was smiling as she leaned in to kiss me softly, pouring all of herself into it.

The depth of Ellie's thoughtfulness and generosity never ceased to amaze me. She was one of a kind. How could I have even considered for a second letting this woman walk out of my life? She hadn't hesitated for a second to do the right thing where I was concerned. My career was important to me but I was learning there was more to a fulfilling life than success and money in the bank.

I'd tell Troy first thing in the morning to call the producers and tell them Ellie wasn't going anywhere and if they had a problem with it they could find someone else to do the show. Business opportunities would come and go but you got one shot with someone like her in your life, and I was determined not to blow it.

chapter thirty-seven

When we arrived at the festival grounds the following day I asked Ellie if she could give Troy and me few minutes to talk in my trailer. She'd gone off in search of Jas and hadn't seemed to mind. I needed to fill Troy in about my decision and I didn't want Ellie around to hear the details. If she knew her presence had caused me not to take the show she'd feel guilty—that's the last thing I wanted.

"I've made up my mind about the show."

Troy glanced around, looking around for Ellie I guessed. "I'm glad to see you've come to your senses and cut her loose." I ignored his comment.

"Ellie stays. You tell those pricks if they want me on the show she'll be around as long as she's around and if they don't like it they can find someone else."

Troy's face grew red. "You're going to throw this away for a temporary piece of ass? Un-fucking-believable."

"You don't know anything about her."

"I'm sure she gives head with the best of 'em, Mason, but she's not worth tossing an opportunity like this away. How long do you think she'll stick around before she floats on to a bigger and better meal ticket?"

"I'm gonna do us both a favor and pretend you didn't just

say that. Go do your fucking job, Troy, which last time I checked is what I tell you to do. Call those producers and deliver the damn message."

"I'll deliver the message but you're going to regret this, Mason. When she screws you over don't come running to me." He stormed out of the trailer, slamming the door behind him.

Troy and I had had disagreements before, but this was the first time there had been any *real* friction between us. He was a terrific manager, great at what he did but I was getting tired of his lousy attitude where Ellie was concerned. He'd never had much respect for women in the past but I'd never seen that side of him. I chalked it up to his disappointment that the deal wasn't coming together. It was easy for me to forget he'd be losing a lot of money, too.

I'd let it blow over for a day or two and act like nothing had happened. He'd get over it.

When I saw Little Mac enter the bullpen where Ellie and I were chillin' backstage, I knew my day was going from bad to worse. I'd had enough dealings with him to know he'd make his way over to us to try to get under my skin.

Sure enough, when he saw me a shit-eating grin crossed his face and he headed in our direction. He stood in front of us and Ellie smiled up at him, having no idea who he was.

"Well, well, Mason. Looks like you're dipping in a pool of higher class girls than you usually go for," he said.

I didn't bother addressing his ridiculous comment. "What do you want?"

He ignored me and grabbed Ellie's hand, bringing it up to his lips for a kiss. She giggled and my balls clenched up—not in a good way. Time to shut this down. I took Ellie's hand from him and placed it on my thigh.

"Ellie, this is Little Mac. You may remember me mentioning him before."

"Oh, I remember," Ellie said, looking abashed.

Mac laughed. "Panties still in a bunch I see, Mason. Don't believe everything he tells you, Ellie. I'm sure it's been exaggerated for dramatic effect."

"I do my best not to talk about you."

"I'm sure it pains you to see my name on the charts. I get it."

"Why don't you be on your way? Aren't you on soon? I've still got a few hours to kill." It was an asshole thing to say. It was well known that the later in the day you performed, the higher up the list you were considered, and today I was on after him.

"Enjoy it while it lasts. When my new album drops you're gonna be the one eatin' crow. Ellie, when you get sick of this second-rate performer come find me." He smiled at Ellie, turned and stalked away before I could say anything. Suited me fine.

"You weren't kidding when you said you two didn't like each other, were you?" Ellie asked.

"Not even a little. Sometimes I think that guy would stop at nothing to try and bring me down."

Mason's performance had been magnificent. No surprise there. The crowd had roared and was totally into it the whole time. After he'd showered we joined a bunch of other people in the bullpen backstage for a party of sorts.

Music was piped in from the band on stage and we all sipped our drinks and mingled. Lights were strung from one side of the makeshift room to the other since the sun had already set. It was a fun laid-back vibe and I realized I was much more comfortable in the off stage environment than the first time I had joined Mason in Atlanta.

Reporters from entertainment shows and magazines were part of the mix. Mason was finishing up an on-camera interview off to the side, while I ordered another rum and

Coke from the bartender. I looked off to my left as I waited for my drink and saw Troy talking to Little Mac between two trailers. It struck me as odd—what would they have to talk about? I shrugged it off. Troy was so protective of Mason maybe he was telling Mac where to stuff it.

I went back to the couch where I'd been sitting before and saw Mason was already there. I sat beside him. "How'd the interview go?"

He shrugged. "Once you've done a couple I swear they could probably just pull tape from the first one and get the same answers. The questions never change."

"Must get monotonous."

"You know it." Mason put his arm around my shoulder and I leaned into his side. He played with the spaghetti strap on my tank top absentmindedly as we sat there.

I was thinking of asking Mason if he wanted to head back to his trailer for some adult wrestling when Troy approached. "Mason, you've got one more interview to do and that's it for the night."

"All right, man. Who is it?"

"Becca."

Mason's body went rigid beside me. He removed his arm from around my shoulders and leaned forward. "I hope you're joking."

"No such luck. She landed a new gig as a co-host on *Star Weekly*."

"I wonder who she had to sleep with to land that."

Before I could ask what that was about a striking woman with blond hair and a short fitted white dress approached. A large V dipped at the front of her dress revealing just the right amount of cleavage to look sexy but not trampy. I caught a number of guys rubberneck as she passed. As she got closer it dawned on me who she was. Mason's ex, Rebecca Stark.

"Mason," she said in a husky voice when she reached us. "Who's the flavor of the week?" She nodded in my direction but didn't remove her predatory eyes from him for a second.

"Congratulations on the new job. How'd you weasel your way into that one?"

She flicked her long hair behind her shoulder then rested her hand on her hip. "Oh, you know me. Never one to let an opportunity pass me by."

"I do remember you being quite the opportunist," Mason said and there was venom in his voice. "Where do you wanna do this?"

"Used to be you wouldn't even ask. You'd take me wherever you wanted me, didn't matter who was around. It's nice to be the one giving *you* direction for a change. Let's head back this way for some privacy."

"Cut the bullshit. Let's get this over with." Mason leaned over and gave me a chaste kiss on the cheek. "I'll be back in a bit, babe. You okay to stay here?"

I nodded and tried to check the impulse to claw Rebecca's eyes out. I knew these two had history and as much as everything they said indicated they didn't like one another, I couldn't help thinking their feelings were too intense to say that they'd both moved past it.

Troy watched them walk away and when they were out of earshot turned to me. "Better watch out for that one, Ellie. She's a viper. *If* Mason comes back anytime soon can you tell him to find me? We have a couple things to discuss."

"Yeah, sure." What'd he mean *if?*

I polished off my drink, got another one and returned to my seat only to see that Little Mac was on the sofa. I glanced around but there were no other free seats. I reluctantly headed over to sit beside him and did so without acknowledging his presence.

"Saw Mason and Becca leave together. Those two hot and heavy again?"

I whipped my head around in his direction and flashed him a bitchy look. "You know they're not."

He chuckled. "I see he didn't fill you in before he ran off alone with her."

I was beginning to see why Mason had no love for this guy. He was an irritating little shit. "Do you have a point?"

"He and Becca used to be inseparable. She went everywhere he did. It was sickening to watch them all over each other. Shit, they must have been together for at least a year or two. He was messed up after they split. Not that we're tight or anything but everyone knew she broke his heart."

"That's in the past."

"You sure about that? I saw her earlier and she was asking me about him. Seemed real interested. Becca doesn't quit easy when she wants something."

Was she hitting on him right now? No. I stopped myself right there before my thoughts turned in that direction. Mason had made it clear that he wouldn't do that to me.

"Aww, don't worry, sweetheart. I'm sure he's not interested in wettin' his whistle in that again. You're pretty hot, too. Though, I gotta say...she was looking pretty smokin' in that dress tonight."

My chest tightened making breathing difficult. I stood quickly. "I need to use the bathroom."

I didn't wait for him to answer, making my way to the bathroom as fast as possible. I sat on the closed lid of the toilet trying to gain my composure and gather my thoughts. I hated that I let that jerk get a rise out of me. It's not that I thought Mason was going off to have a quickie with her or anything...but what if being around her again brought old feelings to the surface for him again? Made him remember the good times they'd shared. I didn't know the details of what had happened, but I knew it had ended badly. Regardless, if they'd been together that long there were a lot of good times, too. Remembering them might make him realize of how much he used to love her, or maybe still did in some way. I couldn't compete with her. She was off the charts beautiful in a way I'd never be.

I leaned forward so my head was between my legs and took some deep breaths. I needed to get myself together. I couldn't let this jerk fill my head with bullshit.

It dawned on me that Little Mac would be good for one thing. He liked to talk...maybe I could get a better idea of what went wrong between Mason and Becca. Mason would tell me if I asked, but I didn't want him thinking I was being a jealous lover—whether or not that was the truth.

I made my way back to where I'd been seated to see Little Mac still there. I sat down beside him and leveled my gaze at him.

"So when does your new album come out? You mentioned it earlier." I figured if I fed his ego a bit it'd be easier for me to pump him for information. It seemed my instincts were right. A big smile crossed his face and he grabbed my drink from the table, passed it to me and leaned back, stretching his arm along the back of the couch behind me. It wasn't so brazen that I could tell him to knock it off—he wasn't touching me—but I leaned forward anyway in the hopes my body language would indicate I was not interested in him in that way at all.

"It drops next month. That shit is gonna be epic."

"How long have you been doing hip-hop?" I asked and took a sip of my drink. I was gonna need more of these if I had to listen to this egomaniac's drivel.

I needn't have bothered—I didn't remember anything after that anyway.

chapter thirty-eight

Yelling. Someone was yelling and the sound beat the inside of my head like a drum. I moaned and covered my head with my hands to drown out the sound. Was that a pillow under my head? I grabbed it and brought it down over top of me.

The mattress beside me moved, bouncing up and down like someone couldn't decide whether they were getting on or off. Still with the shouting.

I might have drifted off for a second again but a hand shoved my shoulder. I tried to ignore it and the queasy feeling the jostling gave me. A hand pressed into the back of my shoulder again but harder this time.

I groaned and rolled slowly over onto my side. I tried opening my eyes but they wouldn't cooperate. Lead weights must've been tied to my eyelids they were so heavy. On my second attempt I was able to open them little more than slits. It took a minute for my vision to focus on what was in front of me.

Mason stood glaring down at me, fury evident on all his features. He grabbed my arm and hauled me out of bed. I stood in front of him and realized for the first time that my pants were missing. What the hell?

"Your playmate's still out cold," Mason said, his voice seething with rage.

I looked around and realized I didn't recognize my surroundings at all. We were in a trailer, but this didn't look like the one Mason had been using. I was pretty sure his had dark wood, not bleached oak like this one. I turned and looked behind me to see Little Mac passed out in the bed, his bare chest visible before the sheet cut off the view at his belly button.

My knees buckled and I slumped onto the ground. What the hell had happened to me? Mason crouched down in front of me to look me in the eyes.

"Was it all a game from the beginning? Did he put you up to it from day one, or you get what you needed and move on to the next sucker?"

"Mason, I—"

"Save it. I don't even want to hear it. I can't believe I ever trusted you. Did you plan to meet me all along once you found out who was renting the beach house? Your mom give you some lessons on how to land a rich guy?"

My heart cracked into a million pieces as I sat there listening to Mason and the venom behind his words. Hot angry tears ran down my cheeks. I couldn't stay in this room any more. I wanted to physically distance myself from whatever had happened here.

I stood and Mason followed suit. My head spun for a moment and I had to take some deep breaths to clear my vision. I looked around frantically for my pants. I needed out of here. I couldn't stand being in that room for one more second.

"Nothing to say for yourself?" Mason spat at me.

"I don't know what happened. I don't remember coming here. The last thing I remember I was sitting on the couch talking to Little Mac."

"Oh, I heard all about you two on the couch. How do you think I found you?"

"Mason..." I croaked out.

"Fuck! FUCK!" he yelled and turned to punch the wall, leaving a gaping hole.

"Someone must have put something in my drink. That's the only explanation!"

"Jesus Christ, Ellie. What are you a fucking teenager? Save your excuses. I'm not buying what you're selling anymore."

"I'm telling you the truth!" I yelled, cringing at the pain it caused.

"Why are you trying so hard to make me believe it? You have a little more planned for me? Feel like pulling the wool over my eyes a little longer? I really didn't take you for an opportunistic bitch but I guess we're all wrong sometimes."

"Stop saying horrible things to me."

"You're right. You're not worth the breath." He started to turn away but stopped and glared at me again. "I hope you weren't counting on this guy being you're next conquest because I gotta tell ya...you couldn't have picked a worse one. This guy's fucked and chucked every girl he's ever been with."

I couldn't form any words around the painful lump that had formed in my throat. I shook my head back and forth as my only form of denial.

"I don't wanna have to look at you ever again." His voice was devoid of emotion now and somehow that was worse than his anger. "Get your shit from the hotel and get out of my life, Ellie."

I couldn't believe that this man who'd been so understanding couldn't find it in himself to consider that I was telling the truth. Not only was I dealing with what felt like a betrayal from him, but I'd been violated. In what way I didn't know yet, but that didn't matter. Instead of supporting me and offering me comfort he was cutting me down.

"Screw you, Mason! You don't want to believe me? Fine. I'm gone!" In a daze of heartbreak and fury, that's exactly what I did.

Skye and Katie were waiting on my front porch when I arrived home from the airport. I'd texted them on my way to the airport and given them the rundown of what had happened—at least what I could remember of it. Thankfully my mom and Ralph were out so I'd be able to put off dealing with them until later.

The skin underneath my eyes was puffy and raw. I'd cried the entire plane ride home, trying my best to do it quietly so other passengers wouldn't notice. The flight attendant probably thought I was an emotionally unstable woman—which might not have been too far from the truth.

"You look like hell," Katie said as I made my way up the walkway.

"Gee, thanks. Kick a girl when she's down why don't you."

"Come on. Let's go in and pour you a nice stiff drink and you can tell us all about it," Skye said.

I burst out crying again. Alcohol was what had gotten me into trouble in the first place. I didn't want to see, smell, think, or hear about it. Skye and Katie took my keys, opened the door, and got my bags inside. They led me to the couch and let me cry for ten minutes without complaint, sitting on either side of me rubbing my back. I had great friends, which somehow made me cry harder.

"I don't know what happened. One second I'm sitting beside this guy and we're talking and the next I'm half-naked in bed with him and Mason is yelling. Someone must have put something in my drink. That's the only explanation."

"Do you think you guys...you know?" Skye asked.

"No! I can tell we didn't have sex but I must have been half-naked for a reason."

"And Mason wouldn't let you get an explanation out?" Katie asked.

"That's the worst part. He didn't believe me. Didn't even try to hear me out."

"Maybe once he cools off he'll listen," Skye suggested.

I shook my head. "You guys didn't see him. He wasn't even that angry when his mom was arrested. After all the horrible things he said to me I don't even want him to try."

"Well, screw him then," Katie said emphatically.

I burst into tears. Skye went to the bathroom to grab me some tissue. I blew my nose and wiped under my eyes.

"It'll be okay, Ellie. You'll be okay," Katie said with confidence in her voice.

"I loved him!" I blurted out without thinking. "How is it going to be okay when I loved him and now I have to be without him? How could he think any of those things about me?"

It was the truth. I was in love with him. I'd been so busy fighting my feelings and trying *not* to need him that I'd been blind to what was right in front of me the whole time.

"We know you're not like that sweetie. It's his loss."

Fresh tears escaped my eyes when I thought I'd had none left. There wasn't anything left to say. Mason was just another in a long line of men who'd let me down. It had started with my dad, continued with my stepdads, and now the only man I'd ever loved.

I laid myself down on the couch surrounded by what was left of my support system until I drifted into a fitful sleep out of pure physical and mental exhaustion.

chapter thirty-nine

My head felt like it'd been split open with an axe when I woke. Not sure if it had more to do with the bottle of Jack I'd polished off last night or the image in my head of Ellie lying in bed with that douche bag. I'd gone and gotten as shit-faced as possible after she'd left, not wanting to deal with crushing weight of betrayal bearing down on me. I think I remembered Troy and Jas stumbling upon me at some point, trying to get me to go easy. Obviously they'd failed.

I hated myself for turning to the bottle to deal, but I hadn't seen any other way to turn off the images of Ellie and Mac scorched in my brain. That was the problem with the bottle that my mom had never figured out; the relief it provided only lasted as long as you had your lips fused to it. The emotions you were avoiding always came roaring back to life the next day.

I didn't understand how I could've been so wrong about Ellie. Was I a complete moron? Had there ever really been feelings on her part or was it all some kind of game to her? I had so many questions scrambling my mind I couldn't think straight. The pain and desolation was unlike any I'd experienced before. Why with him? Why with the one person most guaranteed to ensure that I could never forgive her, regardless of how much I cared for her.

There was a knock at the hotel room door loud enough to wake the people next door. It sent the jackhammer working in my head into overtime.

I peeled my body up off the bed as fast as was possible, which wasn't fast at all, and shuffled to the door. I didn't give a flying fuck who it was I just wanted the banging to stop. For the love of God make it stop!

I unlocked the dead bolt and swung the door open to find Troy standing there freshly showered, looking like he'd gotten his full eight hours in.

"You look like shit," he said. I didn't bother responding. I turned to shuffle my way slowly back to the bed to lay down. "I came to make sure you were still alive."

"You can see I am. You can go now."

"I can see you're technically alive although you might want to consider a shower before we head to the airport."

"Whatever, man. I don't care what I look like right now."

"Right, well, we still have business to discuss even if you're nursing the mother of all hangovers. She's not worth it, Mason. Look what she did to you."

If shouting at Troy wouldn't have split my skull in two I would have let fly, but I'd be the only one in pain for it. "I don't wanna talk about it."

"Well, we have to talk about the offer for the reality show. Have you given it any more thought?"

"Yeah, Troy. I think I thought about it between shot number twenty last night and puking my fucking guts out. Oh, wait. No, I didn't."

"No need to bite my damn head off. I'm the one trying to keep your career on track—not throw you under the bus."

He was right. He'd done nothing but help my career from day one. Turns out he'd been smart to be looking out for me where Ellie was concerned. He'd seen something that I'd been too blind to. "Sorry, man. Just a lot running through my head right now."

"So...should I call the producers and tell them you're in?"

"No. You can tell them I'm not interested in doing the show anymore. Make my apologies. Mac can have the damn show if he wants it."

I was lying on the bed with my eyes closed so I couldn't see him but I heard him stomp closer to the bed. "What do you mean you don't want the show? I figured with Ellie out of the picture for good you'd have come to your senses."

"It has nothing to do with Ellie. I don't want to do the show. I'm not interested in showing the world a fake version of Mason Nash. Some version production has decided the world wants to see. I've had enough of people misrepresenting themselves and I want no part in doing it myself."

"Mason, you'd be a fool to throw this opportunity away. This could open up a lot more doors for you."

"Then I'm a fool. Ellie taught me there's more to life than just work and becoming bigger, better, and richer."

"Why don't I see if I can put them off for a day? You've had a lot to deal with. You should think about it with a clear head."

"I don't know what you're not getting here—I'm not doing the show. Not now, not next week, not next month. It doesn't matter. I want no part of it."

Troy was silent for a minute so I reluctantly opened my eyes to be sure he was still there. He was standing at the end of the bed, his face flushed in anger.

"Don't do this, Mason. Don't throw this away because you got addicted to some pussy and now you're thinking no pussy is ever gonna feel as good. Believe me—they all feel good. After a while you'll forget all about her."

He didn't have the first clue what it felt like to be with someone who was like the other half of you. The missing puzzle piece. What was I saying? It was none of that...that was only what I imagined it to be.

I didn't have the energy or desire to argue with him about it. "Just go, Troy. I don't want any company right now."

"You're making a mistake. A year from now when Little Mac is at the top of the charts and everyone is buying his clothes and cologne in all the department stores you'll wish you'd listened to me."

"Maybe, but I'm okay with that."

chapter forty

Life without Ellie was difficult and dragged on. My feelings for her vacillated between missing her something fierce and loathing her for her betrayal. Either way I was constantly trying to push her from my mind completely.

It was a couple of months later and the morning of the music awards. I still hadn't figured out why she'd done it. I'd racked my brain trying to figure out what her motivation could've possibly been and I'd come up empty every time. It wasn't for money, it wasn't for fame, and it wasn't to get a job. If it had been she would've jumped all over the job at *Session Magazine*. It shouldn't have mattered to me that I couldn't figure it out, but for some reason I couldn't let it go.

A knock sounded at the door to the suite. I was staying in at the Roosevelt Hotel in Hollywood again trying not to remember what I'd been doing and who I'd been doing it with the last time I was here.

I'd had no interest in dating since Ellie and I had broken up so Troy was coming with me to the awards. That must've been him at the door. I'm not sure bringing him was gonna be any more tolerable than a date would have been. The fact that I'd been in a funk since ending things with Ellie was starting to wear on him. At first he'd tried to push other women on me, but I made it clear he needed to stop. As much as I despised it, my heart was still with that damn woman.

I opened the door and to my surprise it was Jasmine. "Hey, Jas. What are you doing here?" She was wringing her hands in front of her and glancing down the hall nervously. "Everything okay?"

"Sorry to show up unannounced," she said.

"It's not a problem but I don't think I'll be needing any powder on my abs for the awards tonight." I'd tried to lighten the mood but she wasn't biting. She looked unsettled.

"I need to talk to you about something."

"Come in." I motioned for her to take a seat. I sat in the chair on the other side of the coffee table. "So, what's going on?"

"First you have to swear that no matter what you'll never tell anyone I told you this. Promise?"

"Promise, sure. What's this about?" I was on edge now. The tone of her voice was serious.

"I mean it, Mason. No one can ever know I told you. If anyone ever confronts you and says it was me you have to deny it."

"Jas, you're starting to freak me out."

"You have to understand what it's like to be a makeup artist. We hear all kinds of stuff we're not supposed to. Half my clients act like I'm deaf and stupid and spill their guts to their friends or managers, and the other half treat me like I'm their psychotherapist. It's an unspoken rule that anything a makeup artist hears doesn't leave the room. If anyone found out I was blabbing I'd never get another job. Never piss off your makeup artist—I can guarantee they've got dirt on you."

"All right, thanks for the warning. What do you have to tell me that has you so jumpy?"

She took in a deep breath. "Last week when your tour had a break for a few days I flew to California to do some work for Little Mac."

I stood up at the mention of his name. "I'm not interested in discussing anything that has to do with that piece of shit."

"Believe me, I feel the same way. I have no love for that guy either but he helps pay the bills and his name looks good on my roster. You'll want to hear this though, trust me."

I sat back down reluctantly in my seat. "You've got my attention."

"I overheard some things I'm sure I wasn't supposed to."

"Such as?"

"He was bragging to his buddy about how he stuck it to you making you think that he'd had his way with Ellie. He was going on and on about how pissed you were over the whole thing. He said it was even better than when you caught Becca with him."

"Is there a point to this?" I asked between gritted teeth.

"I'm getting to it. When his friend asked how he was able to get Ellie to go along with it he said he put something in her drink."

"Are you saying he drugged her?" She nodded. Fury swept through me fast and marrow deep. "Son of a bitch. I'll fucking kill him. Did he touch her while she was out of it?"

"No, he was clear he never laid a hand on her. Made some disgusting joke about how it wasn't fun if they weren't awake to fight you."

"I knew he was a lot of things but even I didn't think he was capable of something like this."

"That's not all," she said.

"What the hell else could there be?"

Her lips pursed before she spoke. "He said Troy asked him to do it."

"*Troy?*" I couldn't comprehend what she was saying; it didn't make any sense. "Why would he do that?"

"I don't know...he just said that Troy told him to do whatever it took to lure her away from you."

I didn't know what to say. It was one thing to see how far a guy would go out of some misplaced sense of competitiveness, but why would Troy be in league with my biggest enemy?

"Is it possible he knew you were listening and only

mentioned Troy's name to cause more trouble?" I asked.

"I was behind a curtain. There's no way he knew I was there. They'd just walked into the room."

"Un-fucking believable."

"My success depends on my clients knowing I have discretion when I'm party to conversations I shouldn't hear. I'll be ruined."

"Jas, relax. This'll never come back to you. You have my word. You've risked a lot coming here. If Mac is bragging that openly then his buddy's not the only one he's told. He's probably told anyone who'll listen. I've always said the guy was out to get me but I never thought he'd go this far to do it."

"I feel better now that you know. As soon as I heard it I knew I'd end up telling you. It took me a bit to work up the courage."

"You're a good friend."

She got up from the couch and came over to give me a hug. "Good luck with Ellie. I hope it works out. She was good for you."

At the mention of Ellie's name, guilt for all the repulsive things I'd said to her came crashing down on me. She'd said someone had put something in her drink and I'd dismissed it as an excuse. How could she ever forgive me?

"Thanks. You should get going. Troy is on his way over."

She hurried to the door of the suite, waved a quick good-bye in my direction and left the room.

She definitely needed to leave before Troy got here. I didn't want any witnesses to what was about to go down.

By the time the next knock at the door came I knew what I had to do. I was primed and ready as I swung the door open to see Troy standing there in his suit.

"I wish they could film these bloody things at night instead of the middle of the afternoon. It's killer wearing these suits in the California sun, man," he said. I didn't say a word but stepped back and swung the door wider so he could enter. "How come you're not ready to go? You're not wearing that are you?"

"Have a seat." I directed him to the couch that Jas had sat on when she'd filled me in on what a duplicitous piece of shit the person in front of me was. The person I'd trusted to help build my career and look out for my best interests for more than five years.

"You're going to need to get a move on if we're going to make the red carpet," he said glancing at his watch.

"I won't be making the red carpet and neither will you." He arched a brow. "Did you think I'd never find out? You got in bed with the wrong guy if you thought that fucker would ever be able to keep quiet about screwing me over."

"What are you talking about, Mason?"

"I want to know why you did it."

"Look, I don't know what's going on here but you're going to have to fill me in." He sounded more agitated.

"That's how we're going to do this then? Okay, I'll play." I stood up and walked behind the chair, white-knuckling the back of it to contain the fury that consumed me. "You set Ellie up. Why?"

Troy stood from the couch with his hands in front of him in a placating gesture. "Mason, please. I don't know what you've heard but—"

"Stop lying to me! I know you got Mac to try to steal Ellie from me. What I want to know is what you said to him and why you did it."

Troy's face paled and a brief flicker of panic crossed his features. There. That's what I was looking for. Any doubts or hopes I'd still harbored that the man I'd come to rely so much on hadn't done such a terrible thing were erased.

He was silent for several long beats. "She would've ruined you in the end anyway."

"What the fuck does that mean?" I said low and menacing. Gone was the ashen color, replaced by cheeks heated in anger and blazing eyes. "Please. You were so god damn pussy-whipped by that broad you were already doing her bidding. Joining social media when I'd been trying for years to get you to do it? Putting her on a track so she could collect royalties, turning down a TV show because it meant you two couldn't get your cuddle time in for a few months. It was disgusting to watch you hand over control to her."

"You sound like a jealous girlfriend."

"I've worked hard to get you where you are today and I wasn't about to watch you fuck everything up for some bitch."

If I'd been any closer to him I would have punched him square in the jaw. "So you decided to get Mac involved."

He shrugged. "He served a purpose. I knew if she was with Mac there'd be no chance of you taking her back or hearing her out."

"Do you know what he did? He roofied her!"

Troy shook his head back and forth looking panicked. "I never told him to do that. I simply told him to—"

"What if he'd raped her?" My voice cracked at the end of the statement.

"He's not a complete idiot. He never would've done that. He'd lose everything."

"He still could. I don't understand why he would've helped you anyway. I can see you'd hoped I'd take the TV show contract after Ellie was out of the picture. He was second in line for that, why would he help you make that happen for me?"

"You're underestimating how much contempt he has for you. You're like the bigger, smarter, more successful brother who gets all the attention from mommy and daddy to him. He feels like he's always living in your shadow. I knew if I went to him with some story about how you and I were falling out and I wanted him to help me get revenge on you before I bailed, he'd go for it. Besides, he had no reason to think you wouldn't take the show. It was just pay back to him."

I'd gotten what I wanted from him. It was time to finish this. "You're fired."

"Nice try kid. You can't fire me—we have a contract."

"My lawyers are already working on a loophole to get me out of it. If you fight me on this I'll drag it out in court so long it'll take all your money to defend yourself. Not to mention what it would do to your name in this business if what you did gets out."

"You little shit! After everything I've done for you? You wouldn't even be in this business if it weren't for me."

"And I couldn't be more grateful to you for everything you did for me up until a couple of months ago. I can't trust you not to go behind my back and try to orchestrate things to your liking. And if I can't trust you—I can't work with you."

"We can get past this, Mason. We've had a difference of opinion on how to handle a situation, nothing more."

"I've made my decision. I'm not changing my mind. Get out of here. I can't stand to look at your face anymore."

Troy stood and stalked towards the door with his fists balled at his sides. "You'll be hearing from my lawyer."

"I expected no less. Now get out."

He nearly swung the door off the hinges, but he walked out slamming it behind him.

That'd gone the way I expected. It seemed odd that I wouldn't see him again...at least not while he was working for me. He'd gotten me into the business and guided me for years. Without his influence I knew I wouldn't be the success that I was. I owed a lot to him. But knowing what he did...going behind my back to manipulate me...I could never believe anything he said again. I didn't believe he'd ever meant Ellie harm—he likely had no idea how Mac had planned to break us up. But I could never forgive him for putting her in jeopardy like that. I still had one asshole to deal with, and I'd do it, in time.

As I left the room to head for the airport I had mixed emotions. On one hand it felt like a new start, on the other I was sad to see an end to what used to be. Only time would tell whether all the changes would be good ones.

chapter forty-one

Heartbreak had made me a masochist. That was the only explanation for why I'd turned on the music awards in a lame and pathetic effort to catch a glimpse of Mason on TV.

It'd been months since he'd kicked me out of his life and I still couldn't make sense of all that had happened and how quickly it had fallen apart.

I'd gotten my first lesson in real love—it sticks around. Although I hadn't seen Mason in fifty-eight days—not that I was counting—it hadn't diminished my feelings at all. Love was like a beach made up of a million grains of sand. When a wave rolled in a single grain was washed away, but it would take an eternity before all my love for Mason ended up in the sea.

I still held anger toward him for all the terrible things he'd said to me. I also told myself that I did know him, and for him to have acted like that, he must have been in a great deal of pain.

It was a solid month before I started functioning again. For a time I'd only gone to work, come home and made my way through the throng of photographers then laid in bed staring at the ceiling night after night. Yes, the press had camped outside my house for a few days. They'd started doing it at work, too. It turned out that Jeff's asshole tendencies came in handy when you needed them because he'd managed to get them to leave. After a few days without a Mason sighting they must have figured they wouldn't be getting any income-producing shots from my boring life and so they left.

The girls invited me out over and over again but I always refused. I stopped applying for jobs. It's like everything stopped, and I repeated the same day over and over again. Eventually Skye and Katie performed a mini-intervention. It was the wake-up call I'd needed. I realized life was still going to exist whether I participated or not. Since then I'd gone out a couple of times with the girls—my evening still consisting of me checking my watch repeatedly to see when I could leave, but it was a start. I'd even begun applying to jobs again.

That didn't mean Mason wasn't still on my mind every day. He'd blocked me on all social media so I'd taken the pathetic step of opening an anonymous account to follow him. It gave me a sad kind of comfort to see his career doing well. I was becoming adept at inflicting pain on myself.

I had the house to myself so I sprawled out on the couch, tucked under a blanket like a child, as the awards show started. Amber opened the show with a song that'd been nominated for an award. Seeing her on stage sent a small pang to my chest remembering how she'd welcomed me so completely.

An hour into the show and the award for Best Hip-Hop Album was being presented. I still hadn't caught a camera shot of Mason yet, which seemed odd but I figured maybe he'd been backstage for some reason. I knew it was inevitable that they'd cut to him when they announced his name as a nominee. Nerves slammed into me. What if he'd brought a date? What if it was Becca? I realized at some point I'd see something online or in a magazine about him with someone new. He'd move on and forget all about the girl he thought had betrayed him. I didn't know if I was prepared for that moment to happen tonight.

I held my breath as they called his name. A stock photo of Mason flashed on screen. Was he still backstage? Seconds later they announced Mason Nash as the winner of the year's Best Hip-Hop Album.

I jumped off the couch, clapping my hands together. I was overjoyed. It took me a moment to realize that I had no right to be excited for him anymore. I sat back down and scolded myself mentally. I would've done anything at that moment to be able to pick up the phone and offer him my congratulations. To still have that connection to him, hell, any connection to him.

I focused my attention on the TV and watched as Amber went on stage to accept Mason's award. I grabbed the controller and turned up the volume so I wouldn't miss what she had to say.

"I'd like to accept this award on behalf of my friend. He couldn't be here tonight. He had an urgent matter to deal with but he wanted to thank his fans most of all, without whom, none of this would be possible. He'd also like to thank everyone else along the way who helped him get where he is today. Thank you."

There was only one reason Mason would've missed such a huge night. Something must've happened with his mother again. Before we'd split she'd been doing pretty well. My heart squeezed for him. I knew he struggled with his feelings for his mother and more issues would only complicate the matter.

It wasn't my place to worry anymore. He had other people in his life to do that, but my damn stubborn heart refused to let him go.

The shrill ring of my cell phone from the kitchen counter interrupted my thoughts. I figured it was one of the girls who knew me well enough to know I'd be watching the show and was calling to check up on me. I was surprised to see Jeff's number on the screen when I picked it up.

"Hello?"

"Ellie, I need your help. What are you doing right now?"

"Um...I'm at home." Why was he calling me on a Sunday night? What couldn't wait until the morning?

"I need you to head over to the Oceanfront Avenue property. I don't know what it is with this place but the renter is having trouble getting the door open using the key in the lockbox. Since you've been there and are familiar with the place I want you to go see if you could help him out."

My stomach heaved at the mention of the house that held so many memories for Mason and me. I had no desire to set foot in that house ever again. I didn't bother confessing to Jeff that the last time I'd had to open the place I'd ended up sprawled half-naked under the bathroom window.

"Could I just call them and walk them through it? It's not hard at all." It was just a lock for Pete's sake. What couldn't they figure out?

"I already tried that."

"I was just about to head to bed," I lied. I knew I was pushing but I didn't want to go out. I was perfectly content to wallow on my own.

"Ellie, I might have made it sound like a request when I called but don't mistake that this is very much in fact an order."

There was the Jeff we all knew and loved. I rolled my eyes for my own perverse pleasure.

"Okay, let me change into something more appropriate and I'll head over there."

"You do that," he said and hung up.

I dragged my ass upstairs like I was headed to the electric chair and not a multi-million dollar beach house and changed into a pair of dark skinny jeans and a green v-neck t-shirt. It'd be cooler by the ocean and I wasn't taking the time to press a pair of dress pants. If the client didn't appreciate my lack of professional attire then they could pull up a deck chair and sleep in that. It was Sunday night for God's sake and they couldn't figure out how to put a key in a lock and turn it.

I grabbed my purse off the bench at the front door and

made my way out of the house, steeling myself for the onslaught of emotions sure to come when I reached my destination.

It was just a house I told myself. It might have been where the memories were made but it couldn't cause me any more pain than I was already in. Those memories were trapped inside my heart and I carried the pain they caused with me everywhere I went anyway.

chapter forty-two

I paced the darkened beach house waiting for any sign of Ellie's arrival. My chest was tight with anticipation both at seeing her again and concern for her reaction to everything I had to tell her.

Car tires crunched on stone and sand a moment later and I heard it turn onto the driveway. I waited to hear her footsteps on the deck but they didn't come. Had the car pulled into a neighbor's driveway? Maybe her boss hadn't been able to get her out here. I'd had to agree to offer free publicity for his Brokerage in exchange for his help but it was a small price to pay. It was somewhat devious to get her here under false pretenses but this was where our story had begun. It's where I hoped we could start writing the next.

We had a lot of great memories here and hell yes, I wanted to remind her of that.

Wait. There. She was on the deck now. I'd left the outside lights for her to see and I heard her opening the lockbox and putting the key in the lock. The door opened and I saw her blackened silhouette against the outside lights.

"Hello?" she called out. A moment later she flipped on the lights. She turned and looked in my direction. Her body went rigid and the car keys fell from her fingertips to crash to the floor. "Mason." My name came out in a rush with equal parts pain and relief.

She was as gorgeous as the day I'd foolishly thrown her out of my life, but was thinner than when I'd seen her last. Was she not taking care of herself? I took in her features one by one like an archeologist examining the most precious of treasures. I committed them all to memory in a way I hadn't before in case she couldn't find it in her heart to forgive me for believing her capable of the worst.

"I needed to see you," I said because it was the truth. It was the truth before I'd even found out she hadn't betrayed me. I'd been working so hard to make myself believe it wasn't the case but she was a need so deep in me it was undeniable. My body needed oxygen to survive but I needed Ellie to really live—live a real life full of joy, happiness and love.

Her eyes were wide with unshed tears. It twisted my guts to see the pain I'd put there.

"Mason, if you're here to rehash everything I don't think I can—"

"That's not why I'm here, Ellie. Will you stay and hear me out?"

It was hard to fathom. Mason was actually standing in front of me. I'd dreamed it, wished it for months but now that it was happening it didn't seem real. I couldn't imagine what he wanted to talk about but I owed it to him to hear him out.

"I'll stay," I said softly.

Relief appeared on Mason's face. "Will you come sit down?"

I nodded and walked over to the couch. As I passed he grabbed my wrist. I stopped. The feel of his fingertips pressed lightly against my skin almost undid me. I wanted so badly to take refuge in his strong arms.

He dropped his hand and I went to sit on the couch. He

sat beside me but not as close as he once would have. The emotional distance between us had translated to physical distance as well.

He looked good in his dark jeans and white Henley. As fit as ever. What I wouldn't give to feel that five o'clock shadow tickle my neck again. I pushed the thought down. Thinking like that wasn't going to help me get through this conversation with Mason.

Mason took my hands in his. His warmth seeped into me and I felt more at peace than I had in months.

"There's a lot I need to say. A lot I need to apologize for. I'm hoping you'll let me explain."

"What is this about?" I asked.

"I found out what happened the night you were with Mac."

I couldn't do this again. He had every right to hate me but I couldn't rehash this. I'd barely patched myself together the first time. His cruel words would break me a second time. I started to stand but Mason pulled me back.

"I'm not here because I'm angry. I'm here to tell you what an ass I was. But you already know that." I looked at him warily. "I know it wasn't your fault. I can't tell you how I found out but that doesn't really matter. I know for a fact Mac put something in your drink that night."

All the oxygen left my body. I felt sick and violated again. It was one thing to assume that had happened but to hear Mason confirm it reminded me how easily I could have been taken advantage of that night. Mason was still, carefully taking in my reaction.

"I didn't know for sure it was him, but I knew someone had to have done it. I told you that when you found us." Nausea swam through my stomach at the thought of what could've happened.

"I'm sorry I didn't believe you. I never should have questioned it. I have no defense except when I saw you laying in the same bed as him, I snapped." Mason's hands came to either side of my face, stroking my cheeks. "Are you okay? Tell me what you're thinking."

I looked into those green eyes that had captured me from the moment I first saw them. They were full of concern and if I didn't know better, glistening tears waiting to fall. "I don't know what I'm thinking. I've been doing my best not to think about it since it happened."

"It's a lot to process."

"I'm angry. I'm upset. I feel violated even though nothing happened." I brought my knees up to my chin and wrapped my arms around my legs, rocking myself back and forth.

Mason hugged me, his cheek pressed to my back. "I'm sorry. I'm so sorry, Ellie. This would never have happened if it weren't for me."

I pulled up to look at him. "It wasn't your fault," I said with conviction.

"There's more you don't know. Troy was the one who put Mac up to it. He had no idea Mac was gonna drug you but he instigated the entire thing."

"Troy?" I sat there dumbfounded. I knew he hadn't liked me but I couldn't believe he'd gone to such lengths to get me out of Mason's life.

"I fired him as soon as I found out. I can't believe I let this happen." Mason scrubbed his hands over his face.

"You didn't do anything wrong, Mason. This isn't on you."

"I did. I did do something wrong." He paused for a second and looked at me with so much pain in his eyes that I wanted nothing more than to take that pain away. "I didn't believe in you. I didn't trust that nothing added up. I took the situation at face value without questioning it when you'd only ever shown me loyalty. I said horrible things to you. Things I can't forgive myself for, never mind asking you to forgive me."

This time a single tear did escape his eye. It was too much to bear, watching the man I loved in so much pain. My own tears joined his.

"The things you said to me, Mason." My voice hitched and it took me a minute to compose myself. Mason shut his eyes tight. "It hurt me. Those words cut me deep." I broke into an ugly cry and Mason wrapped his arms around me, squeezing me tight. I told myself I should push him away after how badly he'd hurt me, but it still felt like home being in his arms and I couldn't do it. After a while I was able to compose myself and told him what I'd been regretting since the incident. "I shouldn't have put myself in the position for it to happen in the first place."

"Stop it. You're not at fault here, you're the victim," he said, his voice fierce.

"I know, but if I hadn't been feeling insecure because of Becca I never would've sat with him. I wanted him to tell me how you and Becca broke up. He was going on and on about how into each other you used to be and when you went off with her... I let him get the better of me."

Mason stroked some stray hairs back from my face. "Ellie, you had nothing to worry about where she was concerned. If you wanted to know why we broke up why didn't you just ask me?"

"I was embarrassed. I didn't want you to think I was being crazy or a jealous lover."

"I wouldn't have thought that, and I would have told you. There's no big story really. We were together, I found out she was cheating on me with multiple people. Mac was one of those people. I caught them in the act and that was the end of our relationship."

No wonder Mason flipped when he saw us in bed together. "I didn't know. I'm sorry."

"I'm over it. Honestly. I haven't have feelings for Becca for years. Nothing except for disgust. I wish I'd known you were feeling that way."

"My insecurity had more to do with me than with you. Every man has left me." My voice broke at the end and I took another minute to calm myself. "My whole life. My dad left after I was born. My mom never kept a husband long enough for any of them to have a relationship with me after they split.

I realized after we broke up that I've been waiting for you to leave from the moment this began between us."

He cupped my jaw. "I'm not leaving you. Not ever again...if you'll have me." His face was pleading.

"As much as you hurt me, that's all I've wanted since the moment I walked away."

Mason wrapped his strong arms around me and gave me a crushing kiss full of desperation and remorse. Our tongues danced in rhythm like we'd never been apart. I wanted to stay this way forever for fear it wasn't real. I poured all the emotion, all the love and loss I'd felt into that kiss telling him without words exactly how I felt.

"I love you, Ellie. I think I always did. From the moment I found you on the floor I was yours. My heart had been caged for so long. And you...you had the key. You picked the lock open and I haven't been the same since. The inside of you is as beautiful as the outside—which is saying a lot. I love your mind..." he kissed the top of my head "...your body..." he kissed down my neck to my shoulder "...and your soul." Finally he placed a single kiss over my heart.

I wrapped my hands around his head and brought him to eye level. "I love you. I admitted it to myself after I'd left. After everything happened I was so upset because I never told you."

Mason brushed a tear gently off my cheek. "It's okay, El. I know now."

There was compassion and forgiveness in his voice. I melted into another kiss. This one was better than any we'd shared before because this was the first kiss with our feelings laid bare for the other to see.

Mason pulled away as our kiss moved from love into lust. "There's something else we have to discuss and I want you to hear me out."

"I don't think I can take anymore revelations tonight."

"This isn't bad news but I know you're going to fight me on it."

"Okay..."

"I want you to come and work for me."

"You can't be serious," I said, eyes wide with a slackened jaw.

"Totally. I want you to oversee all my social media stuff, my website. I want you to implement any other ideas you might have to improve things. Anything that has to do with me and the public I want you to handle. You've got great instincts. I know you have lots of ideas tucked inside that brain of yours you haven't shared with me." He tapped the side of my head with his finger.

I couldn't deny what he said—it was true. When I'd worked on Mason's website I'd had a bunch of other ideas running through my head but I hadn't wanted to overwhelm him so I'd kept them to myself.

"I appreciate the offer but I can't work for you. I want to make my own way in the world, Mason. It's important to me. I grew up watching my mom rely on men for everything and I don't want that to be me."

"This would be a legitimate job. You'd get to use your skill set. Answer me this: If it was anyone else offering you this job would you consider it?"

I thought about that for moment and tried to think past my knee-jerk reaction. Grudgingly I said, "Yes."

"Then why is it so bad that I'm offering you the job? Think about it...you already know that I loved all the stuff you did for me before. So you know I like your work. I'd rather have you working for me than against me if you're working somewhere else. You'd get to travel with me so we wouldn't have to be apart for long stretches of time when I'm touring."

I felt myself caving. Truth was, it was a great opportunity and if it *was* anyone else I'd jump all over it. Beyond any hope I'd gotten my second chance with Mason. I was the one standing in my own way. Maybe there was a way to maintain my independence and work for him.

"If I take this job I'd only be trying it temporarily to see if it's working for both of us," I said.

"That's fair."

"And you'd only pay me the going rate—no more."

"I can live with that."

"And we agree that we keep business separate from personal. If we have a disagreement on a work level I don't want it seeping into our relationship."

"Deal." He knew he had me. A slow grin spread across his face putting his adorable dimple on display.

"And you're going to have to let me pay for things once in a while. You can't always be footing the bill for everything."

"Fine," he said between his teeth. He didn't like that concession.

"I'll do it then."

He brought me into a tight hug. "You're not going to regret it. I promise."

"I wouldn't regret any time I spend with you." He kissed my forehead and just like before—goner.

Mason's face grew serious. "What are we going to do about Mac? How do you want to handle it? I'll be damned if he gets away with it."

"I'm not sure what we can do. So much time has passed there's no way to prove it. Besides, I don't want this situation playing out in front of the media. What do you think?" This was the one dark cloud hanging over top of our reunion.

"If you trust me to handle it I have a few ideas of my own. I'll deal with it. I don't want you involved and I don't want you thinking about it every day."

His plan sounded ominous but I trusted him. For the first time I wholeheartedly, completely and without question trusted someone. "Do what you need to do. I trust you."

"The greatest gift you could ever give me is your trust."

I leaned in to kiss him but pulled away at the last second. "Oh! I almost forgot. You won tonight. You're a winner!"

"I'm a winner, Ellie, but it has nothing to do with my music and everything to do with you."

As we melted into each other the message I'd delivered in my YouTube video came to mind. There really was always hope. I'd woken up that morning a broken woman and when the sun rose tomorrow I'd have the job I always wanted and the man my heart couldn't live without by my side.

Life was a wonderful, tumultuous, exhilarating journey and I couldn't wait to see what it had in store for us.

– THE END –

You'll see more of Mason and Ellie in future Limelight books. Coming spring 2014, get a glimpse into the life of Ellie's best friend Skye...

PICTURE PERFECT
(Limelight #2)

Being the daughter of a big-city mayor, twenty-one year old Skye Summers has giant shoes to fill in her first real job out of college. With the public spotlight on her family, and her dad's expectations running high, she jumps at the chance to work side-by-side on an important project with her sexy new boss.

Playboy entrepreneur Landon Steele has built a successful entertainment PR firm and broken more than a few hearts along the way. He's counting on his enthusiastic new assistant to help him expand his business into LA... until he discovers she's a pampered rich girl who's in the public spotlight as much as his famous clients. Still, he agrees to give her a chance, and soon the two are heating up the bedroom as well as the boardroom.

But when Skye's ex-boyfriend threatens to reveal a dangerous secret from her past, her job, relationship with Landon, and her father's career are suddenly all on the line. Will she be forced to leave Landon? Or will she pursue her heart, regardless of the cost?

Elisabeth has a soft spot for happily ever afters and a hot spot for alpha males. If she's not curled up somewhere with a romance novel in one hand and chocolate in the other you can probably find her typing madly on her keyboard creating her next story. She currently lives outside Toronto, Canada with her husband, two small children, and killer cat.

A Note To Readers:
One of the best ways to support an author is by leaving a review! If you enjoyed Mason and Ellie's story I'd appreciate it if you'd consider leaving a review, whether short or long, on the retailer you purchased the book from or on Goodreads if you are a member. I'd be extremely grateful!

Questions? Comments?
I love to hear from readers! Feel free to connect with me via e-mail at authorelisabethgrace@gmail.com or via anyone of these social media platforms. I love talking books—even if they aren't my own!
Website: Elisabeth-Grace.com
Facebook Profile: facebook.com/Elisabeth.Grace.790
Twitter: @1elisabethgrace

Want to know when the next book of the Limelight Series comes out? Sign up for my newsletter here by visiting my website! I take your privacy seriously. I will not sell your e-mail address. I will only contact you with important news like cover reveals, special giveaways for newsletter subscribers, and to tell you when a new book is available. I won't be spamming your inbox every week!

acknowledgments

There's so many people to thank, but the first person I would like to thank is you. You the reader. You chose to spend a few dollars of your hard earned money, and more importantly, invested precious time out of your busy life to read something I created. For that I am not only humbled, but extremely grateful. I hope the story lived up to your expectations and provided you with some level of enjoyment.

I'd like to thank my crit partners in 'The Clubhouse'. Lisa & Mary—I've learned so much from you and truly consider you lifelong friends.

To my ladies in the 'Indie Chicks Rock' group...to the grave. Enough said. It's wonderful to be a part of such a positive and supportive environment!

My betas...Shawna, Kat and Faith. Your messages along the way about how much you were enjoying the book meant so much! It's so nerve-wracking as throwing your work to the wolves for the first time. LOL Shawna—so glad to have you as a fellow 'book geek'. Thanks for putting up with my never ending phone calls asking for your opinion on one thing or another.

To the fabulous and wonderfully talented Rachel Van Dyken...your willingness to help out a newbie author and take time out of you busy life had me gob smacked and speaks to the giving and generous person you are. I truly can't say enough about what a thoughtful and wonderful woman I think you are!

A big thanks to Monica Murphy for reading my story, e-mailing me to let me know how much she enjoyed it, and giving me a blurb for the cover. She was nothing but encouraging and supportive!

To my editor, Laura Shin...you're input was invaluable in strengthening my manuscript. Thanks for ridding me of all my excessive words! I look forward to working on many more projects together.

To author Misty Evans...thanks for helping me with the back cover blurb. A marketing copywriter I am not, but you certainly could be!

To the bloggers that love reading and support the indie community...I hold a special place in my heart to all of you. You work tirelessly to expose big and small authors alike. I've followed book blogs for years and would never have discovered some of my own favorites if it weren't for you guys! A special thanks goes to all the bloggers who agreed to take a chance and read 'Rumor Has It'. I know how many requests you get, so you have my deepest appreciation. Even the bloggers too busy and declined, thank-you for doing it in such an encouraging way and with such class. You ladies all rock!!

To my family and friends...all the support, encouragement, and inquiries as to where I was in the process of writing the book were appreciated. Believe me when I say it never went unnoticed! If I was tightlipped it's only because I didn't want to bore you to tears...I could drone on about writing for hours!

Lastly, to my hubby who spent many a night alone on the couch because I was too busy typing on the computer...I hope I've made you proud of the end result and that you think it was worth the sacrifice.